What

The Alber Mysteries

"Albert is one of my all-time favorite sleuths."
New York Times bestselling author Tess Gerritsen

"(The Albert Mysteries)...shine with comic brilliance. Crossman has a gift for creating characters...who should show up in further adventures of Albert. And there should be more."
Chicago Sun-Times

"If you have ever aspired to be a private detective, here is some hilarious inspiration. Crossman's delightfully offbeat tale of wacky academic politics contains a host of bizarre characters and an inexplicable homicide. Albert is indeed a unique, likable operative. I certainly look forward to an encore."
St. Louis Post-Dispatch

"The (novels are) an exercise in the comic style, defying disbelief. To his credit, Crossman brings it off nicely. Albert is clearly a survivor, likely to be heard from again."
Los Angeles Times Book Review

"Crossman...creates an offbeat, sympathetic sleuth who meanders innocently through this tale like a lamb through a pack of wolves. Bravo. Encore!
Publishers Weekly

The Winston Crisp Mysteries

A Show of Hands
"Crossman is a skilled mystery writer with a knack for suspense, clues, local color, and a flowing story. "
Times Record

"The writing is fast-paced and full of enough twists and turns to engage the most avid of mystery readers. Crisp is a delightful, plausible sleuth."
Maine Sunday Telegram

The Shroud Collector (formerly *Dead of Winter*)
"As clever as (this) premise is, as satisfactory as the complex plot may be to the mystery buff...it is the peripheral characters that make this book shine. ."
Ellsworth Weekly

"Crossman has created a delightfully unique detective in Winston Crisp, who uses his brains, not his brawn. With the help of a charming cast of supporting characters, both author and sleuth triumph with panache."
Tess Gerritsen, *New York Times* best-selling author.

Justice Once Removed
"It is the author's intimate portraits of life on a Maine island that pull this book together and give it character. Neither Nero Wolfe, nor Columbo, nor most of the rest of the thousands of storybook sleuths ever came close."
Brunswick Sun Journal

"David Crossman is a wizard. This is a charmingly crafted, magically airy book, not to be mistaken for a lightweight."
Kennebec Sunday Journal

The Bean and Ab Mysteries

"These well-structured tales never loses momentum. Bean and Ab are likable characters who move through the story, unearthing clues that take them closer to solving a mystery that has existed for more than 100 years. Their youthful enthusiasm, investigative prowess, and endearing friendship make for interesting characterization. The carefully orchestrated chapters and the fast pace will hold children's attention throughout."
School Library Journal

"Impossible-to-put-down Maine mystery. Suspense builds neatly from chapter to chapter, and the ending is richly satisfying."
Bangor Daily News Sunday

"Crossman's SECRET OF THE MISSING GRAVE is a gripping and well-imagined adventure mystery."
The Horn Book (Boston Globe)

"Be warned...you'll find this suspenseful volume as fascinating as your youngster will."
Portland Press Herald

Requiem for Ashes
The First Albert Mystery
by
David Crossman

Alibi-Folio Publishers
Palm Coast, FL, U.S.A.

Published by Alibi Folio Publishers
24 Blakeport Lane
Palm Coast, FL 32137

Printed in the United States of America

Library of Congress Control Number: 2012903471

ISBN 978-0-6155-1254-9

All characters in this book are fictitious. Any resemblance to individuals, living or dead, is entirely coincidental, or at least highly unlikely.

Cover design: CiA

Dedication

To Mom and Dad - for roots and wings.

Requiem for Ashes
The First Albert Mystery
by David Crossman

Chapter One

1983

Albert ignored the knocking. He exhaled a cloud of smoke through his nose and tucked the cigarette behind his ear. His yellowed fingers stuttered nervously across the staff in a race to keep up with the sounds in his brain. Dots, bars, and flags appeared over the heads of the notes like an Impressionist's drawing of a Memorial Day parade.

From behind his thick horn-rimmed glasses his black eyes stared into the soul of the scribblings, filling the room with music.

The knocking came again. It wasn't until he'd twice written the contrapuntal triplet into the cello line that he realized someone was at the door. The triplet worked; he left it.

He removed the cigarette from behind his ear, where it had singed a few hairs, and dowsed it in an inch or so of congealed coffee at the bottom of a cup; one of many that littered the room. The odor of burning hair had the effect of smelling salts.

He answered the door.

"Your head's on fire," said Dr. Tewksbury, letting himself in.

"Oh. I was working. I was just . . . "

"Did you hear about Glenly?" Tewksbury - Professor of History, Head of the Archaeology Department, Honorary Senior Research Fellow of University College, London and one of colleagues of whose existence Albert was hazily aware - entered the room with his titular entourage as music gave way to archaeology and closed the door on the World Outside.

"Glenly?" Albert echoed. He was struggling to keep from forgetting the next two measures. If only he hadn't spilled beer on the tape recorder. They said that's why it didn't work anymore, though he couldn't see what one thing had to do with the other.

If only Tewksbury hadn't chosen this particular time to unburden himself of gossip. "I don't know . . . "

"You must," said Tewksbury. He dropped his Irish walking hat on the white plaster bust of Rimsky-Korsakov and sat down. Albert wasn't offended. The bust had been a gift from one of his classes and he didn't know who it was any more than he knew who was behind any of the awards he'd been given over the years; little golden statues with their hands in the air, strange contortions of clear plastic on heavy black bases, plaques with records you couldn't even play. He'd tried. Fortunately the school took most of them off his hands. Except the one he prized, a little bronze disc with somebody's face on it. It made a good coaster and comprised his one concession to housekeeping. There was a blue-and-gold ribbon attached to it which made it easy to find amidst the rubble of his room.

To Albert, people were objects that confused and complicated life. He didn't understand them, and didn't really care to. Music was his refuge, the sword and buckler with which he held the World at bay.

"Justin Glenly," said Tewksbury. "Middle Ages and Classical Languages."

"Middle Ages," Albert echoed again. Long experience had taught him echoing things made people think he was listening, and that's all they really wanted; the tactic left his mind free to dwell on music. Most of the time it worked, but Tewksbury seemed determined to make this a two-way conversation.

"He's dead."

The bucket hit bottom. "Dead?" said Albert, not echoing, but exclaiming. "What do you mean?"

"Dead. As in 'as a doornail' . . . or duck. Take your pick. They found him in his office."

Glenly. The name prompted a memory. "He's the one you had the fight with."

"An 'altercation' is the academic term, Albert." Tewksbury dug through the darkened interior of Albert's refrigerator. "We just happened to altercate to the point of a sprained wrist and a bloody nose. Don't you have any St. Pauli Girl?"

Albert, still operating in a fog, suspended a sextuplet of dead Professor Glenlys in their proper places on his mental staff and rummaged through a heap of laundry on the kitchen table. He disinterred a six-pack and handed it to his visitor. "It's warm." He brushed the clothes from the table and gestured Tewksbury to take a seat. "Dead?"

"Heart attack, apparently. As if he had one."

Albert studied the free-form layer of smoke in the air. This was the kind of news about which he should be very concerned.

"Heart attack," he mouthed.

"He was only forty-eight or forty-nine. Less than fifty, anyway."

Albert lowered the last of Glenlys half a step to a B flat. "B flat . . . "

"What?"

"Oh, nothing. Forty-eight?"

"Or fifty."

As host, it was Albert's duty to pick up the conversation when it lapsed, which it did now. What could he say? "What was it you fought about?"

"You don't remember? That's what you get for living like a mole, Albert. It was the talk of the campus. My paper on the Etruscans." These few words were meant to crystallize the subject, a state of mind Albert's expression did not reflect.

"Steidigger's funerary finds in Tuscany last summer? Conclusive proof that they evolved from the native population."

Albert wondered why they would do that. "Who did?"

"The Etruscans," Tewksbury snapped. "Wake up and smell the coffee."

"Etruscans," Albert replied in a whisper. "Oh, yes."

"'Yes,' my aunt Fanny's foot. You wouldn't know an Etruscan from a Pekingese." Accepting this, Tewksbury proceeded to elucidate. "There's always been a debate about their origins."

Albert declined the impulse to point out that the statement was unsupportable. Assuming Etruscans hadn't been present at Creation, there couldn't 'always' have been a debate. "Oh."

"Some think they were autochthonous."

The word raised Albert's left eyebrow.

"Native," Tewksbury explained. "Indigenous."

Albert's eyebrow settled back into its autochthonous position.

"Others side with Herodotus, who says they came from the Aegean . . . Asia Minor . . . one of the waves of Sea Peoples who were making a nuisance of themselves all over the eastern Mediterranean at the time."

"Does it make a difference?" asked Albert. All the while his hands had been combing his apparel in search of a cigarette. One was finally extracted from his shirt cuff. The search for matches extended to a nearby pile of sheet music that cascaded to the floor at his touch and stayed there. "That was a long time ago." With a subconscious cock of the eyebrow Glenly the Sixth was reinstated as a B natural.

"Archaeology tends in that direction," said Tewksbury, his derisive tone absorbed entirely by the clutter. "Of course is makes a difference. I published a paper supporting the 'native people' theory. It appeared in the CVA, remember?"

Albert lit the cigarette. "CVA. Yes."

"The *Corpus Vasorum Antiquorum*, Albert - organ of the *Union Academique Internationale*?"

Making a listening noise, Albert found a fingernail that hadn't been bitten in a while and bit it and wondered silently what organs had to do with archaeology. The danger in asking the question, though, was that Tewksbury might be prompted to answer, and Albert's ears were filling too rapidly as it was.

Tewksbury shook his head in exasperation. "Glenly refuted it in the *Journal of Archaeology*." Mention of the affront disinterred Tewksbury's academic indignation. "A professor of classical languages refuting me in print about Etruscans!

"He selected some arbitrary facts, entirely out of context, and contorted them into evidence suggesting they were Canaanites. Canaanites! The overflow of those squeezed out of the Fertile Crescent by the Sea Peoples; the flotsam that Tyre, Sidon, Byblos, and Akko couldn't accommodate!

"As if that wasn't enough, he based all these archaeological gymnastics upon a totally fatuous connection with Mari religious practices! Of course, he disregarded the inconvenience presented by the fact that the Mari empire had been dead and gone over a thousand years by that time. Then there's the trifling problem of the singularity of the Etruscan language. Bah! And he called himself a scholar! Mari!

"They might as easily have come from Poughkeepsie." He crushed the can, even though it was still half full. He reacted quickly, so the beer fell harmlessly to the carpet where it wouldn't be noticed.

"He wanted my slot."

"Archaeology?" said Albert. It was time he said something.

"Not the chairmanship. Too much administration for the likes of him. No. He wanted Ancient History. Mediterranean and Middle Eastern," Tewksbury amended. "Coveted it. Of course the man wouldn't know a Sumerian from a Scythian's backside." Tewksbury slammed the dented can into Albert's laundry. "He was trying to make points with that paper; create a controversy, make a fool of me.

"That's what scholarship's come to these days, Albert, all about generating some kind of controversy that will resonate among the unwashed, get them clamoring. That's when the foundations take notice and apply a little oil to the rusty hinges on their purses. Scholarship be damned.

"He expected to get a lot of mileage by advancing an unprovable hypothesis. Don't be surprised." Albert wasn't surprised; he hadn't the vaguest idea what Tewksbury was talking about. "It's not that uncommon. Mind you, he never expected to be proven wrong."

"That's what you fought about?"

"That's when it started." Tewksbury, a reformed smoker, was one of those people who fanned the air flamboyantly in the presence of smoke . . . held his breath and pointed to "No Smoking" signs and tattled to headwaiters. Theatrics were wasted on Albert. "What really got me, though, was that some people in the community . . . respected archaeologists . . . were treating his conjectural . . . ejaculations . . . as if they constituted serious scholarship! I couldn't believe it!"

"So you fought?"

"Not at the time. That was a while ago," said Tewksbury. "Ancient History." He snorted as if he'd made a joke.

People were always doing that. Albert knew they expected him to laugh, but it was a response he was unable to manufacture at will.

Some stale popcorn had dropped from the table onto Tewksbury's trousers. He brushed it away. "I decided to ignore him. Figured anything less would have dignified his . . . warblings. But I knew, because the public had taken notice - however sheathed in ignorance - Administration had taken notice. That's what they do."

"So you fought?" Albert restated. It had worked once. The triplets were being a nuisance. They changed the whole texture of the composition.

"It came to a head month before last. I could only take so much, after all. It was like having somebody stick pins in me every time we met. There's a limit."

"So you hit him?" It was a variation on a theme.

"In the hallway outside Administration."

"And now that he's dead, you're sorry?"

Tewksbury was thinking about bumming a cigarette. He was nervous. "Hardly. I haven't seen him since the Steidigger Paper was published. I hardly had time to launch the first volley in my gloat campaign." Tewksbury interpreted a twitch of Albert's eyebrows as a sign of interest. "Just a letter." He winced. "I really let him have it. Even went to the thesaurus for some really despicable adjectives."

"And you mailed it?" Albert was on auto-pilot, dropping comments into conversational openings at appropriate intervals. He pretended to doodle on a paper bag. What if he made them eighth notes with a dotted whole?

A cigarette protruded from a discarded pack under some papers. Tewksbury's eyes kept wandering to it. He loosened his tie. "Yes, I did. Together with a copy of the Steidigger Paper. That's what worries me."

Albert stopped doodling. "What? You think the letter gave him a heart attack?"

Tewksbury was astonished. "What? Of course not . . . it never occurred to me!" The awkward silence that followed was punctuated by a dry laugh. "Wouldn't that be ironic?" He had to hitch in his seat to reach the cigarette. He removed it nonchalantly from the pack. "No. I was disappointed that he might not have read it. The thought that he might have died with that supercilious grin on his face . . . " He put the cigarette between his lips, ran his tongue against the stubbly end of the filter, "still thinking he had the upper hand . . . it was almost more than I could bear.

"Of course, now that you mention it . . . " He laughed again.

"Wouldn't that be ironic?" Pause. "Got a light?"

Albert turned his black eyes on Tewksbury and put the matches in his pocket. "No."

Tewksbury smiled with half his mouth, sighed, and dropped the cigarette on the pack. "You smoke too much."

There was a pause.

Albert managed to scratch out three more measures. He realized the whole piece was starting to take place around the accidental triplet. The mystical workings of serendipity always amazed him; but the unexpected results were often enjoyable.

"I'd better go. I've got a class in fifteen minutes," said Tewksbury. But he didn't go. He sat searching the apartment for his thoughts.

Taking his cue from the silence, Albert looked up. "Forty eight's young."

"I'm fifty."

It amazed Albert when people spat out their ages like that, as if it was foremost in their minds all the time and required no calculation whatsoever.

Tewksbury stood up, retrieved his hat from Rimsky-Korsakoff, and scuffed to the door. "Death is real, Albert," he said, puffing an imaginary cigarette. "Take care you don't catch it."

Albert was already scratching furiously on the brown paper bag.

Tewksbury left the room.

That evening Albert found a tin of sardines and some peanut butter for supper. There wasn't any bread, but the combination worked well as a dip. He found some milk and some Ding Dongs, too. Several day's debris had fetched up on the Naugahyde recliner; he pushed it aside, made room for his feet on an upright trumpet case, and began his dinner.

The TV took a long time to warm up. It was an ancient black-and-white tube type that someone had given him; so old it should only show reruns. He turned it on whenever he sat down to eat and watched whatever was on, then, when he had finished eating, shut it off. It was fulfilling a social obligation; a nod to the world of which he seldom felt a part.

The news was on. He hated the news, but the sound was off so he didn't bother changing the channel. The bright blue light poured the world into his room, spilling staccato shadows of violence and rage all over his music, his instruments, himself. He didn't watch. He felt violated and embarrassed, the way he'd felt at a Dukakis rally he'd been dragged to once.

He looked at the ceiling while he ate. When he'd finished, he dislodged himself from the chair and reached for the TV, shutting it off just as a familiar face flashed on the screen. He turned it back on. The little pinhead of white light immediately burst into a full-screen picture of Tewksbury. Albert dropped the glasses back onto his nose, squinted at the screen and turned up the sound. A crisp young lady was speaking from the ether of electronics behind the grainy, ten-year-old snapshot of the Head of Archaeology.

"Dr. Andrew Tewksbury was discovered in the dead man's office late this afternoon," said the woman, her voice brittle and a shade contemptuous.

"Andrew," Albert repeated. He'd never thought of Tewksbury as having a first name.

Another face took the place of Tewksbury's. The caption identified it as belonging to Police Lieutenant William Craig, Jr. The lieutenant was not any more comfortable being watched than Albert was watching him. That seemed to speak well of him, somehow.

"I saw a light on when I returned to Dr. Glenly's office. I'd made arrangements to go back that night to clean up, make sure we hadn't overlooked anything. Just routine. There wasn't any reason to expect foul play, up to that time. So the place wasn't guarded. Then I found Tewksbury . . . Dr. Tewksbury in the office, going through the papers and things of the deceased subject." Did that sound as awkward to everyone watching as it did to him? "The place had been neat as a pin earlier. Now it was a mess."

"And you found something incriminating in Dr. Tewksbury's possession? Something that cast a new light on the death and made you suspect foul play?" said someone with an arm and a microphone.

The lieutenant moved his mouth nervously, evidently to accommodate the words that had been put there. He moon-lighted security at the Stop and Shop; he wasn't media-wise.

"Yes," he said. "We think there might be more to it. It's just speculation at this point." He swallowed, darted a shy glance full into the camera, wondering if it was over. The lit-tle red light was still on. That meant the camera was still running. It wanted more. "It might have been murder." He hadn't meant to say that. "I think you should be talking to my superior . . . "

The lieutenant's picture went away and was replaced by the crisp lady, sitting at a white desk with lots of television screens behind her.

Albert was glad none of them was tuned to the news.

The woman was attractive in an antiseptic, sexless way - like a statue - and talked without using her eyebrows or moving her upper lip. "Sources close to the investigation re-port an ongoing animosity between Dr. Tewksbury and the dead man concerning credit-taking on some fine points of ancient history."

"Etruscan," said Albert.

"Glenly was widely respected in university circles for his controversial theories on the ethnic origins of certain Mediterranean peoples. Dr. Justin Glenly, dead at 48 of un-known causes; though police grant the possibility of foul play. We'll have more on the story as it unfolds."

Albert shut off the TV. Usually the world left the room when he did that. Not now, though. It was still there, palpa-ble in the darkness. The shadows were full of Lt. William Craig, Jr., and the Crisp News Woman, and the disembodied voice with the microphone, all talking at once; all implying that Tewksbury had killed Glenly.

Isn't that what they were saying?

And he'd denied the condemned man a cigarette.

Albert cocked his head as if listening for something. He heard a siren in the distance; footsteps creaking on the ancient floor above. Rain. Traffic. Soft voices in the hall. A world of sounds, but the music was gone. The domineering mistress that commanded all his senses had packed her bags and gone - crowded from his brain newly inhabited by shadows - and no longer there to drown out the world.

Would she ever find her way back?

Chapter Two

The police station represented everything that Albert didn't understand about the world. It had been a grand building once, but several decades of lead-based paint - added layer-upon-layer, like false testimony - were proving more weight than the plaster could bear; tearing it from the wall and exposing it to air and sunlight so that it turned to powder and rained down upon the blindfolded statue of Justice in the foyer. Every night the cleaning crew swept it up in bits and pieces. Someday they'd sweep up the last of it and all the official-looking people in polyester suits and uniforms would have to find a new place to drink coffee and ignore people.

It was going to be one of those uncomfortable times that Albert hated. He went to the biggest desk and waited.

There was a black woman seated in a green swivel chair on the other side of the desk, and an older man, white, with pale eyes; red, watery, and strained by cynicism. She was writing, he was on the phone.

Albert cleared his throat. The woman finished writing one thing and started another. The man hung up the phone and began opening and closing drawers, looking for something. Albert sighed and put his hands on the desk. The woman looked at them out of the corner of her eyes, then sideways at him. It was a territorial warning. Albert put his hands in his pockets. He needed them to play the piano.

The woman returned to her writing. "May I help you'?" she said. Odd how a sentence and the tone of its delivery can so emphatically contradict one another.

"I'd like to see someone . . . in prison," said Albert.

The man and woman looked at each other and laughed by merely flaring their nostrils. Albert reddened. He was a foreigner in a strange land and didn't know the language.

"This is a jail, not a prison," the woman explained. The distinction was lost on Albert. "Name," said the woman, twisting an official-looking form into the laundry ringer of her typewriter. It was a question without a question mark. Albert's heart skipped a beat. He had a fifty-fifty chance.

"Dr. Tewksbury."

"T-o-o-k ." said the woman, typing.

"T-e-w-k . . . " Albert corrected.

The woman scalded him with a glance, ripped the triplicate form from her typewriter, slam-dunked it into the basket, and began again. By the time the spelling was worked out, Albert felt his clothes had outgrown him. "And who do you want to see, Dr. Tewksbury?"

In the end, Albert told them he was Tewksbury's brother-in-law. Whether that got him into the little waiting room or not, he didn't know. Albert was pretty sure Tewksbury wasn't even married. Almost positive.

He hadn't been prepared for the search. He should watch more TV. It was embarrassing and they seemed suspicious when they didn't find anything in his pockets but a sax reed and a tidal chart. It took him a long time to remember where the chart came from, then he realized he must have gotten it when he went to see his mother in Maine last year. He used the sax reed as a guitar pick.

They asked him why he didn't have a wallet or any money. He said he didn't own a wallet. He didn't need folding money or credit cards . . . they didn't fit in cigarette machines. Finally they called the school and got someone to identify him. Apparently it wasn't that difficult.

The waiting room was small, with a wooden table and two folding chairs. The table had lots of scratches on it. The walls were painted to a wavy mid-point with glossy dark brown paint roughly the color of excrement and the rest of the way with a color Albert couldn't imagine a name for.

Most of the linoleum tiles on the floor were torn or warped and there were deep scuff marks in them on either side of the table. Cigarette burns pocked every surface. A thick metal grid covered the room's solitary window which looked out onto the soot-baked bricks of an adjacent building. The view discouraged escape.

The wait dragged on. He couldn't dispel the notion that they'd found him out on the brother-in-law lie and were going to ignore him into confession. Finally the door opened and Tewksbury came in. A uniformed policeman came in, too, and stood against the wall and looked out the window at the bricks.

Tewksbury looked confused and frightened. It was a world he didn't understand, either. He sat on the other chair and asked for a cigarette. Albert gave him one, and a match. Tewksbury looked at them, then gave them back. "It's not that bad yet, is it?"

Albert shrugged his shoulders. "Are you all right?" It was a rhetorical question. The answer was obvious. "It was on the news. What happened?"

Tewksbury leaned across the table. The policeman yawned, looked at his watch and back out the window. Albert leaned in.

"I've been framed," said Tewksbury. His breath was very bad. "I . . . got a call in the office after my last class. I don't know who it was. A man. He said he knew about the letter. He said the police would find it interesting." His hands busily sculpted the air with his tension. "I thought it was a blackmailer. I waited for him to say something . . . make some kind of demand, you know? But he didn't. I heard him breathing for a minute, then he hung up."

"You went to Glenly's office?"

Tewksbury nodded. "It was a mess. There were papers everywhere." Tewksbury's concept of "mess" differed wildly from Albert's. "It looked like your place."

22

Albert nibbled at a hangnail. It tasted like stale ciga-rettes.

"Who'd want to kill Glenly?"

"You can start with his mother and work your way out in ever-widening circles, I should imagine. He was a . . . pesti-lence. I'm surprised the meteorologists haven't commented on the improvement in air quality since he died," Tewksbury bounced a twitching smile off Albert's blank face, "but I did-n't do it." He grabbed Albert's hands and squeezed them tightly. "I didn't, Albert."

Albert instinctively retrieved his hands from archaeolo-gy's grasp. Some leftover sunlight squeezed through the window grate to see what was going on. Albert traced the patchwork of shadows on the table.

"I had a motive," Tewksbury continued. "I don't deny it. But there were others, Albert. Lots of others." He seemed to be struggling not to say what came next. "He was a . . . he manipulated people. No scruples. He knew just what every-one wanted to hear, and said it. They ate it up! Smart peo-ple. The Dean, the Chancellor. Women."

"Women?"

"Girls. Students. He teased them. Innuendo, you know? Sophomoric behavior. Detestable especially for someone in his position. But . . . they'd giggle. He'd giggle. The gargoyle."

Albert had witnessed this kind of unreasoning hatred years before, on the playground. In the classroom. It result-ed from the hoarding of offense and bridled at the slightest provocation.

"People were afraid of him, like they are of sharks. A ter-rible fascination." Eyes downcast, slow deep breath vacates lungs all at once. "It was like he cast a spell on people. I don't know. I never understood it. I mean, intellectually he was a cipher. I'm not just saying that. Everyone on the facul-ty will tell you the same – would have, anyway, if he wasn't dead. Academically his accomplishments were practically nil. Even his teaching abilities were rudimentary; Cliff notes, probably. But he had a way. I don't know."

There was a silence during which the guard had time to look at his watch twice.

"What now?" said Albert after a while.

"They've denied bail, pending arraignment day after tomorrow."

"What's arraignment?"

There followed a brief lesson in American jurisprudence headed by its most recent victim, who understood the subject only in the light of the last few hours' events.

"Do you have a lawyer?"

"The school has lawyers for this type of thing. I'm sure they'll send someone over. I know I can't afford one." Tewksbury exhaled through his nose. "They've assigned me a public defender in the meantime, compliments of the legal system. They said he'd be here, but I haven't seen him yet." He looked where his watch would have been if he'd been wearing one. "I'm sure the school will do something. They have to, don't you think?"

Would the sun rise? To Albert the school was the womb. It defined the parameters within which he lived and breathed. It sheltered him. It abided his imperfections. Forgave him for being clueless. Together with Huffy, his agent at William Morris, it coordinated his life; told him when to be where and got him there. Best of all, it welcomed him when he returned.

He ate free at the cafeteria.

"Of course it will," he said.

Both men studied their fingers for a minute. "I told them I was your brother-in-law," Albert confessed in a whisper.

Tewksbury smiled. The guard smiled, too. "Good idea," said Tewksbury.

"I just felt like I should see you. I wanted to know if there was anything I could do," said Albert. "Does your family know?"

"I just have my father," said Tewksbury, "in Vermont. He's had enough problems in his life since my mom died four years ago. I'm not going to bother him with it." Pause. "He's old." Pause. "Besides, I'll be out of here soon."

Albert nodded. "Who do you think it was who called you?"

"I don't know."

"You didn't recognize the voice?"

Tewksbury replayed the phone call mentally. "No. It was breathy. Almost a whisper. Whispers all sound the same."

It was a ridiculous assertion to Albert. Faces, names, relationships . . . they all congealed in an amorphous mass . . . but voices, sound, that was the currency he dealt in. He never forgot a sound.

Over the next several days Albert poked his head out into the world like a Disney character waking from hibernation. He listened to the radio, watched TV, read the newspapers, inputting all the information he could get on the I.Q. Murder as the press dubbed it. The edges of the story were trimmed with other news, having to do with other lives, other events. They told about a world too big and disturbing to cope with. So he didn't. If the news didn't pertain to Tewksbury, he simply tuned it out.

Things weren't going well for Tewksbury. His fingerprints had been found all over Glenly's office. The incriminating letter had turned up and was reprinted in the papers; combustible material for gossip in a small college town. Blackest of all, the school had decided not to sully itself with the business. Its concern was summed up in a brief statement to the press. "The college will do everything possible to aid the police in their investigation."

Albert had once seen a film run backward. A building lay in ruin amid a cloud of dust and debris, then, magically, reassembled itself. The analogy came to mind as the days passed. From the initial confusion and chaos an orderly array of evidence fell into place, as if by magic, forming an edifice of implications around Tewksbury. A place with no doors and no windows. No room for movement.

The story faded from the front pages. History. There was a touching human interest piece when Tewksbury's father finally visited him in jail. Albert had met him, a confused old fellow who couldn't hear well and didn't understand why his son was there.

Albert stopped reading papers after that. The TV died a violent death. There must be some chemical in coffee that destroys electronic things. A scientist could explain it. He turned the radio back to the classical station but kept the volume low, otherwise he'd hear it.

He visited Tewksbury regularly. He was the only one who did.

The black lady even smiled now when he came to the desk. She'd hand him something to sign, which he did, then a policeman would take him to a room and search him. He'd bought a wallet for the occasion. It had a picture of Howdy Doody on it; a precaution that should keep it from getting mixed up with others.

Tewksbury was an official prisoner now, his life reduced to shades of gray. Albert had brought him the reading matter he'd requested from the school library, Plutarch's Lives, the works of Josephus, Aristobulus, Strabos, Justinian and Herodotus, and various professional journals and periodicals.

At first he seemed to gain some inspiration from them. Then he stopped asking for more. He stopped reading. His mind imploded in helplessness. His words spewed the dust of his internment.

"What about the phone call?" asked Albert. "Didn't you tell them about it?"

"Of course I did," said Tewksbury. "Over and over. They don't believe me."

Albert hadn't thought of that. What could be expected, though, in a world where even the school couldn't be depended upon?

Tewksbury was chain-smoking now. "Somebody's doing this. It's all too perfect."

"What do you mean?"

"It's like I'm trapped under ice," said Tewksbury. "Every time I find some breathing space, it freezes over before I can get to it."

"What's the public defender doing?"

"He's gone, thank heavens," said Tewksbury, tossing the public defender out of the picture with a quick jerk of the head. "He resented the fact I wasn't some drugged-out homeless pariah. I don't think he'd ever defended a taxpayer.

"The school retained a private firm." Tewksbury brightened a little, like a child who has just been told he may keep the light on in the hall and the door open a crack. "Goldstein, Perlman, Quimby and Bowles," he said. It was clear from the look in Albert's eyes that he might as well have recited the phone book. "Connors recommended them."

Albert seized on the one name that had a ring of familiarity.

"Connors?"

Tewksbury's optimism, newly born and self-generated, wasn't proof against the unmasked doubt in Albert's eyes. Somebody shut the door on his little room of hope and it was dark again. If there was a light on in the hall, he couldn't see it. "Professor Connors, Dean of the Law School."

Albert mouthed the words, "The Law School." He was aware of it; an intimidating Secret Society . . . like the Masons or the PTA. Lawyers, his mother had said after losing a boundary dispute with a neighbor, were 'practitioners of dark arts who lick sustenance from the mucousy fringe at the edge of the Underworld . . . where they spend their holidays.'

Mother - at heart a Maine housewife, despite her Brahmin upbringing - would have found it difficult to edit her opinions, had she ever tried.

He'd seen emissaries of the Law School at faculty meetings; older men who always looked elsewhere when they shook your hand; younger men who seemed to be driving fast German sports cars, even when they were sitting still in the conference room, smiling.

"Goldman?"

"Goldstein . . . Perlman, Quimby and . . . " Tewksbury felt as if he was reciting a nursery story about four dwarves. The last gentleman caught on the lump at the back of his throat. He coughed him up. "Bowles. They're supposed to be the best. Reputable."

"Reputable," Albert repeated. "What do they say?"

"About what?"

"About your being framed."

Tewksbury's remaining confidence shrunk like a wool sweater in a sprinkler. "It's hard to say. I told them all about it . . . the phone call. I don't know what they think. They don't talk in straight lines." Pause. Sigh. "I don't think they believe me."

Albert imagined himself in Tewksbury's place. He was sitting at the end of a long table in a windowless room. The table was lined with young lawyers wearing manicured expressions that all shifted in unison. First-degree concern. Shift. Second-degree concern. Shift. Worry. Shift. Mild amusement. Shift. They parenthesized in Latin and refused to commit to so much as the color of their coffee. He shivered.

"Shouldn't they believe you?"

"l don't know," said Tewksbury. "You'd think so, but . . . I don't understand the whole business, frankly. I feel like I'm in the middle of the Nazca plain . . . lines stretching off to infinity in every direction. There must be a pattern somewhere. But it's only discernible from an impossible altitude."

His eyes brimmed with tears.

At the moment it occurred to Albert that a jury would no more convict him than it would a puppy in an orphan's arms. If he could just hold that expression.

"I didn't do anything, Albert! How can it seem I was there at the time of the murder, when I wasn't? How can it seem as though I poisoned him, when I didn't?" His brows were arched upward, like hairy little fists clasped in supplication. "I didn't do it, Albert. How can it seem like I did?"

The building analogy came again to mind. It was nearly reassembled. They were putting in the carpet and the bath fixtures. Pretty soon they'd be turning the keys over to the new owners, who shouldn't mind the tapping within the walls. Seems they'd built an archaeologist into the place. But his room had no windows. No doors. Not to worry, there was never meant to be a way out.

"What is Golderberg doing?"

"Golderberg?"

"Your lawyer."

"Goldstein," Tewksbury corrected. "He's dead. They just kept the name on. They're all dead, as far as I know. Like Sears and Roebuck."

Albert wondered if Mr. Dunkin' was dead as well. "Who's your lawyer, then?"

"I don't have a lawyer," Tewksbury replied. "I've got an ice sculpture named Melissa Bjork."

"A woman?" Albert was cognizant of women. They played violins and flutes. His sister had played the saxophone, but she was exceptional. His mother wasn't musical, so he wasn't sure what she did, besides live in Florida. But she wasn't a lawyer.

"I thought so at first," said Tewksbury. "She sure looks like one. She's got . . . ." he cupped his hands a unnatural distance from his chest. His eyes brightened for a moment. Albert knew Tewksbury was a womanizer; he'd been subjected to any number of his monologues on the subject. They made Albert uncomfortable, but seemed to fill a need for Tewksbury. "She doesn't believe me, either." Tewksbury lowered his hands, and his expectations. "She doesn't care."

"'They said you could get out on bail," said Albert. He'd forgotten overhearing that. He wasn't sure what it was, but "out" had a positive ring to it.

"Out!" said Tewksbury, rising quickly. "Out to what? People pointing at me and talking about me? Reporters in my face twenty-four hours a day? No, thanks." He looked around the room. "That would be hell. This is just purgatory. I'll just stick it out. It's warm and I eat a lot better than you do."

There was another silence. A sudden burning sensation reminded Albert that he'd tucked a lit cigarette behind his ear. He removed it and ground its remains into a peanut-butter jar lid that the state had provided for the purpose. "What do they do . . . lawyers? How do they find out what happened?"

Tewksbury shook his head and rubbed his red eyes with the heels of his hands. "I don't know. I guess they ask questions. Frankly my understanding of the profession doesn't extend much beyond what you see on TV." That explained why Albert's understanding didn't extend at all. "I don't know if she does anything but put in time. She looks at me like . . . I get the feeling she goes home and takes a bath in disinfectant after she leaves here," he said. "I don't think she believes me, either. Nobody does."

"Does she ask questions?"

The beeper on the guard's watch went off. The visit was over. Tewksbury got up from the table. "I guess so. How else would she find out anything?" He turned as the guard led him from the room. "I've been forgotten, Albert."

At the trial Albert learned that "truth," as defined by the law, was a much more abstract and slippery thing than he'd imagined; a distant and ragged relation to his concept of right and wrong. In a court of law, nothing was absolutely true, but anything might be legal, or illegal.

Ambiguity was the byword. He wondered how it was possible to "tell the truth, the whole truth, and nothing but the truth" if you weren't allowed to finish a sentence.

For the most part the proceedings were a blur to Albert. In the end a few important things stood out, and they painted a bleak picture for Tewksbury. The infamous letter was admitted in evidence, the heat of its scholarly indignation parboiling Tewksbury where he sat, especially in the eyes of the men and women of the jury, mostly blue-collar workers from the factory side of town who had little fondness for academics in general and whose patience seemed strained by discussion of the finer points of Etruscan civilization.

There was a lot of eye-rolling and head-shaking.

Albert, standing in line at the water cooler during a recess, was made sharply aware of the popular consensus by the conversation of two men in front of him.

Man number one, a burly blond who stood an arm's length taller than Albert: "Nossir. If you're gonna kill somebody you do it with a shotgun, or a tire iron. That's what I'd do." He took a long, loud sip.

Albert wondered if most people were like that, perpetually prepared to murder.

Man number two nodded. He was a little shorter than Albert, and roughly as tall as he was wide. His cap matched his bright orange hooded sweatshirt, and the ensemble was set off to great effect by black-and-red plaid wool pants and brown boots. "Sulfites." he said disdainfully. "It'd take one've them eggheads to come up with a stunt like that."

"Etruscans," said man number one with a wag of the head as he rose from the fountain. Water dribbled down his beard. He wiped at it with his sleeve.

"Etruscans," echoed man number two, pressing his lips to the spigot. "Who the hell cares?"

Concerning the fight in the hallway with Glenly, three or four coeds were called to witness, each wording their testimony with a mind to how it would look in the papers back home. Scrapbook material. Two young men acknowledged the scuffle. Not really a fight. A slap or two. A sprained wrist and a bloody nose. Nothing broken. No vital organs displaced. Mostly yelling. Comes of being more accustomed to backstabbing than frontal attack.

But there was no doubt who started it.

One thing, though, struck Albert as curious: nobody eulogized Professor Glenly. No one testified about the dead man's services to humanity in general, or the community in particular. Even the school had only the requisite to say. The same as it says for indifferent janitors and cafeteria cooks upon retirement after long service.

Several people, Albert among them, were called to testify on behalf of Tewksbury. For the most part, though, their testimony as to Tewksbury's character was so tepid and equivocal it would have been better if they'd stayed home. Albert wished he'd stayed home. What could he say about Tewksbury? Only that he was sure he hadn't killed anyone. They wouldn't let him say that.

Maybe Tiglath-Pilesir III, Akenaten, or another of Tewksbury's friends would have spoken well of him, but they didn't show up, and nobody suggested they be subpoenaed.

In the end it was proved – at least to the satisfaction of a jury of his peers - that Tewksbury had murdered his academic nemesis, a crime all the more sinister since it was not one of passion, of archaeological ardor, but of cunning. Planning. "Councils held in the secret hours with the changeling shadows of private torment and jealousy," in the prosecutor's words.

Glenly had been killed with sulfites, a common food additive to which a small portion of the population, Glenly among them, is deathly allergic. His allergy was no secret on campus. He'd raised a stink about their use in the cafeteria, and succeeded in eliminating them from the kitchen.

It was effectively demonstrated that Tewksbury had access to an abundant supply of sulfites in the lab where he had recently been working with student-chemists to develop a preservative for what he called "archaeological undies," organic artifacts too delicate to withstand the debilitating effects of exposure to light and air.

So, in the end, Tewksbury was found guilty "beyond a reasonable doubt." Nevertheless, Albert had his doubts.

They'd set aside a separate day to announce the sentence, which Albert thought strange; as if the judge hadn't entertained the possibility during the long weeks of the trial. In the end the going rate for Glenly's life was set at twenty years in Walpole State Penitentiary, with the possibility of parole in seven. Payment to begin immediately.

The sentence was much more lenient than beheading or burning at the stake, which Albert had anticipated as the natural consequence for taking someone's life. Then again, Tewksbury was innocent. Albert was sure of it. Maybe the jury had taken that into account.

It was dark by the time it was all over. A storm that had been threatening all day had worked itself into a frenzy. Albert took a bus back to the school and struck off across the common.

Snow had been falling on Albert's neck for ten minutes before he realized it. A few icy daggers traced his spine. He shivered and turned his collar to the storm. Loud mirthless music thumped through the ancient walls of one of the dorms, like a demon's heartbeat.

His eyes were drawn to one of the lighted windows, the shades of which were closed. Human-shaped shadows threw themselves around with the abandon of the Israelites at the foot of Sinai.

He stood still and looked around the campus. Everything was where it was supposed to be. The snow drifted in the same places it always drifted. Naked veins of ivy held the old brick buildings to earth and, over the edge of the world, its half-shaded windows lit in a self-satisfied smirk, the Law School leered malevolently.

Everything was the same, but something had changed; something fundamental to Albert's foreshortened under-standing of things. How could the world absorb the terrible knowledge of Tewksbury's imprisonment and continue on as if nothing had happened? Shouldn't everything come to a halt until the truth had been got to? Who would keep up with all the latest developments in Ancient History?

Albert released a captive sigh of steam which the wind seized with angry fingers and tore to pieces. Snow had collected on his glasses, obscuring everything from sight. He didn't wipe them off. He bent his head to the wind and let habit lead him home.

Chapter Three

Albert had corn and Nestle's Quik for supper; the corn still frozen, like a popsicle, the Quik dry, straight from the can. As he ate he searched the rubble for a phone book. A xylophone came to light, a sweater he'd forgotten entirely. A pair of socks he'd neglected to put in the dryer that had somehow doubled in size with something fragrant and fuzzy. Other things turned up, too: a desiccated pizza, a few records, several unfinished symphonies, but no phone book.

"Thank you for using AT&T, may I help you?"

The last time Albert had called the operator it was a woman and she just said "operator." Now it was a man, and he gave a speech. Albert fought the urge to hang up.

"I'd like to speak to Miss Melissa Bjork," he said.

"You want Directory Assistance," said the operator.

"Yes, please," said Albert.

"That number is 555-1212."

There was a click on the line and Albert was alone again. He held the phone out and looked at it. "555," he whispered.

He dialed "0" again. This time it was a woman. There was hope. "I'd like a telephone number, please."

The operator interrupted. "Information is 555-1212," she said.

Subconsciously Albert affixed the face of the lady news-caster to the operator's voice.

"555?" he stammered.

"1212," said the operator then clicked and disappeared.

Albert dialed quickly; he had no memory for numbers.

"Information. What city please?" It was a woman again. There were at least two left.

"Ashburn?"

"May I help you?"

Albert wondered if he'd accidentally tapped into an audio loop of some kind. He plodded bravely on. "I'd like the number of Melissa Bjork, please."

"Have you looked in your phone book?" said the operator. He was being scolded. He didn't want to tell her he couldn't find the phone book. There might be repercussions.

"I'm blind," he said, closing his eyes.

"Oh, I'm Sorry," said the operator. "What was the name again?" He gave her the name, she gave him the number. She began telling him about special phone company services for the blind, but he had to hang up or he'd forget the number.

His call was met with hesitation. Yes, of course she remembered him, but she didn't understand why he wanted to see her; the trial was over, there was no more she could do. Within five minutes, though, Albert's gentle persistence had piqued her curiosity.

She would see him at her office first thing in the morning. But he wanted to see her now. Another five minutes wore the edge off her resistance. She had a collection of his recordings, even an old LP of the famous Carnegie Hall concert. How dangerous could a musical genius be?

"I'll meet you at the Dunkin' Donuts on Main Street," she said. Albert was relieved; that's where he did most of his shopping. "Fifteen minutes?"

Fifteen minutes later they were sitting in a booth over coffee and doughnuts. Snow was melting from their hair and clothes, making puddles everywhere. He was befuddled. She was amused.

Albert suffered over small talk. Seeing the pain on his face, Miss Bjork quickly came to the point. "Why did you want to see me?"

At the moment Albert hated only one thing more than small talk, and that was a direct question. He choked on his coffee. Miss Bjork smiled benignly.

"It's Tewksbury," said Albert finally. "They found him guilty."

He looked at her as if expecting to find her surprised by the news. His eyes betrayed a childlike confusion, deep and genuine.

Miss Bjork, whom hard experience had prepared for anything, was not prepared for Albert.

"I know," she said, looking down at her coffee cup. She felt Albert's eyes on her, burning with questions he didn't know how to frame. A spring of words bubbled to her lips, as if they'd been rehearsed. "I did all I could," she said into her coffee. "The evidence against him was just . . . overwhelming."

"But he didn't do it."

Miss Bjork's training overtook her. She'd faced recrimination from a client's family and friends before. She'd minored in inscrutability in law school. "What do you mean, he didn't do it? How do you know?" Why couldn't she look him in the eye? Was it the elephant of fame that loomed behind him, nearly crowding the air from the room but of which he seemed so unaware? She flushed. She never flushed. Fortunately he was looking out the window. "Do you know something?"

Albert kept looking out the window. "Yes," he said. "He didn't kill Professor Glenly. Tewksbury wouldn't do that."

Miss Bjork's whole body sighed. Even her hair relaxed. 'Tewksbury wouldn't do that.' No new evidence. Just feelings. She reached across the table and laid her hand gently on his arm. "Albert may I call you Albert?" He didn't reply. "Professor . . . I understand how you feel." A dreadful thought occurred to her. Was it possible that Tewksbury and . . . ? She withdrew her hand. No. Not Tewksbury. Not after the way he'd come on to her during their first interview. But . . . what about this man? This quiet, nervous, extraordinary man who seemed unable to say what was on his mind? Not all feelings are reciprocal, after all. "I think I know how you feel," she amended. "Sometimes it's hard to believe that those close to us," she tested the ice, "those we care for, are capable of desperate things."

"Care for?" said Albert. It was such an unlikely notion, he said it again. "Care for?"

Miss Bjork tilted her head a little. "Love?"

That was even more unlikely. "Love?" Albert repeated. "Who?"

"Tewksbury."

Albert looked from the window to the table, his heavy black brows tangled in thought. "I don't think anybody did. I mean, his father did, I suppose."

She wanted to make it easier for him. "I mean you."

The expression that spread across Albert's face was a billboard for confusion. He didn't know what she was talking about. She wasn't sure why she was relieved. She backed off the ice. "Why are you so interested in the case?" she asked.

Albert deliberated too long, as he always did. He didn't know why he was so interested. Someone should be. "I know him," he said finally. "He would come up to my place and . . . talk about the school. And drink my beer."

"He said you were friends."

The words had a jarring effect on Albert. He had never tried to define his relationship with Tewksbury. Friendship? He didn't think so. He had no friends that he knew of, and Tewksbury was another of the many who weren't. They knew each other, that was all.

"He wouldn't have done something like that," Albert said in lieu of what he was thinking. Powdered sugar sifted from lips to his trousers. "I know him personally."

Finally Bjork had the key; here was a genuine hermit - a brilliant, breathing, doughnut-eating anachronism - whose existence was circumscribed by a sort of musical cocoon. It quickly became evident that the school sheltered him, its most precious asset.

Early in her research into Tewksbury's case, it had struck her as curious that a composer and performer of Albert's renown had settled on Smethhurst College, until she turned up the fact it had been his father's alma mater. It was at his mother's suggestion - some said insistence - that he had turned a deaf ear to cacophonous, purse-rattling overtures from clamoring battalions of the world's most prestigious universities and schools of music from Vienna to Sydney.

He didn't seem to mind ending up at Smethhurst. In fact, he scarcely seemed aware. Though tiny, Smethhurst could lay claim to well-deserved academic prestige but, more importantly, it offered the reclusive Albert what no other institution could - a womb that he could crawl into.

Suddenly life comes along and shines a harsh light up that tight little academic cervix and the world reaches in with both hands and drags him out into the maelstrom; of course it would be inconceivable for one so cloistered to imagine someone of his own professional acquaintance capable of premeditated murder. That explained it.

"It was Tewksbury who told me Glenly was dead," Albert said.

"I remember your testimony."

So did Albert. He'd never been on a witness stand before. He'd never been in court. He seemed to say all the wrong things, like always. Usually no one paid attention, but they did in court. The memory made him cringe. Most memories made him cringe.

They were sitting in the No Smoking section. Wraiths of fragrant smoke wafted from the counter area. Albert had forgotten his cigarettes. His lungs ached. He inhaled deeply. Miss Bjork's eyes were watering. "He didn't act like someone who'd just killed somebody."

"Who knows what a murderer acts like?" said Bjork philosophically.

It was a rhetorical question. She wasn't prepared for the response.

"Cigarettes," said Albert.

When she looked at him his eyes were riveted on hers, but they were looking inward. She shifted uncomfortably in her seat.

"What?"

"All he could think about was cigarettes."

"What do you mean?"

"When he came to my apartment all he could think about was cigarettes," Albert explained. "He'd quit smoking. Somebody who's planning to murder someone doesn't quit smoking." Albert was sure of that. He'd tried to quit smoking once. He could certainly imagine committing murder in that state, but planning such a thing was out of the question.

"Did he ask for a cigarette?"

"No. He took one. He asked me for a light, but I don't think he would have smoked it. He liked teasing himself."

"'How long ago ... how long before the murder ... did he quit?"

"I don't know. A week?" He nodded. "A long time."

"You didn't give him a light?"

An unfathomable trace of amusement visited the edges of Albert's mouth. "No."

It was Miss Bjork's turn to be jarred. It wasn't evidence, of course. But psychologically it was profound. Would someone who was contemplating murder quit smoking? Would someone who had committed murder "tease" himself with a cigarette?

"Besides," said Albert, "Tewksbury won the argument."

"What argument?"

"The one everybody was talking about at the trial. Everybody said they had an argument."

"A fight."

"But it started as an argument. About Etruscans."

"We went over that at the trial."

"Not really," Albert said quietly. "You just talked about the fight. Nobody mentioned that Tewksbury won the argument, all that about Etruscans. Someone wrote a paper that proved he was right."

Pause and effect. "Steidigger." Miss Bjork wondered who was in the cocoon, and whether the light was shining in or out.

"Winners don't kill losers, do they?" said Albert.

Miss Bjork stood up and threw her coat around her. "Why didn't you say any of this at the trial?"

Albert looked up at her. She felt her hair tense again. Those eyes.

"In court . . . they only let you answer what you're asked. I was waiting for someone to ask."

The phone rang in the middle of the night. Albert sat bolt upright as if someone had spilled herring on him. He blinked and picked at his ears. The ringing happened again. He blinked again, cocked his head like a bemused puppy, and sat cross-legged with one foot caught in the sheets. Eventually the regularity of the rings reminded him of the telephone which couldn't have had more than a ring or two left in it by the time it was disinterred. No one called Albert at night. No one called Albert in the daytime. No one ever called Albert.

A musical emergency?

The phone was cold on his ear. "Hello?"

"Damn you!" said the caller. A woman.

Albert squinted, but it didn't help his comprehension. He frisked the bed for his glasses. "I, h'mm." He didn't know what to say. Even a conventional greeting would have been challenging enough at this hour.

She said it again, with somewhat less vehemence. He found his glasses. "Did I do something? I don't understand. Is this Miss Bjork?" He knew it was. He knew voices.

"I haven't been able to sleep, thanks to you. So I didn't think it was fair you should." She sounded tired. "I've got a confession to make."

He waited. She hesitated. "I shouldn't." He waited. "I thought he was guilty all along."

Albert's glasses dangled from the corner of his mouth. "That's what he said."

"Who said?"

"Tewksbury."

She was surprised; she prided herself on inscrutability, that quality lawyers so prize in one another. "He knew?"

Silence in the affirmative. Maybe it shouldn't bother her, but it did.

"Cigarettes," she said.

He brushed some sleep from his eyes and sucked on his glasses. She draped some random thoughts on the silence and studied them at arm's length. "I don't know if he's innocent," she said. "But ... "

"You don't know he's guilty."

"I don't know he's guilty."

Albert's tongue tasted awful. He wanted to evict it from his mouth. He uncrinkled the butt end of a cigarette from the ashtray and lit it.

She continued. "It sickened me to have to defend him. I figured everything he said was a lie, until you said that about the cigarette." She jumped to the defense of her conscience. "That doesn't mean I let him down. I did everything I could think of to get him off."

Albert probably shouldn't have been struck by yet another oddity in the odd world of law, but he was. "Even though you thought he was guilty?" he said, still mistaking law for justice.

For a long time the only sound was the soft hiss of the open phone line.

Albert put his glasses on. "What happens now? Will they let him out of jail?"

Ms. Bjork wasn't sure what to make of the music teacher's naïveté. "It's not that easy," she said. "We've got to come up with some solid evidence. The fact that he'd quit smoking doesn't automatically exonerate him."

"It would if the judge smokes," Albert suggested.

"I'm afraid not," Miss Bjork said. "We need something a lot more concrete than that."

Albert couldn't imagine anything more concrete. "Like what?"

"I don't know," she said. "If he's really innocent, we have to find someone else with a reason for wanting Glenly dead."

"Someone else?"

"What do you know about Glenly's lifestyle?"

Albert had hardly been aware of the man's existence. "Nothing," he said flatly. "I'm not . . . I don't know many . . . "

"You need to find out."

Albert took his glasses off and looked at them closely. He wasn't hearing properly. "Find out?" he repeated.

"Chat up your colleagues. Get them talking about Glenly. About Tewksbury. You'll be able to get a good idea if anybody had something against him or something to gain by his death."

Albert protested. "But isn't that your job?"

"I'm a lawyer, not a detective," said Miss Bjork.

"And I play piano!"

"Besides," she continued, ignoring him to City Hall perfection, "you're less likely to arouse suspicion than a stranger would. People will talk more freely to you."

Albert could think of nothing half as suspicious as him going around "chatting people up." There was something unnatural in the very suggestion. Some eternal balance would be upset. Surely Albert would be. He was honing the words of his rebuttal when she terminated the conversation.

"I feel better already," she said. Albert's lips moved like a fish's but nothing came out. "Tell me as soon as you find out anything," she concluded, "and if it's something backed by solid evidence, I'll get the police on it." Sigh. "I think I'll be able to sleep now. Thanks. Good night, Professor." Click.

Having deposited her demons on his doorstep, Miss Bjork vanished into the ether. She would sleep better; Albert would sleep no more.

Only one thing terrified Albert more than talking to people; the thought of talking to them. He hung up his glasses, put the phone in his slipper, and laid down. For a long time he stared holes in the ceiling, unable to fend off the memory of another night like this.

Early in his career, The New England Conservatory of Music had invited him to lecture and give a recital of original work. Lecture? The shock inverted Albert's entire nervous system. He couldn't imagine what hat his name had been picked from, but they assured him he had been selected on purpose. By committee. That partway explained it. Still, he felt there was some misunderstanding. He knew that when he showed up they would say "You're not the Albert we wanted. You must have got his mail by mistake."

Perhaps they'd turn him in; there was a penalty for opening other people's mail. "We don't want you." It would be high school athletics all over again. Nobody wanted Albert except to play the piano.

Four days before the lecture he had lost his appetite. Three days before the lecture he lost control of the index finger of his left hand and his right eye started twitching. He lost his lunch. He lost his nerve. Nevertheless, thanks to the school - which had apparently entered into some dark, Satanic agreement with the annoyingly persistent Huffy - he found himself alone on stage at the appointed time. The auditorium was packed to the rafters . . . with people. They applauded, even though he hadn't done anything yet. When were they going to realize their mistake?

He mumbled some words into a microphone. People laughed and applauded, as if he'd said something funny; on purpose. His face felt like a voodoo doll, tingling with pins. He felt faint. He said something else. Something about music. He couldn't hear what it was; his ears were plugged with his heart. He couldn't lecture. The words he'd been rehearsing all week long sounded like a foreign language in his brain. His fingers went to the keys for comfort. His lover was at hand. He closed his eyes and began to play. The music was alive, a river of melodic mathematics in which he immersed himself. It surged across the keys, washing the world away.

He played as long as the music came. Not a note of it had ever been heard before. Not by him. Not by anyone. The audience tingled in the presence of raw creative power. They were baptized.

No one coughed. No one stirred. Some wept. They were spellbound. Dumbfounded. Albert didn't notice. He only became aware of the audience again after he'd finished playing. The last note trailed off for fifty-eight seconds, embraced by silence. Then somebody started clapping.

He realized he wasn't in his apartment.

As the wave of adulation intensified, so did his awareness of himself. He managed a feeble bow, raced from the stage, left the auditorium, and hid behind the tinted window of the limousine that whisked him to the hotel. It was always like that after he played.

As lectures go, well, it hadn't been one, had it? For years he'd been haunted by the notion that, one day, the phone would ring, or there would be a knock at the door. Someone would have tumbled to the fact that the advertised lecture had never taken place. They'd want their money back, and he didn't know where it was.

But tomorrow he would have to talk to people. And he wouldn't have a piano.

Albert got up early. He filled the sink with freezing water and stuck his head in. The resulting shock usually got the music started. Not this time. When he opened his eyes the cold went straight to his brain, etching there a portrait of Tewksbury, innocent Tewksbury, languishing in jail, his cell peopled with mummies and littered with broken artifacts. No musical instruments among them.

He put his glasses on and looked in the mirror. The water streamed down his face. There was a lot of white in his hair now. He hadn't realized that. He hadn't shaved in days. He grimaced. His teeth were yellow with nicotine. Below the purple whisker line on his neck, his body was chalk white, almost transparent. His veins showed through. He was scrawny. Anemic. For the first time in a long time ... maybe ever ... he was embarrassed. This is what Miss Bjork had seen. That bothered him. He wasn't sure why. That bothered him, too.

Albert was usually late to class. Customarily he would go directly to the board, or the piano and, without directly addressing the semi-circle of students, begin thinking aloud in a sort of musical stream-of-consciousness. If someone asked him a question he would turn, eyes on the floor, and, pacing back and forth, exhaust his knowledge or opinions on the subject. The process often took the whole period.

Albert's presence had allowed the school the luxury of selecting from among the best and brightest. They were not insensitive to his genius and were economical in their interruptions.

Today Albert was early; meaning not nearly as late as usual. He was clean-shaven. He'd had a haircut and his skin was almost ruddy with washing. He wore his suit; the tweed outfit his mother had bought him for high school graduation, the one he wore to every formal occasion other than those requiring a tux, which the school rented for him. It had gotten a size or two small, but that's not what the students noticed. Nor the wide paisley tie or the white socks.

It was a suit.

There are places in the world that devout people dream of; places to which they must travel at least once in a lifetime, though it cost them all they own. The true pilgrim is not content to stop at the gates of the City of David, to cease walking with Mecca in sight, or stand at the foot of some Iberian hillside while others crawl to the summit on bloody hands and knees, achieving sanctification. Such a place was Albert's class. Its pilgrims were talented young musicians from around the world. Here, they were anointed. Here they were in the presence of the Gift.

Albert hadn't a clue.

It is too much to say Albert's class that day was normal. That would be impossible. Wonderful things would take place; there would be miracles. But not as many as usual. It wasn't just the clothes. Something was different about Albert. Speculation tended toward romance, since there was no overt sign of a religious awakening.

After class, as the students left the room, he stopped the last two, one of each sex, shut the door, and asked them to sit down.

"I'd like to ask you a question," he said. The brevity of the words belied the difficulty with which they were formed. He'd been phrasing them for fifty minutes. "Professor Glenly is dead."

The girl was a flutist. The boy, a pianist with a lazy left hand. They looked sideways at each other. Perhaps he should rephrase the question.

"I really didn't know him. What was he like?"

"Slime," said the pianist. The flutist said nothing.

"Did you take any of his classes?" Interrogation wasn't so hard, after all.

No, he didn't, but he'd heard. The girl hadn't had him, either, but ... she confessed hesitantly, he'd made passes at a friend of hers. "Not just passes ... with words," said the girl. "You know what I mean?" Even Albert understood. The study of history seemed to excite the testosterone.

"He was always after someone," she said. "A lot of the girls thought it was just in fun. Flirting, you know? I guess it's all right to say, now."

Albert was struggling to get his knee on the next step. The bell rang in the hall.

"Look what happened to Joanne Alter," the boy said as he collected his books.

There was something familiar in the name. "Alter?" said Albert.

"Professor Alter," said the girl. "Biology?"

"Joanne's his daughter. She was a junior, and Glenly got her... "

"You don't know that," the girl protested.

Got her what? Flowers? Candy? "Got her what?" Albert asked.

"Pregnant," said the boy with a defiant sneer at his classmate.

Pollyanna had just arrived at Peyton Place. "Pregnant?" echoed Albert, "with a baby?"

"That's why she changed schools last year," the boy continued.

"You don't know what you're talking about," said the girl. "She hated Glenly."

"He was all over her!"

"That doesn't mean she liked it. Besides, her father would've killed ... " The refrigerator door swung open and the light came on. "Oh, come on, Professor. You don't think .. . *Tewksbury* killed Glenly."

"Is that what this is all about?" said the boy, standing. "That's old news, Professor. It's a done thing."

After they left, Albert felt oddly triumphant. His very first interview had turned up a possible suspect. He did feel, though, that he was lacking something in interrogatory style. What did detectives do? His brain rifled through the contents of its "Detective" file, and turned up only two examples: The Hardy Boys and Sherlock Holmes.

A cursory search of the school library came up blank on the *Hardy Boys*, despite boasting several million volumes. Nevertheless, they had a copy of *The Complete Adventures of Sherlock Holmes*. Ten hours later they wanted to close the library. They insisted. It never occurred to Albert to take the book home. He tucked it back on the shelf. He'd read *A Study in Scarlet, The Sign of Four*, and all the short stories from *Scandal in Bohemia* through *The Musgrave Ritual*. The lights went off as he stepped into the night.

The stories all began with an impossible crime for which Holmes always found an equally impossible solution. Mysteries solved by an enigma. Albert gained nothing by osmosis. He did, however, stumble upon the fact that he and Holmes had something in common: they were both designed to do one thing to the exclusion of all else.

One other thing was clear: successful detection lay in observation, an art that was as foreign to Albert as skydiving. He walked to the bus terminal, bought some candy from a vending machine, and sat down to observe. Try as he might, he couldn't determine a person's profession from his attire. It helped if they wore uniforms, but who knew what uniforms signified?

Failing this, he began to study faces. Hands. Motions—expressions, and gestures—to the point where he could perceive someone who was late for something at twenty paces. Beyond that, if there was an ax-murderer among the patrons at the bus terminal, they needn't have feared detection by Albert. He did enjoy watching people, though. That was a surprise.

It was late by the time he got home, and he still had no idea what to do next. He took off his suit, put the flimsy plastic dry-cleaner bag over it again, and hung it up. The suit hadn't been dry-cleaned in over ten years, but it could take another decade's wear at the present rate before laundering was necessary. Besides, the bag had held up well.

In his T-shirt and boxer shorts he banged around the darkened kitchen, preparing supper. He had meant to buy a light bulb, but they didn't sell them at Dunkin' Donuts. In the past he had simply transferred bulbs from room to room. Now there was only one left, by the bed.

He'd have to move soon.

He grabbed a bag, some cans and jars from the refrigerator, and took them to the other room to see what supper was going to be: half a can of beer, flat, some frozen chocolate-chip cookie dough, and pickled onions.

As he ate, he recalled his conversation with the two students. What would Holmes have made of it? Pregnant girl, irate father . . . and the guilty party? Dead. Even more incriminating, Alter was a biology professor. He'd know all about sulfites; and he'd have access to them. It was all there: motive, method, and . . . opportunity? That wouldn't have been a problem.

Perhaps he had learned something from Holmes after all. Something uncomfortable suddenly occurred to Albert: in order to prove Tewksbury innocent, he'd have to prove someone else guilty. If Alter did kill Glenly, he'd have to go to jail. What would happen to his daughter and her child?

What would it be like to have your grandfather in jail for the murder of your father?

Albert felt an overwhelming urge to sit down at the piano; to escape into his music, bathe himself in it. Life had always been a dilemma to him. Crime and passion and intrigue only made it impossibly complex. Everything affected someone. What was good for one person was bad for another; what would help one would harm another and everyone had other people, other lives in orbit around them who - in turn, had lives in orbit around them. Soon everyone would have to be affected, somehow.

The bare bulb tossed shadows on the wall. The farther from the light, the more distorted the shadows became. There was an analogy in there somewhere, but Albert was too tired to dig it out. He fell asleep in the chair, the essence of pickled onions and cigarette smoke wafting through his brain, giving an edge of immediacy to his dreams.

Chapter Four

The next morning, following his new routine of personal grooming, Albert put on his other tie . . . the white one. It would be impossible to say what he thought of himself as he walked across the common, but he held his face right out front, his hands thrust purposefully in his pockets. His step - yellow woolen socks in black patent-leather shoes - was jaunty, and he cut an irresistible figure against the ice and snow. He wanted only directions to the nearest windmill.

The recent change in Albert was the topic of no little speculation in the faculty lounge. The tropical fish of indeterminate species might have crawled out of their tank in the corner and taken up hairdressing at reduced rates and attracted less attention. Some things just didn't change. Yet there he stood in the doorway . . . suit, tie, matching socks. For the first time in his life, Albert was making a fashion statement of sorts. What, exactly, he might be saying was anybody's guess, but he was saying it unequivocally.

Conversation dissolved like venom in water. Everyone watched him through their eyebrows and over their glasses. Academic surveillance.

Albert had never been in the lounge before. He bobbed and nodded in the doorway for a few seconds, prompting an anthropologist in the group to launch into a monologue on the mating habits of albatross in the Galapagos. Albert grinned at people whose eyes he met. Pretending to recognize them, he nodded harder.

As he crossed to the coffee urn, the ponderous gears of conversation creaked and groaned to life again, resolving to a steady hum by the time he'd added his forth or fifth sugar. He smiled inwardly; blending in wasn't as difficult as he'd imagined. He was the soul of anonymity. He helped himself to a powdered doughnut.

"You were a friend of his, weren't you?"

Albert spilled hot coffee on his hand, but was too busy choking on his doughnut to notice. Someone slapped him soundly on the back, fixing the foreign object a little more securely in his throat. "Of course you were. Sorry, Maestro," said the Slapper. "Didn't mean to startle you."

Albert managed to get the doughnut down the right hole finally and casually rearranged a small puddle of coffee with wax paper while he caught his breath. Sweeping up after social disaster was not unfamiliar to Albert. He hated being surprised. He hated the fact that everything surprised him. And he hated the silliness of acting as if nothing surprising had happened.

"No, not really," he sputtered. "It wasn't your fault, I was just . . ." He turned to the speaker. The raspy basso profundo combined with the thrashing he'd just undergone had inclined Albert to suppose his tormentor was a man. He was, therefore, further disoriented to find it was a woman; very large and squat with a tiny head that seemed pressed down into the mass of flesh like the cherry on a sundae. Oddly enough, he had some remote sense of having met her before. His brain began a frantic search of its coffee-stained archives in an effort to turn up the name that went with it.

"It's the artificial sweetener," said the woman. Miss . . . Miss . . . He almost had it. Agatha? Persephone? "It's a depressant, you know. Lord knows what else it does. Deadly to marine algae, no doubt. They put it in everything these days." Seeing Albert had nearly recovered, she peered into his contorted face with exaggerated concern. "Better?"

He nodded. Who was this woman? He intentionally coughed and sputtered a few more times, like an airplane in a stall. Bertha? Melody? Juliet? Juliet! English! She was Geraldine Abercrombie, English Lit. He nosed over and the horizon spiraled into sight. "I'm well, Miss Abercrombie," he said. He'd remembered! He was ecstatic. Who knew what other nuggets lay hidden in his memory?

"Moodie," said the late Miss Abercrombie.

Then who was Miss Abercrombie?

"You've seen this, I suppose?" said Miss Moodie. She had an English accent, but it wasn't real. Albert knew accents. It was a familiar affectation in academic circles, music circles, too, come to think of it. She thrust a newspaper at him and indicated an article on the front page.

Albert had developed a revulsion for newspapers. He held it by the corners, as if had recently been extracted from a birdcage, and let it fall open. The same old photograph of Tewksbury stared dully from the page. Why didn't they use a more recent picture? They'd taken thousands at the trial.

The arrangement of letters that captioned the picture went straight to Albert's stomach. "I.Q. Murderer Attempts Suicide in Cell." His knees seemed to give way. He tottered to a chair and eased himself into it. The newspaper fell to the floor.

"I'm so sorry," Miss Moodie proclaimed as she picked up the paper. "Seems I've given you a double dose." She refilled his coffee cup and brought it to him. "I assumed you'd heard."

"No," said Albert. "Is he . . . ?"

"Oh, he'll survive," said Miss Moodie, folding the paper. "I doubt if he really wanted to . . . " she continued, filling in the blank with her eyes. "I expect he just wanted some attention. He must be very . . . yes. I should think that's what it was."

Moodie had the habit, common among academic women somewhat beyond middle age, of failing to finish sentences, leaving the listener to complete the thought for himself. True or false? Multiple choice? Life was a pop quiz. Albert hadn't done well in English.

"When?"

"Last night. He's at the hospital now."

Miss Moodie waited for the music teacher to ask the modus operandi. He didn't. "Razor," she volunteered. He looked at her blankly. His eyes were still thick with tears from choking on the doughnut. She nodded in mute agreement with something she imagined in his expression.

"Razor?"

She slit her wrist with her fingernail. "Lord knows where he got it. I guess in prison ... well ... " That sentence, too, picked up its lantern and tottered off in search of an ending.

General conversation among the faculty had taken a decidedly Albertian turn in consequence of his choking and shock at the news of Tewksbury's suicide attempt. Art class had convened and everyone was drawing conclusions. Curious fellow, this former prodigy. Must give the Administration a great deal to overlook in their determination to boast a genius in residence.

"Men don't normally do that," Miss Moodie said. "They jump from great heights or shoot themselves. Hari-kari, that sort of thing. Much more dramatic. Women slit their wrists. Take pills. Stick their heads in ovens. It leaves lots of time to be found before it's too late. Sympathy factor, don't you know."

Albert didn't respond except to look at her as if she was a visitor from a distant and frightening planet.

"It's all in Agatha Christie," continued Miss Moodie, determined to supply the questions that never came with all the answers she could muster. "He was going to be shipped to Walpole tomorrow. Must have been depressed."

"I'll have to go see him," Albert said at last.

"He's at St. Mary's, I think," Miss Moodie offered, sifting through the article. "Here it is. Yes. St. Mary's." She read on. "But he's in Intensive Care. You won't be allowed to see him till he's out of there, I shouldn't think. I'm sure, in fact."

Albert felt impotent. The situation seemed to be slipping from doubtful to hopeless. Holmes would know what to do, but Albert didn't.

"I wonder what they'll end up doing in ancient history?" said Miss Moodie, taking up both sides of the conversation. "Young Strickland's taken over for the time being."

Albert didn't know young Strickland. He had been Glenly's protégé, said Miss Moodie and, "strictly entre nous he's shown more than a healthy interest in Glenly's daughter. In fact, at this moment they're ... "

"He had a daughter?" Albert interrupted.

"Stepdaughter, really," Miss Moodie replied, not unaware of the eyes upon them. Her company would be a coveted commodity that evening. "They didn't get along." Her sturdy fingers wrestled a rebellious bra strap into place. "Not that anyone got along with Glenly much in the first place. Strickland did, it seems, but ... "

Another nugget wriggled loose from Albert's store of knowledge. "Mrs. Glenly died, didn't she, Miss Moodie?"

"Goodness, yes," said Miss Moodie. "Call me Gert," said Gert. "Just after homecoming three years ago." Pause, eyes on the ceiling. "Or was it four? No. Three years. Yes. Three years, I'm sure. Not more than four."

Albert looked at the ceiling, too. He half expected to find something written there. Moodie waited for him to ask how she died. "Hit-and-run driver," she said when he didn't, "just as she was getting out of ... goodness, you just never know, do you? One minute you're here and ... " She brushed some doughnut crumbs down the precipitous slope of her ample bosom. "You remember, don't you?"

He'd forgotten but, once reminded, it came back vividly. It was impossible to keep everything out, no matter how hard you tried. Now and then things seeped through. Vietnam. The Kennedy assassinations. Men on the moon.

Mrs. Glenly had been much younger than her husband. Very pretty. Sad and misplaced. Even Albert noticed. He didn't know the daughter, though. There were so many girls, and they were all the same. They talked the same, dressed the same, giggled and talked behind their hands and always went to the lady's room in bunches.

Tewksbury could tell them apart.

"I remember."

"Poor child," said Miss Moodie. Her sympathetic voice was even deeper than her normal voice, musty from late nights in one-sided library debates. Albert imagined it got that way from overuse. Actually, she'd smoked long, thin, black cigars once, much in vogue among liberated ladies of her generation. She gave them up when her doctor predicted throat cancer. A relief, it was, since she'd always hated the damn things.

"What happens to her now?" asked Albert. One question was leading to another all by itself. All one had to do was pay attention to the conversation.

"Who, dear? The daughter? Catherine?" Moodie sat back in her chair, tucking in her chin till it all but disappeared and elevated her nose and her eyebrows at once, as if to get them as far from the following words as biologically possible. "I hear she's taken up residence at Strickland's," she said. "Not the kind of behavior that's likely to do much for the school's reputation, should it get out. Tuition-paying mummies and daddies back in Newport or what-have-you take exception to the notion of their daughters being deflowered by the hired help."

"No," Albert agreed, not bothering to wonder what gardening had to do with anything. "She's all right, though?"

"If you mean is she grieving . . . you needn't trouble yourself on that score. There's no black crepe on the windows, if you take my meaning. Nor 'round her heart."

Albert's coffee was cold, so he drank it at a gulp. "They didn't get along?"

"Nobody got along with Glenly." Either Gert had taken up ventriloquism or someone else had joined the conversation. The latter proved to be the case. A tall black man in gray pinstriped pants and multicolored suspenders was leaning on the back of Albert's chair. Albert began to stand.

"No, no. Sit," said the man, adding his name and subject in response to the desperate look in Albert's eyes. "Walter Lane, Political Science." Albert responded in kind. Lane smiled at Miss Moodie, but she didn't smile back. Her franchise was in jeopardy.

"I was just getting some coffee and couldn't help overhearing," said Lane. "May I?"

He took a seat next to Albert, across the table from Miss Moodie. "Nasty business, that," he said, nodding at the paper. "Poor Tewks couldn't take the heat."

Miss Moodie twisted herself into an exclamation of reproof at the remarks, but Lane took no notice. Neither did Albert.

"Heat?"

"From Glenly," said Lane. "He was an ass."

"Glenly?"

Lane shook his head and blew an exclamation point through his nose. "How well did you know him?"

"Glenly?" said Albert. His mental pants were around his ankles. "Not much," he said. "Not at all," he confided. "I don't remember exactly who he was, I mean, what he looked like. The pictures in the paper didn't look familiar."

Lane and Moodie exchanged a look that Albert wasn't supposed to see. He did. But it was a familiar look. "I'm not very good with faces," he explained. "I remember what his wife looked like." Come to think of it, he didn't really. All he remembered was that she was blondish or brunette, and that she'd struck him as pretty. "She was pretty."

"They weren't very good pictures," said Lane.

Miss Moodie remarked that he'd been dead in most of them.

"He wasn't a nice person," said Lane.

"You shouldn't say that," said Miss Moodie. "The man's dead, after all."

"And there's joy in Mudville," said Lane unapologetically, then, seeing Miss Moodie inflating herself to object, added: "Come on, Gert. You can't tell me you're brokenhearted to see him gone."

Miss Moodie became the personification of offense. She lowered an eyebrow and examined the hem of her skirt. "I'm not going to say Glenly was an Apostle, if that's what you mean, Professor Lane," she said frostily. "Neither do I find it necessary to defame him."

"What she's trying not to say is that you were fortunate not knowing him," Lane interpreted. "He was overbearing, arrogant . . . loved to play with people's brains."

"Brains?" said Albert.

"You know," Lane replied. "Mind games. His favorite trick was to connive his way into your confidence - get you feeling he was as empathetic as Dear Abby, then he'd subtly prod, pry . . . "

"Cajole," Miss Moodie said, without looking up from the hem of her skirt. "Insinuate."

"That's the perfect word, Gert. He'd insinuate himself into your confidence and search out your secret."

"Secret?"

"We all have our secrets, Professor. That little peach pit of sin that makes us human," said Lane. His eyes settled on something that wasn't there.

"We all do," Miss Moodie affirmed softly, still not raising her eyes.

"He had a talent for recognizing people's weak spots; their greatest embarrassments, biggest failures, fears . . . "

like a maggot in an open wound. He'd wait for the most damaging possible moment to turn the screws, then he'd sit back and watch you fall apart."

"Like that Special Ed undergrad," said Miss Moodie, who was making a noble effort to overcome her aversion to speaking ill of the dead.

Lane shot Miss Moodie a searching glance which she didn't seem to notice. "Daphne Knowlton," he said, his voice suddenly quiet.

"Daphne Knowlton! That's it!" said Miss Moodie. "I've been trying to remember it ever since Glenly . . . It's a good thing she wasn't around when it happened, or she'd be the one in jail."

Two suspects in two days. Albert's heart added a jazz riff at the possibility.

"Don't be absurd," Lane snapped.

"Nothing absurd about it," Miss Moodie protested. "After what he did to her? I think she's to be commended for not well . . . setting him on fire."

Albert had lost the tail of the kite, and it was sailing away without him. "What happened?"

Moodie and Lane conferred with their eyes. Lane turned away.

"It was unforgivable, really," Moodie began. "I mean, the last thing I want to do is speak ill of the dead but . . . " She lost her chin entirely in the folds of her neck. "Surely you heard? It happened not a year ago, in this very room. There was a party, I forget the occasion . . . lots of grog. Unfortunately. Most of the faculty was here." She quizzed Lane. "You were here, weren't you, dear?" Lane grunted, stood up and walked to the coffee urn with his hands in his pockets. He was agitated. "Yes, of course you were. I remember now. You got there later. Glenly, as usual, had had too much to drink. That's when he was worst.

"I can see him now, sitting by the fire being witty and charming."

Albert's ears caught on the discord. "Witty and charming?"

"Oh, he could be the most ingratiating."

"That was the set-up," said Lane, who had meandered back into the conversation. "That's how he wheedled his way into your confidence."

"He was a very charismatic man. People gathered round him like flies around ... Well, that's what he was, if truth be told." Miss Moodie formed a flying buttress of her elbows on the chair arms, to support the sagging bulk of her edifice. Her shoulders were thus elevated to her ears and her neck disappeared altogether. "That's what made him all the more horrid. It wasn't as if he didn't know what he was doing."

"He'd build people up, set them on a pedestal then take a sledgehammer to it," Lane said. "It was sport."

"We digress," said Moodie, reigning to the narrative's inside rail and applying the whip. "She was an intern. Very shy. Not a beautiful girl, I wouldn't say, but very . . . pleasant?" She tossed a silent question mark at Lane for approbation. He declined comment. "Full bodied, she was," said Moodie, who was about as full-bodied as was permitted by the atmosphere in an enclosed space. "Anyway, Glenly paid her special attention that night. He was ingratiating and gentlemanly, coaxing her out of her little shell ... by degrees. Plying her with drinks. I'm sure she'd never been made such a fuss of. Well, before long . . . I'm amazed we didn't see it coming . . . aren't you, Walter?" There was a moment of self-conscious silence. "The upshot was, she ended up on the coffee table, with her shirt unbuttoned, dancing as they clapped and goaded her to undress. Glenly at the head of the percussion section, naturally. Of course, she had no idea what she was doing. Probably the first wine she'd ever had outside communion."

Albert was shocked. Things like that didn't happen in his world. "Didn't anyone try to stop it?"

"Of course we did!" Moodie exclaimed. "Goodness, you don't think that all of us were parties to such a ... the poor child ... but, there you have it. If we'd spoken up, we'd just have become anathema to those who were egging her on with their laughing, clapping. Would've just made it worse. Though I don't know how much can be held to their charge. They were all knee-deep in their cups by that time."

"That's no excuse!" Lane protested passionately.

"Oh, of course not, but ... " Aside. "I should mention that Professor Lane wasn't here while all this was going on. He arrived toward the end ... broke it up, actually, if I recollect aright."

"I offered to take her home," said Lane. "In the end she went with someone else. Next morning, I heard she was gone. Her resignation letter arrived at the school a few days later.

"Can you imagine what that did to her?" Lane sat down slowly. "That kid was straight outta, I don't know ... Mr. Rogers's neighborhood. Innocent as they come, and an idealist to boot. She was in Special Ed because she really wanted to help people." The look in Frank's eyes when he raised them was the nearest thing to cold blood Albert had ever seen. "He died too easily."

Three suspects?

The thread of conversation was run through the needle's eye and tied off at the loose end as Dr. Strickland entered the room. "Haven't seen him here since ... " Moodie commented under her breath. "He looks three days dead."

The six eyes at their disposal followed Dr. Strickland as he crossed the room and joined a knot of people near the fireplace.

The first thing Albert noticed, perhaps due to his own awakened sartorial acuity, was that Strickland, though appearing tired, was impeccably dressed. Albert adjusted his tie and ventured a slight smile, but any similarity he had begun to entertain in that regard was nipped in the bud when he saw how easily Strickland fell into conversation with his colleagues.

"Hasn't slept much lately, it would seem," Moodie diagnosed. Lane concurred. "Things aren't very peaceful at his place, I warrant. Lice in the lovenest, eh? I don't see why Administration allows it," Miss Moodie huffed on the exhale as she inflated her dignity. "She is a student, after all."

Albert was observing. Strickland was probably in his mid-thirties. His hair was dark and, though it overhung the collar of his black wool greatcoat, seemed in general retreat elsewhere. His smile was frequent and insincere, mirroring those around him. His eyes were keen and clear and rarely fixed on anything, but were full of expression. Now and then a word straddled a peal of laughter and rode across the room.

"Tenure," said Miss Moodie.

Albert stopped observing. "Pardon?"

"They're talking about tenure," Lane elucidated. "Always brings back memories.

"I remember when I was up, there were two or three others . . . Glenly was one of them. That's all we talked about." He smiled as if the thought awoke a melancholy.

"A pox on modern education," Miss Moodie sighed from atop her heap of years. "Tenure is a sin." The conversation laid down tracks in a scholastic direction, so Albert went away. He had a lot to ponder. He ducked into a rest room, shut himself in one of the stalls, and lit a cigarette. He paced back and forth around the bowl, two and a half steps in each direction.

He was agonizingly uncomfortable with the picture he had gotten of Glenly.

It had been Albert's experience that when someone dies, all their shortcomings were buried with them; they became candidates for sainthood. Everyone suddenly had nothing but wonderful things to say about them; it was amazing the world had gotten along before them and it seemed unlikely to survive their passing. It was always like that, for politicians, teachers, plumbers, churchmen, even artists who lives had been a wasteland of sin and self-satisfaction.

Yet, no one mourned Justin Glenly, despite his brutal and untimely demise. That's what really bothered Albert. Were the things he'd been hearing true? Was it possible that such a person existed? Even more bewildering, what accounted for his hold on people? Why hadn't they just ignored him?

He'd smoked half a pack of cigarettes by the time his train of thought derailed. All his effort had netted him was a headache. He must be hungry. He groped his way to the door and into the hall. It was dark. The building was closed and locked.

It was a different place at night, with the lights off, and Albert - unfamiliar with all but his territorial swatch of it in the light was day - was a complete stranger to it in the dark.

A row of tall, small-paned windows sliced squares off the moonlight and laid them in neat regiments on the floor. The darkness was deeper by contrast, and Albert's footsteps saluted them in passing. Something moved in the shadows at the end of the hall. He stopped. Somebody must be locking up.

He overcame his instinctive surprise and continued down the hall with his face at full mast. "Hello!"

There was no response. Albert slowed in his tracks. "Who's there?" He stopped and announced his name. Still no reply. Maybe he hadn't seen anything after all. His glasses were dirty. He squinted. There was no distinction between the shadows. This was silly. His heart sent white-capped waves of blood to his temples. He'd never heard his heart-beat before; it was out of time. He proceeded slowly.

The shadows stood between him and the door. Some words tested the waters, but found his throat suddenly too dry to float them. He coughed and said "hello" again.

Albert had never been frightened before. He'd been embarrassed, Lord knows. He'd been painfully nervous. He'd felt inadequate in social situations. But he'd never had that "tiptoe up to the windows of the spooky old house at the end of the street" kind of fear. It was new, and it wasn't pleasant. It made him feel doubly silly.

He stood a little straighter and quickened his pace.

The shadows in question were twenty feet ahead on the right, and the closer he got the more it seemed there was someone standing there, cloaked in black, pressed into the corner. The clearer the image became, the harder he worked to imagine it into a coat on a hook or a window curtain.

At the instant he was able to deceive his eyes no longer, the shadow burst from hiding and threw its full weight into him, slamming him into the opposite cinder-block wall with a skull-splitting crack. Albert's hands immediately went to his head as he dropped heavily to the floor. The pain was instant and aggressive. In the final blur of reason before the lights went out, he saw the shadow flying down the hall, a cape billowing in its slipstream like a demon on its back.

Chapter Five

It was still dark when Albert awoke. His hand went immediately to his throbbing head. He half expected to find a gaping I hole in his skull and all his brains spilled on the floor, except the segment that registers pain; that bit was intact and functioning perfectly.

Blood from his nose had crusted on his face and formed a warm, sticky puddle between his cheek and the floor.

He peeled himself off the flagstones, sat up, and lit a cigarette. The burst of match light adhered itself to the inner walls of his eyelids. The neatly ordered platoons of moonlight were marching up the wall opposite. Must have been an hour. Maybe an hour and a half.

He'd never considered the speed of moonlight.

There was a curious smell in the air. Perfume? Chemicals?

When he was young, Albert had gone to Mt. Washington with his mother. There was a car park near the top, and a telescope you could look through for five cents. While his mother was getting her nickel's worth, he persuaded his head between two rails of the wooden fence and looked over the edge. It was a tight fit, but a glorious view seven hundred feet straight down. One of the men from the weather station finally had to break the rail to get Albert's head out. It all came back to him now.

At least his memory worked.

"One and one is two," he said. His voice echoed eerily through the halls. "A dotted half gets three beats in four-four time."

Basic logic intact.

He ground out the cigarette, collected himself from the floor, and stood up. Instantly his brain seemed adrift in some volatile fluid. There was a brief but brilliant display of flashbulbs and Molotov cocktails in the confines of his cranium. The floor rushed up at him. It should be an easy thing to stop the fall. But his limbs ignored his brain's commands and crumpled beneath him like beanstalks.

For the next several days Albert's chief activity was waking up, experiencing delirious pain, and falling asleep again. The hem of his consciousness was laced with voices. Men and women. Some familiar, some not. He couldn't tell what they were saying. There were dog barks, too. Train whistles. Gunshots. A whole library of grotesque sounds and voices that, orchestrated by the pain, coerced fantastic things from his subconscious. He couldn't tell if he was awake or dreaming.

Something seeped through, though. It was the general impression of whiteness; the smell of bleach embedded in the stiff linens against his face, rubbery white hands that lifted, and rolled, and wrapped, and soothed, and performed a host of duties that only his hands had done before. He'd be embarrassed when he felt better.

Somebody lifted his eyelid. He could feel his eyeball contract.

"Ah, somebody's home."

Albert tried to respond but only succeeded in producing a raspy grunt.

"Don't try to talk," the doctor said. "If not for your sake, then for mine. I hate trying to figure out what people are saying. Doubly hard since most folks recovering from your condition don't make sense anyway."

After a while Albert managed to arch his eyebrows high enough to pry his eyes open. The doctor had seated himself on a bedside chair and, leaning forward with hands on his knees, regarded Albert over the tops of his reading glasses with the expectancy of a baker waiting for the pastry to rise.

"You're in hospital," said the doctor. He had an accent. Not quite English. Not Irish. "I'm Dr. Williams." Not Scots. "I'd've laid money you'd never see the light of day again."

Not Jamaican or Bahamian. "But there you are." He was Welsh. Albert had always had the ability to identify accents, sometimes in minute detail. It was a faculty that embraced his only other interest in life besides music: geography.

Dr. Williams would be called "stout" in polite company. His reddish hair was streaked with white and stood out like wings on either side of his linen cap. "I know two young ladies'll be glad to see you."

Albert didn't know two young ladies. He knew his sister, who was in Florida, and he knew Miss Bjork . . . but she was more lawyer than lady.

He lubricated his throat with a drink of water and made some sounds similar to an old Volkswagen bus starting on a cold day.

"Two?" Albert said creakily. All his life he'd hardly noticed the sex, now they were popping up everywhere.

"One's a lovely little thing. Nose like a pixie," said the doctor. "Bit frostbit, though."

"Frostbit?" Once again Albert found himself conversing in questions. He became aware of the bandages, traced them gently with his fingertips.

The doctor finished scratching some notes on Albert's record and hung it back on the bedside. "Eighteen stitches there, my friend. Don't go poking at my handiwork.

"She's more GQ than Cosmo, if you take my meaning." The doctor laughed.

Albert summoned the same dull smile he always did when he didn't understand the joke. What was a GQ? It often seemed there was an entire vocabulary that he wasn't privy to hidden somewhere in the English language. There were so many things he didn't comprehend. He'd never much cared before. He'd been a sickly child. Missed a lot of school. Those must have been the days they taught all the important things.

"What I call a 'no-frills woman.' All business."

It was Ms. Bjork. Albert suddenly felt unkempt. He wanted a tie.

"And the other one?"

The doctor deposited a buttock on the end of the bed. "A real treat, there." He tapped his temple with a forefinger and lobbed another knowing glance over the rim of his glasses. "It's not till after you've been talking to her for two or three minutes that you realize the record has a skip in it."

An analogy Albert could understand!

"You'll be going along, right as rain, when all of a sudden skip, skip you're in another groove." He paused. "Sometimes phwip!" his hand skidded through the air, "clear off the turntable altogether."

"Crazy?" Albert ventured.

"Well," said the doctor, slapping his knees as he stood up, "one of us was. Who is she, sister? Cousin?" His conscience pricked itself in retrospect. "I say, I hope I didn't ... "

"No," said Albert, knitting his eyebrows in confusion. He paged through the half-dozen women of his acquaintance; all had their peculiarities, being women, but none was crazy. Not what he'd call crazy, anyway. "What did she look like?"

"Oh, early twenties, thereabouts. Flaming red hair. Not what you'd call 'slim as the mayor's reputation,' but not fat. Painfully shy. Quiet, for the most part. Not unattractive, either. Like I said, took me a while to realize." The doctor tapped his temple again. "Those kind are more worrisome than your Napoleons and Teddy Roosevelts. A little scary. She sits there in the corner, watching. Hums, sometimes."

A shiver thrilled its way across Albert's back. He looked at the empty chair in the corner.

"Well, if there are no complaints, I'll pop in again this afternoon. Need anything? Pillows? Painkiller?"

Albert hesitated. His head was throbbing. He'd been so glad to be conscious he hadn't noticed. "Maybe something for this headache?"

Dr. Williams extracted a tiny knot of round white pills, wrapped in cellophane, from his pocket. "Happen to have just the thing." He handed three of the pills to Albert, together with the water glass from the bedside table. "Not very professional," he said as he retied the bundle and slipped it back into his pocket. "But I make up for it in bedside manner, don't you agree?"

Albert nodded as he took the pills and water, dribbling on his gown in the process.

"Right, then," said the doctor with a smile as he headed for the door. "Anything else?"

Albert wiped his chin with the back of his hand. He shook his head. The doctor opened the door.

"Doctor?"

Williams turned in the doorway and grunted.

"That woman . . . the second one . . . does she come often?"

"Oh, every night . . . about eight. They turn her out at nine; end of visiting hours."

The doctor left in his wake a profound and troubling silence, one that was shattered suddenly by an ear-splitting whistle, an explosion, and the same hideous laughter that had plagued Albert's dreams.

Whoever was in the bed on the other side of the curtain had turned on the TV, full blast, in the middle of a Bugs Bunny cartoon. No wonder he'd had such strange dreams.

"Could you turn that down, please?"

The mayhem continued unabated.

"Please turn that down!"

Albert's feeble objection was swallowed whole by the sound of a piano falling on a duck. Nevertheless, his meager effort had exacted a painful price. He closed his eyes and massaged his temples.

A nurse swept into the room on hospital feet, shut off the TV, and began scolding the person in the next bed.

"I told you to keep that TV down, Jeremy. The Professor's a very sick man. Needs his rest. Do you understand?" Albert's lately acquired appreciation of nurses was elevated at once to veneration. "Now if I have to tell you again, I'll take the remote control away."

The nurse reappeared from behind the curtain. "So good to see you back among the living, Professor! Sorry about the noise," she said, mechanically tidying Albert's bed as if he wasn't in it.

"He's a teenager," she explained in a whisper.

"Oh," said Albert.

"Normally, we'd have someone like you in a private room, but we're packed to the rafters. Never seen the like.

The nurse left the room.

Albert wondered what that meant, 'someone like him.' Were there others? Did they keep them in special rooms?

"You the friend of the guy down the hall?"

It was the Teenager. Albert waited for someone to answer. The room could go on forever for all he knew; there could be row after row of invalids beyond the screen. Perhaps they all had remote controls.

"Hey!" said the Teenager. "You asleep?"

"Are you speaking to me?" said Albert.

"Yeah," the Teenager replied. "You're a friend've that guy down the hall, aren't you? You know the guy who tried to you know, like, the guy who killed the guy?"

"Tewksbury?"

"Yeah. Tewksbury."

"He's here?" said Albert, remembering at the same time.

"Yeah, he tried to ... "

"I know," said Albert peremptorily.

" ... kill himself ... "

"I know," said Albert with finality.

"Slit his wrists."

Albert became aware of the boy's shadow on the curtain; he was enthusiastically sawing at his wrists.

"I know," said Albert pleadingly.

" ... with a razor blade," the boy continued.

Albert's repeated broadsides had struck a denser substance and fallen harmlessly into the brine.

"What's he like?" the boy asked. He didn't wait for a reply. "There's this guy in the movies who hacks people up with a weed whacker. He's really dead, but, like, he keeps comin' back to life on Arbor Day, you know?"

Albert didn't know. "He's not like that," he said. He fingered his stitches and studied the boy's shadow. He had the distinct impression that if he swept the curtain aside suddenly, there wouldn't be anybody there. "Tewksbury didn't kill anyone."

The boy blew an indecipherable comment through his nose.

There was a brief, blessed silence. Perhaps he'd lapsed into a coma. A mild one.

"That woman's weird, though."

The icicles played on Albert's back again. "The one the doctor ... ?"

"Yeah," said the silhouette with a shudder. "I mean, like, I try to ignore her, you know? Just watch TV. It's like tryin' to ignore a ghost, or a troll, or something. I don't think she even knows I'm here. I think I'd pass out if she ever looked at me! Man!"

He savored a delicious fear for a moment. "She just sits there. I mean, I heard you tell Doctor Williams you don't know who she is, or I wouldn't've said anything." Pause. "I'll be sittin' here and my eyes start driftin' over to her 'cause I feel like she's lookin' at me. But she don't.

"I mean, she ain't hard to look at, you know? But she acts like some crazy person from one of them weed-whacker movies."

72

Albert wanted to change the subject. "How many people are in the room?"

"Here? Just us. Just two beds."

The conversation lapsed. Albert felt drowsiness about to overtake him again, probably the pills.

"The other one's real pretty," said the boy. "For an older woman. She should be here any minute. She reads mostly, you know? She talks to me sometimes." The boy's voice was getting fuzzy and hard to hear, taking the long route to Albert's brain, and rattling all the way.

"She told me all about Tewksbury, and everything." There was a very long pause. "She said it's too bad you have to die."

Albert's brain was too overtaken by sleep to rouse itself, despite there being something startling and terrible in the words that vibrated in his ears. Had he heard what he thought he heard, or were his roommate's words simply mingling with the speaker in a dream?

Albert's dreams were more troubled than usual. He dreamt his head hurt. If that wasn't enough, he dreamt that he woke to find the Crazy Woman in the corner. The lights had been turned off, but the door was open and a soft light from the hall fell across her hands. Her fingers were busy with something; she was knitting long sheets of music, and humming. It took no time for Albert to realize that as the woman hummed, her hands knit the notes. Her head and shoulders were in shadows. Then she looked up. Her eyes sparkled in the darkness and fixed on him, widening, pulling the corners of her mouth back in a malevolent grin.

She stood up, slowly. The knitting slid off her needles and each note sounded its swan song as it crashed to the floor. Suddenly she lunged at him, clutching knitting needles in each hand. He tried to scream, but could only moan. His mouth couldn't voice his terror. His body wouldn't respond to his panic.

He awoke with a start, beaded in cold sweat with the sound of a shout dying in his ears.

Chapter Six

Everything was dark and quiet. Albert shot a terrified glance at the chair in the corner, but couldn't see anything. He turned on his light. The chair was empty. He realized he hadn't exhaled since he had awakened. He did now.

There was a stirring on the other side of the curtain. Was she hiding there, ready to burst through the curtain, needles upraised with murderous intent?

"Professor?" said a tired voice. It was the Teenager; lesser of two evils. Albert breathed again. "You okay?"

Albert's voice cracked as he responded. "Yes." He cleared his throat. "Just a dream, I guess." Beat. "Must've had a bad dream."

The boy's breathing suggested he was almost asleep again.

"Did that . . . was that woman here tonight, the odd one?"

The Teenager mumbled something; either "Yes, like always," or "My goldfish eats prunes" and dissolved into a rhythmic snore.

Even Albert's limited understanding of marine life, such as it was, argued against the likelihood of prune-eating goldfish. The Crazy Woman, he deduced, must have been there again. His bewilderment was almost too much to bear. But he wanted a cigarette . . . and his head didn't hurt anymore. Not much.

A police guard was sitting outside one of the doors in the hall. Albert had found a cigarette amongst his belongings and was now wandering about the corridors on enfeebled legs, an honest man in search of a light. He wore his old plaid robe and a pair of paper slippers the hospital had supplied, designed by committee.

The guard had been dozing, but at Albert's approach he sat up. Even the pleat in his trousers straightened itself out until he recognized Albert.

"Professor!" said the guard warmly. "What'd you do to yourself?"

It was the guard from the jailhouse, the one who had stood by the grimy window when Albert had visited Tewksbury.

"I'm not sure." said Albert, smiling hesitantly. He wanted to say something else, but, after a moment, just repeated, "I'm not sure. Do you have a light?"

The guard conducted a thorough search of his pockets. "I quit smoking," he said. Albert sighed. "But I might have a match. Ah, here we go!" He produced the tattered remains of a matchbook to which one bent, pathetic match clung with waning resolve - too many times through the washer. Nevertheless, Albert was past master at nursing spark and flame from recalcitrant matches and was soon drawing the tobacco's genie deeply into his scorched lungs and his brain.

He coughed and choked and his head floated five or six inches above his shoulders for a second or two in a rush of dizziness and pain, yet the insipid smile of a true addict lay upon his lips.

"You better not let the nurses catch you smoking in here," said the guard, with the compassion of one who remembers. "They'd haul out the thumbscrews."

Albert pointed at the door. "Tewksbury?"

The guard nodded. "Funny you guys being here at the same time." Albert nodded. "I feel sorry for the guy, you know?" said the guard. "Gotta be pretty low to do something like that."

"Well," said Albert, "I guess going to jail for something you didn't do . . . something like . . . " The rest of the thought wrapped itself in silence, but the guard understood.

"Mmm."

"Can I go in and see him?"

"Afraid not," said the guard. "No matter what you think . . . or I think . . . the law says he's a murderer. My job's to keep this room closed so tight only air can get in." He shrugged his shoulders. "Sorry. Orders, understand?"

Albert nodded, said good night and shuffled the paper slippers back toward his room. He didn't understand. He wanted to talk to Tewksbury, even though he had no idea what to say. His thoughts were running together again. He needed sleep.

His roommate's light was on, his shadow was sitting up on the curtain, reading.

"Professor?" said the Shadow, putting the book down.

Albert grunted a reply. He was too tired to negotiate the suspension bridge between generations.

"Where've you been?" asked the Teenager with a sniff. "You shouldn't smoke. It's not just bad for you. Other people have to breathe, too."

Albert felt genuinely guilty. The thought had never occurred to him.

"Did you go see what's his name?"

"I went down there," said Albert. He slipped off his slippers and got into bed. "But there's a guard. He wouldn't let me in."

Albert's eyelids closed like sandpaper over his eyes as his head hit the pillow. He felt very strange; his thoughts weren't quite connected to the world around him. Despite his fatigue, he was suspicious of the extended silence. It filled like a water balloon over his head and finally burst.

"I can get you in there, if you really want to," said the Boy.

"There's a guard," said Albert.

"So? I can still get you in there."

Albert didn't reply. He wanted the boy to think he'd fallen asleep.

"Don't you wanna get in?"

Albert propped himself on an elbow and glared at the Shadow. "There's a guard," he said almost sternly. "He won't let me in. I told you."

"You don't watch much TV, do you, Professor?"

"Not much."

"If you did, you'd know there's hundreds've ways to get in somewhere . . . climbin' through air-conditioning vents . . . except they're never, like, big enough for people in real life. Not strong enough to hold 'em if they were. But we could get some sleeping pills . . . or you could dress up like doctor or a nurse . . . "

"Nurse?"

"That'd really throw 'em. A woman nurse. You'd have to shave your legs, at least from the knees down. Or a delivery man with flowers. Or you could climb through the window. Or . . . hey! Did you try callin' him?"

Albert sat up. See what he missed not watching TV? He picked up the phone and dialed the operator. "Professor Tewksbury's room, please."

"There is no phone in that room." There was no "good-bye," the voice was just suctioned into the hiss at the other end of the line.

"Hello?"

Nothing. Albert hung up. "He doesn't have a phone."

"No problem. I just figured out a way!"

Albert lay back down. He didn't want to hear it. "Tell me tomorrow."

"We need a diversion," said the Teenager. "I know! I could go out in the hall and throw a fit, like something's wrong!"

Albert must be nearly asleep again, the silhouette was making less sense than usual. "Then what?"

"'Then, when the guard and everyone come to help me you slip into Tewksbury's room!"

"It wouldn't work," Albert proclaimed. "People always need help in a hospital. Nobody would pay any attention."

"Yeah, they would," said the boy. "I got a secret weapon."

Even the shadow grinned.

"Crazy," said Albert, or maybe he just thought it loudly. He went to sleep.

It was late morning when Albert awoke again. As he came to his senses he heard a familiar voice. Just a few words and a tag note of polite laughter . . . but enough. It was Miss Bjork, talking to the teenager.

He felt instantly unkempt. He sat up and tucked the covers under his chin. He could feel his whiskers growing and knew his hair was pointing more directions than Scarecrow at the crossroads.

As he reached to smooth it down, his hand hit the bed tray, sending a water glass to the floor.

The splinters hadn't settled before Miss Bjork appeared.

"Most people prefer an alarm clock."

Albert's embarrassment segued into bewilderment. Miss Bjork was smiling as if she had a sense of humor; it must be her day off.

She sat beside him on the bed and calmly rang the nurse's bell. "We were worried there, for a while."

"We?"

Miss Bjork looked at her nails. "I was worried," she said.

When she looked at him again, Albert's interior telegraph system went haywire. What was it his roommate had said last night? Something terrible something . . . he remembered. Was it just a dream? And why was she here? And why didn't she look like a lawyer anymore? The teenager's description of Miss Bjork came to mind, unbidden. Immediately on its heels was Tewksbury's pointed appraisal. Albert could feel himself blush. What was happening to him? He put his hand on his heart so she wouldn't see it beating through the sheets.

Miss Bjork had developed an easy familiarity as a result of her visits, but already she was realizing it was much easier communing with Albert when he was asleep. The nurse appeared and began cleaning up the glass. Albert stuttered an apology.

"Don't worry about it. Professor," said the nurse. "Two-thirds of being a nurse is cleaning up after patients." She tipped the dustpan into a plastic bag and stood up. "The other third we're cleaning up after the doctors." She smiled with her mouth, but not with her eyes. "How're we doing today?"

"Better," said Albert. His tongue tasted awful. He covered his mouth with his hand. "Better."

There was a sudden cry and the cascading crash of a loaded table being knocked over. Miss Bjork and the nurse disappeared behind the curtain followed by a doctor and an orderly who ran in from the hall. Albert leaned forward breathlessly.

In the rush to make space, the curtain was swept aside and Albert saw the Boy for the first time. He was being lifted back into bed. His left leg was missing from the knee down.

He was pale and lean with bright red hair and freckles. About fourteen or fifteen. Smaller than his shadow had suggested. He winced with grim determination as the nurse drew the sheet over him. Albert's heart was in his throat until the boy tossed him a mischievous glance and winked.

Albert was stunned. A well of sympathetic mist was stillborn on his lids. This was the boy's secret. A diversion would work! It was all he could do to keep from laughing.

Once the clamor subsided, Miss Bjork put the screen in place and was about to resume her seat at Albert's side when the doctor placed a preemptory hand on her shoulder.

"I think we've had enough excitement for one morning." He said. "Let's let the Professor and our young friend get some rest."

"But I ... "

"You can come back this afternoon," said the doctor, extending his arm toward the door.

Miss Bjork looked furtively at Albert as she was conducted gently from the room. "I've got something to tell you," she said. "You'll never guess ... "

Albert had no doubt of that.

"This afternoon," the doctor said sharply then, softening his demeanor. "They need their rest."

Once the room was cleared, class segued from diversionary tactics to lock-picking, 101. Jeremy Ash re-situated himself in his wheelchair, tucking his good leg under the stub.

"This is the kind of lock on my old room," he said with a twinkle in his eye. "I've been pickin' it for years."

"At home?" said Albert. The boy indicated the affirmative with a slight nod. "Why would you need to pick the lock to get into your own room?"

The boy's demeanor changed suddenly. He dropped his eyes to the bobby pin that twirled between his thumb and forefinger. "I wasn't getting in."

There was something dark in the words. A depth of tragedy that Albert couldn't fathom.

Albert's musical dexterity proved commodious to burgling. Within half an hour he was able to perpetrate a felony in five seconds. He was proud. He'd never been proud before. Certainly not of his musical accomplishments. They were part of his physiognomy, like burps and heartbeats. But now, with a simple bobby pin, new, forbidden worlds were open to him. He was exhilarated. He beamed and the boy cheered.

The performance went off as scripted. While on his customary rounds of the halls, Jeremy Ash upset his wheelchair and spilled himself onto the floor to the accompaniment of anguished screams. As predicted, everyone in earshot came to his aid ... including the guard.

Albert pressed himself to the wall and made his way against the onrushing tide of compassion to Tewksbury's room. A moment later he was inside.

It was dark in the room. The shades were drawn, the lights off.

"Who's there'?"

The voice was feeble. but still recognizable as Tewksbury's.

"It's me. Albert."

"Albert!" cried Tewksbury.

"Shh!" said Albert. He groped for the light switch. "Where's the light?"

"Over here!" Tewksbury whispered sharply. "Over here, on the headboard."

Albert felt his way to the bedside. "Where?"

"The little round switch on the cord. Feel along the ... "

"I found it," said Albert. The little light over Tewksbury's head clicked on. Tewksbury flinched. The sight of the prisoner was Daguerrotyped on Albert's brain.

Under three or four days growth of beard, Tewksbury's face was sunken and yellow. His eyes were embedded in poster-child depressions and the veins stood out on his forehead.

His arms lay tightly at his sides and were held in place by straps of some kind. His feet, just visible at the edge of the light, were similarly bound. He was dressed in a T-shirt and light-blue boxer shorts from which his limbs protruded like hairy sticks.

By degrees his eyes became accustomed to the light. Albert stepped back in shock.

"C'mere, Albert," said Tewksbury with a wag of the head. "I can't see you. C'mere."

Albert stepped into the halo of light. "How did you get in here? What happened to you?"

"My head," Albert stammered.

"I can see that, you idiot. You look like a friggin' genie."

Something of the old bravura in Tewksbury's voice was reassuring to Albert. "Forget that for a minute. Scratch me, will you?"

"Scratch?"

"Scratch! Scratch me . . . I feel like I'm crawling with bugs."

Albert began to scratch Tewksbury's torso tentatively.

"Scratch, man, scratch! Use your nails. Oh, thank you, Lord! My legs. Do my legs." Albert did his legs. "And my shoulders. Ah! That's it." He sighed. He looked five years younger. "And my back . . . get as far under as you can."

Albert applied himself vigorously to the task and soon, under the combined influences of the physical exertion and apprehension of the criminal act, had worked up a sweat and his head was throbbing.

"Undo my arms, Albert. I'm going to go completely crazy if I don't get out of this thing for a few minutes."

Albert hesitated.

"You can strap me up when you leave."

Having come this far, Albert was resolved against half measures. He undid Tewksbury hand and foot. The prisoner sat up and went through an awkward series of calisthenics which Albert subconsciously scored with The Dance of the Marionettes. At the coda, Tewksbury collapsed in exhaustion.

"I'm so weak." He massaged his arms. "How did you get in here? Isn't there a guard outside?"

"He had to go away for a minute," said Albert, still aghast at the ruin that Archaeology had become. "He's probably back now, so just whisper."

"But the door's locked," Tewksbury whispered.

"I picked it," said Albert through a grin he could not contain.

Tewksbury was dumbfounded. "You picked the lock?"

"My roommate showed me how."

"Your roommate?"

Albert nodded.

"Sounds like some of my roommates. Lucky for me he's not an ax murderer," said Tewksbury. "You're on this floor?"

"Down the hall," said Albert, "and over that way a few rooms."

Albert's eyes had inadvertently fixed on Tewksbury's bandaged wrists.

"I don't know what made me do it" said Tewksbury. "I was shaving, and nicked my chin." He paused. "It's so easy, I thought. Just a couple of quick cuts across the wrist . . . if it gets me out of the damn cell, away from those other men . . . well, good enough. If it kills me, so much the better." He picked absentmindedly at the bandages. "So, I just did it. Real slow, it seemed. Like a dream. I didn't feel it, really-just watched as the blood pumped out. Like it was somebody else. I just watched." He looked at Albert. "I fainted in no time. Next thing I knew, I was here." He flipped the buckle on the restraining straps. "With these."

He looked hard at Albert from the recesses of his soul, deep behind his sunken eyes. "Don't put them on me again, Albert. I feel like I'm just holding on to sanity by a thread as it is. If I have to be tied up like that . . . "

Albert was equipped to release, not to bind.

"I won't," he said quickly.

Tewksbury fell to his knees beside the bed and wept silently, like a hopeless man whose final prayer had been answered. Albert stared, wide-eyed, at the bandages.

"What now?" he said finally.

"I've got to escape," said Tewksbury through his tears. "I've got to hide. I can't go back to jail, and they say Walpole is worse. Much worse." He searched Albert deeply. "I never imagined what life was like in jail, Albert." He shook his head. "I never imagined." Pause. Shudder. Sniff. "I'd rather die out there somewhere," he nodded toward the world, "than live in prison." He wheezed an ironic sigh. "The worst of it is, I'm innocent. Completely innocent." He raised his eyes from the floor. "You know that, don't you?"

Albert was emboldened by compassion for his former colleague. "How do we get you out?"

A spark of hope awoke in Tewksbury's eyes. "Do you mean it?" He shook Albert by the shoulders once or twice. Hard. "Do you mean it? Will you help me get out of here?"

"You can't stay here . . . like this," Albert replied flatly. "What do we do?"

"I don't know," said Tewksbury, like the man who'd been playing the lottery for seventeen years, five one-dollar cards every Friday until it became a habit. He no longer thought about winning. It was five dollars he'd spend on beer, other-wise, and he didn't need the weight. Then he won, and had no idea what to do with the money. "What floor are we on?"

"Second, I think," said Albert. Something was already forming in his mind. He crossed to the window, pulled the blackened shade aside, and lifted the curtain. "There's a roof right below us. Five or six feet." He slid the window open. "It's almost dark."

Tewksbury had found his clothes in the closet and was almost dressed. "I've been praying, Albert. Can you believe it? Me, praying?"

Albert surveyed the area below. There was a delivery van of some kind, lots of lights on, but no one in sight. There were several dumpsters.

"You can go to my place and hide," he said. "There's a key in the planter at the top of the stairs."

"My agnosticism doesn't run as deep as I'd thought," Tewksbury continued.

"So I prayed . . . and here you are. Albert the angel."

"There's some beer in the fridge. And some cereal some-where, I think," said Albert, not sounding much like a brochure for a bed-and-breakfast. "Cocoa Puffs or Wheaties. Dig around."

Being familiar with the typical bill of fare at Chez Albert, Tewksbury's salivary glands remained dormant. "They'll be 'round any minute with supper," he said. The prophecy was immediately self-fulfilling. The meal cart rattled at the far end of the hall.

"I'll wrap the sheet around the radiator here," said Albert, "and you climb down it."

He hadn't finished speaking before Tewksbury was at his side. "Then I'll pull it up and close the window."

It occurred to Tewksbury before Albert.

"Then, how are you going to get out?"

Something very like panic seized Albert by the solar plexus and gave it a sharp squeeze. Everything had been going so smoothly.

"I'll have to go out the window, too."

"And have us both missing? Your house is the first place they'd look!"

The dinner trays rattled again in the hall, much closer this time.

"I could go around and come in the front."

"That might seem a little suspicious, don't you think? A patient wandering in off the street, all dressed for bed?"

It would. Albert looked around the room frantically. "I could hide in the bathroom. If they came in and saw you gone, and the window open . . . "

"They'd look. They'd look." Tewksbury, too, was scanning the room. "I've got it! The ceiling!"

Albert looked blankly at the ceiling, which looked blankly back. He leveled his gaze at Tewksbury. Perhaps the restraints had been on too long already.

Tewksbury climbed up on a chair by the bathroom door and gave one of the ceiling tiles a push. To Albert's amazement, it lifted, revealing a space about eighteen inches deep between the old original ceiling and the new.

"It's a drop ceiling," said Tewksbury excitedly, his eyes flashing with rekindled spirit. The dishes rattled across the hall. The guard could be heard exchanging words with the nurse's aid.

"Quick! Climb up there!"

Tewksbury got off the chair.

"It won't hold me, will it?"

"No. But the old plumbing is still up there. Grab on, pull yourself up and hang there till the coast is clear."

Albert had never hung anywhere 'till the coast was clear.' He had never hunkered or slunk or shadow-to-shadowed. He'd never played hide-and-seek, perhaps for fear that nobody would look for him. There was nothing in Albert's repertoire of emotions with which to compare his feelings as he climbed awkwardly onto the chair.

"I'll call you at my house," he said. "I'll let it ring three times, then hang up and call again." Paganini was dueling the devil on his heartstrings. Exhilaration raced through his being like a five alarm fire.

"Okay, okay," said Tewksbury. "Climb!"

Albert pulled himself through the hole and wrapped himself around the pipes. One of them was very warm. He hung there like a bat as Tewksbury pulled the panel back in place.

"Albert," said Tewksbury. "Thanks."

There was another rattle in the hall. The guard would be inspecting the tray. Tewksbury dropped the panel back in place, leaving Albert suspended in the dark with only his heartbeat for company.

He heard Tewksbury lift the chair back into place, click off the light, then tie the sheet to the radiator. His breathing was labored as he let himself down. No sooner had his feet lighted on the gravel of the roof below than the door opened.

"Here we go, Professor," said a young lady. One of the pipes to which Albert clung was no longer warm. It was hot, scortching the length of his pajama-clad body. The nurse hadn't noticed the escape at once; Tewksbury must have lowered the black curtain over the window. A second later, though, a click of the headboard light prefaced a sharp scream that nearly shook Albert loose from his roost. He held tighter.

He could feel his flesh searing against the pipe. He grit his teeth and held on for dear life.

"He's gone!" said the nurse as the guard rushed in. Albert followed the sound of the ensuing search, first to the bathroom, as Tewksbury had prophesied, then under the bed— that had been Albert's second idea. Then to the window.

"He got out here! Look! He used this sheet." The guard reported the escape into his walkie-talkie. Albert wondered if he'd be betrayed by the smell of his burning flesh. The guard signed off.

"I don't understand," said the nurse. Her voice came from directly below Albert.

"What?"

"How did he get out of these? They're not cut, or ripped. They didn't come loose, I did them myself. They're just laid aside. Like the Shroud of Turin."

"Well, it's not your fault," said the guard. He realized at the same time that if it wasn't her fault, it was his. "You couldn't help it," he added. "We've got to find him."

They left the room. Albert let out a sharp sigh of anguish, pulled the ceiling tile up and aside and dropped to the floor. It was a long fall, and his paper-slippered heels smacked loudly against the old wood floor. He pulled out the chair, climbed up, readjusted the tile, and jumped down.

For half a second he considered going out the window. It was still open. The sheet was still there, but the sound of voices coming up from outside made up his mind. With one last glance at the ceiling to make sure the tile was straight, he left the room.

Already there was excitement in the hall. Elevator doors were opening and closing. An army of officials rounded the corner just as Albert stepped into his room and shut the door behind him.

"Well?" said Jeremy Ash excitedly. "What happened? What's all the noise? I thought they caught you!"

Albert stumbled back to bed. "He escaped," he said.

"Escaped!" said the boy. It was hard to tell which was wider, his mouth or his eyes. "He tricked you?"

"No," said Albert.

"He beat you up?" That wouldn't have been hard.

"No."

"You didn't . . . did you . . . did you let him go?" Jeremy said with rising enthusiasm.

"I helped him," Albert replied softly.

"You helped him!"

"Shhh! I couldn't leave him there like that." Pause. Consider. "He knows about Etruscans." That had made more sense in his brain than in his mouth.

"This is intense, man! I'm like . . . I never knew you were gonna let him go!"

"I'm tired," said Albert. He was also in pain. A wide red stripe marked his body in several places. "I'm tired." The wave of adrenaline subsided, beaching its musical flotsam on the linen shore.

"Let him go! Geez!" The words wrapped themselves around Albert's advancing dreams where they would alternately commend and condemn him throughout the night.

Chapter Seven

It was just after five in the morning and still dark when Albert awoke. He reached for the phone, dialed Directory Assistance, got the number of the phone in his apartment and called. He began counting the rings.

"Albert?" said Tewksbury in a whisper.

"You weren't supposed to answer yet," said Albert. The best laid plans.

"I know, I know," said Tewksbury. "But I knew it was you. Who else could it be?" There was a pause during which Albert didn't answer. "Besides, I couldn't sleep."

"Is everything okay?"

"Fine. Fine. What happened after I left? I take it they didn't find you."

"No."

"Good! How long did you hang up there?"

"Everything went okay." Beat. "I burned myself on the pipes."

"Hot water . . . I forgot about that," said Tewksbury. "Sorry." He was. "Don't you have any cigarettes?"

"Look around."

"I'm not that desperate. What happened?"

Albert told him. "What now?"

"I don't know," said Tewksbury. "It's all happened so fast. I need time to think. When will you get out?"

Albert hadn't thought about it. One day they'd tell him, and he'd go. "I don't know."

"Well, find out. You need some groceries . . . and fungicide."

Albert slammed the receiver down in response to some stirrings on the other side of the curtain. Unfortunately his finger was in the cradle at the time. It worked well as a mute.

"Professor?" said Jeremy Ash. "You talkin' to me?"

"No," said Albert with his fingers in his mouth.

"Tewksbury?"

Albert said nothing.

"Where is he?"

Albert shrugged on his side of the curtain.

"Your place?"

Albert sighed.

"Escape! Geez! I can't believe it! And I helped! That makes me an accessory." There was a half-second's silence. "How'd you do it?"

Albert replayed the details, step by step, omitting nothing. By the time he'd finished he'd won a new place in the boy's estimation.

"Geez! You could go to jail for that!" Jeremy said breathlessly. "I mean, I'm like . . . not many people would do that for somebody, you know?"

Jail? For freeing a trapped animal? It was ludicrous; a possibility that hadn't occurred on the most distant horizon of Albert's imagination. Scolding, yes. But . . .

"Jail?" he repeated beneath his breath.

For the remaining hours 'til breakfast he dozed on and off, his thoughts wandering the foggy realm of semi-consciousness; half-shaped dreams stumbled into one another, colliding in stillborn ballets at the wobbly edge of his reason. Unrelated elements orchestrated by the distant sounds of the waking world and joined by a single common thread: jail.

A wave of relief swept over him when he awoke to find the dreams weren't real, followed by a wave of bleakest misery at the possibility that they could be.

Somebody had to find Glenly's killer.

The rattle of the breakfast cart over the threshold made him salivate. He sat up and drew the lap table in front of him. Worry was hungry work.

"Ah, good morning, Professor."

It was a strange voice. Albert put on his glasses and brought the speaker slowly into focus. It was a man in a suit; a gray suit that matched his eyes, a white shirt that matched his teeth, and a dark tie that matched . . . darkness. Either the shirt or the tie was much too big for the man, Albert couldn't tell which.

He was probably over forty. Maybe fifty. Or sixty. His black hair came to a sharp point in the middle of his head, but retreated some distance on either side. He was about Albert's height but powerfully built, with a straight, lipless mouth and restless eyes that searched the room like a gerbil looking for the toilet paper roll. He took off his overcoat and folded it over the footboard.

"How are you feeling this morning?"

"Fine," said Albert. The nurse took the covers off the breakfast plates and set them in front of him. Albert looked hungrily at the food, then worriedly at the man who had now pulled up a chair, seated himself next to the bed, and was staring at him.

"Go on, Professor. Eat your breakfast," said the man. He produced a leather folder from his inside coat pocket, opened it, and held it out. It was a badge. "I'm Detective Naples."

"Inspector?" Albert said.

"Detective."

"Mm." To Albert, there was no distinction. Inspector Naples was fixed in his brain like a burdock, and so he would remain, world without end, amen. He took the wallet from the policeman and studied the badge carefully, at the same time trying not to betray his vain attempts to swallow the knot that had tied itself in his throat. "Number 564."

Naples was momentarily nudged off-center by this curious new animal. He took his badge back.

"I'd like to ask you a few questions, if you're up to it. Won't take a minute. Are you going to eat that bacon?" Albert proffered the bacon, which Detective Naples crunched noisily as he spoke. It must be very crisp. Just the way Albert liked it.

He had the presence of mind to know that if he tried to drink his coffee or juice he'd spill it. He nibbled some toast.

"You know Tewksbury escaped last night?"

The dry toast settled like dust on the knot in Albert's throat.

He wanted a drink, but his hands were shaking.

"There was a lot of noise in the hall last night," he said. "I heard them yelling."

"You were here when all the excitement was going on, then? Here in bed?"

Albert moved his head in a sort of circular nod.

"Because one of the orderlies said he happened to look in and you weren't in bed. Don't you like grapefruit?"

Albert pushed the tray toward the inspector.

"He was in the bathroom," said Jeremy Ash.

Naples folded the curtain back. Anticipating the policeman's predatory tendencies, Jeremy had crammed most of his breakfast in his cheeks, to be consumed later. Otherwise he was as cool as hospital coffee.

"And you are ... ?"

"Fine, thanks," said the boy through his breakfast.

"I mean your name."

"Jeremy Ash," said Jeremy Ash, dispersing partially masticated fragments of breakfast on the bedspread.

"You say the Professor was in the bathroom?"

The boy took his time chewing and swallowing his food. "Off and on, he was. He gets, like nauseous from his headaches, y'know? He barfs a couple of times a night. If he was anywhere, he was in there."

Naples smiled lengthwise and turned his attention once more to Albert and the grapefruit. Albert had managed a sip of coffee during the preceding exchange.

"You're friends with Tewksbury, I understand."

This was one question Albert was ready for. "I know him. He's a colleague. He visited me sometimes."

"That's it?"

"Yes."

"Mmm." The inspector held the empty grapefruit up and squeezed the juice down his throat. Albert winced. "The guard said you tried to visit him."

"I saw him in the hallway."

"You saw Tewksbury in the hallway?"

"I thought we were talking about the guard."

Something unpleasant flashed in the Inspector's eyes. "I was talking about Tewksbury."

"Oh. Yes, I did try to get in to see him," said Albert. He was breathing easier. "But the guard wouldn't let me." He braved another sip of coffee quite successfully. "He's a colleague. Ancient History. I heard what he did . . . You know." He pointed at his wrists. The inspector nodded with his eyes. "I thought well, if it was me . . . "

The inspector helped himself to some toast and jelly. "What happened to your face?"

"My face?" Albert's hand went immediately to the red racing stripe along his cheek. His mind was going a million miles a minute, leaving his mouth hopelessly behind. "My face?"

"Your face. That's a burn, isn't it?"

"Yes, I . . . I burned it somehow."

"Your hands, too," said the inspector.

Albert sat in the presence of a Discerning Brain.

As if on cue, a gush of warm, word-heavy air from the hall heralded the arrival of Miss Moodie and Professor Lane.

"You see, Lane?" Moodie was saying. "That nurse was as balmy as a night in Bermuda. We needn't've awakened that elderly gentleman in the body cast." She turned to Albert. "Well, you don't look any the worse for . . . well, here we are." She thrust an oversized bouquet of flowers at him. "This will speed the recovery. Flowers. From the school. The faculty."

"And the students," added Lane, lest mention of that contingent be scratched from the credits.

"You'll need something to put them in. Let's ring for the nurse," said Miss Moodie, so doing.

"How're you feeling, old man?" Lane shook Albert's hand.

"This is Inspector . . . " Albert stuttered.

"I'll be back some other time, Professor," said the Naples. "Thanks for the breakfast." He picked up his overcoat and, with an odd tap on the side of his nose with his forefinger, departed.

"And up the chimney he rose," chuckled Miss Moodie. "What was all that about? Ah! Nurse. Some water please, for these flowers. And a vase, or a bedpan, or what-have-you."

"Was he here about? Tewksbury?" said Lane who had taken the inspector's seat. "What happened last night?"

"You've heard?"

"Heavens, yes," chimed Miss Moodie on the hour. "It's everywhere. Old Tewksbury escaping, can you imagine!? What a lot of excitement we've have in our little . . . my, my, yes."

"Where will he go?" Lane wondered.

"He has no family."

"His father," Albert corrected. "In Vermont."

"Oh, my, yes. That's right. He was at the trial. You remember Walter, the poor old fellow who sat in the . . . Yes. That's right. Very sad."

"I doubt he'd go there. Besides, they've got police all over the place. Roadblocks, too, I should imagine."

"You should see!" said Miss Moodie, tasting just a morsel of scrambled egg and toast. "They're everywhere. Like a police drama on the telly. Nurse, these eggs are cold. Where did she go?"

Albert looked at Jeremy Ash with thanks in his eyes, but cartoons were on, and real life got no notice. He looked at his plate. It was almost empty, but he was still hungry.

"How's the old head?" Lane said.

"Better," said Albert.

"Everyone's asking after you," Miss Moodie continued. She spoke much more succinctly with her mouth full than Jeremy had. The benefit of practice. "This is really terrible. Hospital food." She cocked her eyebrow in judgment of the universal malady. "But you're back to your old self, and that's what matters.

"Of course . . . it leaves certain questions begging . . . "

"Before Gertie wears herself out beating around the bush, Professor, what happened to you? That's what everyone wants to know."

Albert told them. Even cartoons paled momentarily by comparison.

"Gracious me!" puffed Miss Moodie. "Who's ever heard of such a thing!"

"Any idea who it was?"

Albert shook his head.

"This is positively thrilling! I mean, it's terrible, of course, but . . . " said Miss Moodie. "We thought it was just an accident."

"You're sure you didn't see anything?" said Lane. "I mean, there's nothing at all you remember that might give a clue as to who it was?"

Albert thought carefully. He remembered the figure running down the hall, the black cape flowing behind it. That was all.

"That's all," said Albert. "Maybe I've forgotten something."

He looked from one to the other of his visitors. Miss Moodie was consuming the last of the toast. "Can't let this go to waste," she said. But Lane seemed suspended in midair. "I don't usually remember things." Lane dropped gently to the ground.

Miss Moodie coughed. "Toast is dry as the Serengeti," she said. "Glad I et before I came." She dusted the crumbs of Albert's breakfast off her hands. "I suppose you've heard about Strickland?"

Albert remembered Professor Strickland and wondered why he wasn't connected with the Law School. "What?"

"He's been named to head Ancient History."

"Just temporary," said Lane.

"Means he'll be taking over the digs in Crete, though, once spring rolls around."

Albert was struck by something quite apart from the conversation. "You live alone, don't you?" He was looking at Lane. "You're left-handed, and you cook with gas."

The sudden turn down a narrow side street nearly threw Lane off the turnip truck.

"What? Gas?"

"Gas."

Lane looked at Miss Moodie who was busy helping the nurse arrange the flowers in a vase to the accompaniment of a lecture on crisp toast and hot eggs. "As a matter of fact, yes, I do cook with gas."

A thrill of revelation rattled through Albert. "And you live alone?"

"Yes, but," Lane was suddenly uncomfortable under Albert's unabashed gaze. "What, Albert? You're looking at me like I forgot to put my pants on."

"There's no light on your right side when you shave," said Albert aloud to himself. What could that mean? He related the observation to his own experience. "Your bathroom light isn't working. There's a window on your left."

Lane shifted on the bed. "Do you hear this, Gertie? I think the concussion's made the Professor a mind-reader."

"What?" said Gertie as the nurse departed, freshly weighted with orders for the cook. "Who?"

"The Professor," said Lane. "He's a psychic."

"How do you mean?" said Gertie, bending close to Albert and studying him over her glasses as if he'd just come down with spots. "He looks all right to me."

"A psychic," Lane repeated. "How did you do that?"

"Do what?" said Miss Moodie.

Albert's excitement doubled. "Was I right?"

"Right as rain, except about the window," said Lane. "There are lights on either side of my bathroom mirror. The right one blew out a few days ago. Haven't had the chance to put a new one in. How did you do it?"

"What did he do? What's all this about plumbing?" said Miss Moodie, a little offended that the conversation should have gotten so far without her.

Albert had withdrawn to a separate level of consciousness, one where pleasant thoughts resided, if the smile on his face was any indication.

"Remarkable," said Professor Lane. "I think we'd better let him get some rest. He's tired."

"Well, I shouldn't wonder, what with . . . " Lane guided Gertie from the room by her elbow. "But he'll have to water the flowers regularly."

"The nurse will take care of them," said Lane, who had been discomfited by Albert's scrutiny. "Let him rest."

After they left the room, the sounds of the cartoons subsided. "Professor?" said Jeremy Ash. He'd pulled himself to a sitting position. "Professor?"

Albert regarded his roommate distantly.

"Professor?"

Albert focused. "Yes?"

"How did you do that?"

"What?"

98

"I was listening. What you said to that man about gas and the bathroom and living alone. How did you do that?"

"I'm not sure," Albert said. "He was rubbing his hands together, and I noticed he had a lot of hair on the fingers of his right hand, here," he added, pointing to the first joint of his finger. "White hairs. But there was hardly any on the left hand, and what there was burnt, just like mine when I put the tea kettle on and turn on the gas. Poof! It stinks."

"And since it was on his left hand."

"He must be left-handed."

"Unless he put the pot on with his left hand, because he was right-handed . . . and used his right hand to turn on the gas."

"I hadn't thought of that," said Albert, who hadn't. "But I was right."

"What about the bathroom light?"

Albert stroked his growth of whiskers. "Something I read somewhere. Dr. Lane is a very well-dressed man; clothes are important to him. But there were places he missed shaving . . . only on the right side of his neck. So he must have had good light on the left, and bad light on the right."

"Makes sense."

"And he must live alone. He had no wedding ring. Besides, his wife would have told him to shave again." Miss Bjork came suddenly to mind. "Miss Bjork would have told him."

What, Albert wondered, would the burns on his face and hands have told the very observant Detective Naples?

Chapter Eight

It was late afternoon when the doctor came in. Jeremy Ash was trying to explain I Love Lucy to Albert.

"Well, everything seems all right here. Everything under control, young man? Let's have a look, shall we?"

The color drained from Jeremy's cheeks. Even Albert noticed. His face became set and determined. The doctor unfolded the curtain between them. A moment later Albert realized that not all the moaning he'd heard had come from the TV. Sympathetic tears welling in his eyes, he took off his glasses and stared at the wall.

The doctor squeezed himself around the screen when the examination concluded. "We'll let young Mr. Ash get himself together. How's the head?" Without waiting for an answer, he began unwinding Albert's turban.

Albert was not encouraged by the rows of rust-red stains surrounded by pale-green haloes that marked the trailing cloth. Dr. Williams pressed for a nurse. "Beautiful job of stitching, that," he said. "I got the design from a sewing book." Albert didn't laugh. "That was a joke."

Albert thought the doctor's manner was forced and unnatural. He had something on his mind.

The nurse came in with new bandages. By the time the Williams had finished applying them, Albert had discovered that he was right-handed, smoked a pipe, drank beer, had been married a long time, and had a son who lived at 25 Highland Avenue in Terre Haute, Indiana. Furthermore he was farsighted and regarded with affection by the hospital staff. All this information had been acquired without a word of reference to any of it. It was amazing how much could be learned if one just looked.

Righthandedness was easy to figure out. The smell of smoke on his breath combined with the lack of nicotine on his fingers made him a smoker from a distance - a pipe. His wedding ring was deeply embedded in the supple flesh of his finger. It had been there a long time.

The doctor's physique suggested a penchant for beer, an impression greatly reinforced by the glow on his cheeks and nose. It had a Pavlovian effect on Albert's salivary glands.

As for the son, each time the doctor leaned forward his coat bulged aside revealing a letter in his shirt pocket, from "Dr. John Williams, Jr." Finally, the pen with which he scribbled his notes on Albert's chart was gold and inscribed "to D.J.W., with love, from the staff of St. Mary's."

Albert decided to take a bold step. "I'm sorry your son's not going to be a doctor."

Dr. Williams started as if he'd been slapped in the face.

He rolled back in his chair with the loose ends of Albert's bandage in his hand, like someone about to start a lawnmower.

"I beg your pardon?"

"Your son, in Indiana," said Albert. "He's decided not to be a doctor, hasn't he?"

Williams's hand went quickly to the letter pocket. "You know my son?"

"No." Albert was ashamed. In playing his game he'd struck something deeply personal, and painful. "I'm sorry," he said, lowering his eyes. "I saw the envelope . . . the letter. It must be your son, 'Dr. Williams, Jr.'. But the 'Dr.' was crossed out in pen."

For a moment Williams seemed unsure how to respond. The gaze he settled on Albert mixed confusion and wonder. It was a lesson Albert was never to forget.

Williams let go of the loose end of Albert's bandage, so it hung from his head like the shroud on Marley's ghost. He took the letter from his pocket and turned it over in his hands. "Well, you deduced a hell of a lot," he said. "And you're right. He's dropped out of med school. I'd given him this stationery as a gift a year or so ago. Counting my chickens, I suppose. He never was too keen on the idea. My wife and I . . . well, I thought seeing 'Dr. Williams' in print like that might, you know, inspire him . . . but it didn't."

The doctor raised his watery eyes to Albert's. "You deduced a hell of a lot," he said again. He put the letter back in his pocket and resumed his work in silence. "I'll drop in tomorrow, Professor," he said as he left the room.

Albert called after him. "Doctor!"

"Yes?"

"When can I go home?"

"Well, you could go now, if you wanted. I mean, we can't keep you here, you know. But I wouldn't advise it. Not for another two or three days. I want to keep any eye on that – "

"Could I go home, then come back? I need to take care of some things mail. Messages." Albert didn't remember the last time he'd had mail, or a message. Huffy handled all that.

"Do you feel up to it?"

"Yes."

The doctor deliberated. "I don't imagine you'll do yourself much harm. You'll have to sign yourself out, you know. You're not under our care while you're gone."

"Where?"

"At registration downstairs. Just home and back, mind."

Albert nodded. "Home and back."

"Good."

Once more the doctor turned to go. Once more Albert stopped him. "Dr. Williams I'm sorry . . . I'd like to . . . I mean I didn't mean to . . . I'm sorry."

Williams looked at him for a moment in silence, nodded with a half-smile and disappeared down the hall on soft-soled shoes.

On his way out of the hospital Albert passed Tewksbury's room. The yellow police ribbon was stretched in front of the door, but the police were gone. Tewksbury was gone.

It felt strange to be outside. The sun was out, but the air, instigated to indiscriminate acts of aggression by the winter wind - was bitingly cold. It felt good. Albert pulled his turbaned head a little further into the upturned collar of his coat and struck off through the shadowless waste of midday.

First he went to the school to get some money but the person who usually had his envelope full of change wasn't there. They sent him to the bank where he had direct deposit. He'd never been to the bank before. He'd never had to. His rent was automatically deducted and someone else got all his bills. Huffy, he suspected. Maybe an accountant at the school. Someone.

The bank reminded him of the Law School; a row of women stood behind a counter and thick windows of bulletproof glass. There were no lines, but Albert still had to wait until one of the women finished telling the other women a story about somebody named Claudette.

"I'd like some money, please," said Albert. He never forgot to say please.

"I can't hear you," said the woman behind the glass. Albert could hear her perfectly.

He bent down and repeated his request through the narrow gap between the window and the counter.

The woman tapped a slotted metal disk in the middle of the window. "Up here," she said without further explanation. Albert pressed the disk firmly and waited for the money.

"No . . . talk here. What do you want?" She'd heard what he wanted when he spoke under the glass, but that wasn't the right place.

Albert pressed his lips to the disk and reiterated his request for the third time. He wondered how anyone ever managed to rob a bank.

The tellers seemed a happy crowd, all smiling very actively at one another. And at Albert.

"Account number?" said the woman.

"I don't have it with me."

"You don't remember it?"

Albert couldn't tell if this was a question or an accusation; in either case it was preposterous.

"Of course not."

"Checking or passbook?"

Honesty was the best policy. "I don't know," Albert said into the disk. It was cold on his lips.

The teller had descended to the bottom of her very short rope.

"What is your name, sir?"

Finally, a sensible question! He told her and she entered it into the computer.

"Here it is." Suddenly her demeanor changed. "Goodness! When was the last time you made a withdrawal?"

"A what?" said Albert, afraid he'd done something wrong. "I didn't do it." He probably did.

"You've got a substantial balance in your savings account!"

"I didn't know that," said Albert. "I just need some groceries."

Usually he just charged groceries to the school, but they'd be suspicious if he charged all he'd need for both him and Tewksbury. "How much are groceries?"

The woman looked at the other women who had gathered around the computer screen to admire Albert's assets. "Well, I spend a hundred and twenty-five a week and I've got three kids."

Tewksbury would equal three kids. "I'll take that," said Albert.

"A hundred and twenty-five."

"I'll need to see your driver's license."

"I don't drive."

"You don't drive?"

"Ask for his Social Security number," said one of the other ladies. Albert heard her perfectly, too.

"Does it have it in there?" asked Albert, pointing at the computer.

"Yes, it does," said the teller.

"Then that's it," said Albert. The Age of Reason hadn't passed.

The teller went into a little glass room and said something to her supervisor, who replaced her minion at the window. "May we help you?" said the lady with an arch of the eyebrow.

Even Albert's patience had a limit. "I've said all that to the other lady. I have money here, don't I?"

"If you're who you say you are, yes," said the woman. "But you must appreciate that we can't just give you the money because you say you're you."

Who should he say he was? Albert was just going under for the third time when he heard someone call his name.

"I didn't recognize you for a moment, Professor," said the dark-eyed man. The voice was familiar. Professor Strickland. "You look like an Arab in that headgear."

In response to Albert's bemused stare he said, "I don't think we've been properly introduced. I'm Michael Strickland, from Archaeology." Recognition wasn't immediately forthcoming in Albert's expression. "Ancient History? Tewksbury's colleague." The light was slowly coming on in Albert's reddened eyes. "I'm a great fan of yours."

People often said that to Albert. Complete strangers would stop him on the street and ask for his autograph. He knew it had something to do with music, the records he'd made. One of music's unpleasant side effects. "Thank you," he said, etching his name on a deposit slip at the teller window and handing it to Strickland whose turn it was to be bemused. He looked at the paper and tucked it in his pocket.

"Thank you, Professor," he said. He extended his hand. Albert had an idea. He took Strickland's hand and pulled him to the teller window.

"He knows who I am," he declared.

"Doctor Strickland," said the supervisor, a little abashed. "You know this man?"

"Doesn't everyone, Mrs. Bridges? The Professor's the most illustrious member of our faculty. A national treasure."

Strickland excused himself with a handshake. "I'm sure they'll help you now, Professor." He went about his business at another window. He knew where to talk.

"Fill this out, Professor," said Mrs. Bridges. He did. "You have a lot of money in this account, Professor. It should be in separate accounts. Separate banks. The FDIC only insures accounts up to a hundred thousand dollars. The records show we've written you about it."

They should write to Huffy. Albert was watching Strickland. He'd written something on a piece of paper and slid it under the glass. Albert scratched in the amount and did the same. "How would you like that, sir?"

Was this a test? "I'd like it very much."

"No, sir. I mean, would you like five, ten, or twenty dollar bills."

"Quarters." Albert was comfortable with quarters.

"Quarters?"

"Yes, please."

The teller assembled rolls of quarters.

"I'll be happy to take care of that for you, Professor. We could transfer the overage to an IRA or Keogh," the supervisor suggested.

"A keyhole?"

"Keogh it's a ... "

She described what it was and Albert struggled to look as if he was paying attention. He was thinking about poor Tewksbury with no cigarettes, no beer, no donuts, at the same time he took an almost subconscious survey of the supervisor. She was probably attractive. He wasn't sure. Over forty. A grandmother ring, like the one his sister had given their mother, indicated she had three grandchildren, two of one and one of the other. He couldn't remember which colors were for which sex.

What else? A permanent indentation on the ring finger of her left hand suggested she had worn a ring there for a long time, but hadn't been doing so recently. She was widowed or divorced. His mother had been widowed for years, but she still wore the ring. He decided this lady was divorced. Unless she'd just lost it. She wore contacts, and as she spoke she leaned on the counter, revealing grandmotherly cleavage and a transparent bra with "Tuesday" written on the lace trim.

So it was Tuesday.

She was right-handed, spoke with a definite Connecticut accent, and dressed like Miss Bjork. Albert was glad he'd shaved.

Just as the supervisor finished her speech and Albert was putting a great deal of effort into his facial expression, he overheard Dr. Strickland, two windows over, saying he'd like to put something in his safe-deposit box.

Glancing in that direction, Albert saw the teller lead Strickland, who was carrying a black shoulder bag, into another room, and out of sight.

Mrs. Bridges had stopped talking. Albert looked at her, smiled, and nodded.

"Well?" she said. "Which do you want to do?"

Albert continued smiling and nodding. "The last one," he said finally.

"The Keogh," said Mrs. Bridges approvingly. "Excellent choice." Albert was relieved. "I'll take care of the paperwork and get it out to you by the end of the week." Albert smiled more broadly, stuffed the rolls of quarters in his pockets, signed a piece of paper, and backed out of the bank. He had to hold his pants up.

The grocery store, being somewhat more familiar territory, was not as much of an adventure. Why couldn't banks operate on the Redi-Mart principle? He placed his eclectic selection on the conveyor belt and tried to ignore the monotone G-sharp beep as his items were dragged across the little light by the gum-chewing girl behind the counter who was talking to another gum-chewing girl behind another counter as if Albert wasn't there.

"That's thirty eighty-six," she said.

He had a hundred-twenty-five dollars. There would be a lot left over.

Albert knocked three times on his apartment door, waited four beats, knocked twice, waited four beats, knocked once. The door opened and light fell upon the archaeological remains of Professor Tewksbury, who pulled him in and slammed the door. "Cigarettes!" he said, taking one of the bags from Albert and pouring its contents on the kitchen table. He found them, tore open the carton, tore open a pack . . . like Russian dolls . . . at last extracting a slender, pure-white weed of delicious poison.

He lit it on a burner of the gas stove, searing his eyebrows, and drew the entire thing deep into his lungs in several noisy drags. He lit another, and one for Albert.

"Oh, that's good!" he said.

Albert started unloading the other bag. "I got light bulbs. Seventy-five watt, is that okay?"

"It'll be nice not having to sleep here in the dark," said Tewksbury. "It's bad enough in the light. Place is an oversized petri dish. A bacteriologist would have a field day rutting around in here. You could probably get the CDC to underwrite it for research purposes. What'd you get to eat?"

Albert wanted to know himself. He was hungry. He called off each item as he took it from the bag. "Pizza, Parmesan cheese, spaghetti sauce, fetuccini noodles - that's spaghetti, isn't it? Black olives, taco sauce, burrito shells, hot peppers, a hardboiled-egg slicer, coffee, milk, two new coffee cups! Pita pockets? Fried pork rinds, Eskimo pies, peanut butter, and beer."

He stood back and surveyed the little mound of edibles with the approving eye of a connoisseur. He glanced at Tewksbury.

He'd seen that look somewhere before . . . the creature that buzzed through trees on the Bugs Bunny cartoons came to mind.

Tewksbury made no effort to couch his dismay in civility. "That's it?" he said. "We're supposed to live on this stuff?"

Albert's culinary balloon was burst. His habit had always been to push his cart quickly up and down the aisle - before anyone had a chance to recognize him and ask for his auto-graph - tossing in whatever came in reach. Sometimes the outcome was disappointing, leaning heavily toward hard-ware and paper products. This time, though, there was a certain theme to the selection, most of which was edible!

He put a new light bulb on the shelf in the refrigerator.

"It's for you," he said. "I'm going back to the hospital. Three more days."

Tewksbury looked at Albert. "You mean they didn't let you out yet?"

"No. I just came out for a few hours, because . . . "

"Because you had to do a favor for an inconsiderate ass." Tewksbury put a hand on Albert's shoulder. "I'm sorry, Al-bert. I appreciate it. Really. Thanks."

"A policeman was at the hospital this morning. He asked me about the escape."

There had been a spark of life in Tewksbury's eyes. It was gone in an instant. Extinguished by the blunt return to reason. "So soon."

"What?"

Tewksbury enveloped Albert in the abyss of his eyes. Albert had never seen death before. "They'll be here any minute."

"How could they?" said Albert. "Nobody knows."

"It doesn't take much to figure it out." Tewksbury replied softly, dropping to the arm of a chair. "We're friends. There was all that disturbance last night then you check yourself out for the day?" He sighed. "They'll be here any minute. I'm sure they had someone follow you."

Albert hadn't seen anyone at the bank or the Reddy Mart but, since his practice was to avoid eye-contact whenever possible, he didn't say anything.

"What did he say? What did he ask you?"

Albert didn't remember, exactly.

Tewksbury released a mouthful of smoke that seemed in no hurry to ascend. Like the smell of a lost love's perfume it brought tears to his eyes, curled in milky tresses, and teased away. "It's not important."

It wasn't. Albert was thinking, or a thought had come to him. Sometimes mail came the same way. "Will I have to go to jail?"

Tewksbury's expression made room for the possibility. "Good Lord, Albert! I'd never given it a thought." That was all the answer Albert got. He wondered if he'd be allowed to take his piano. And all these groceries.

He had no idea what to do with the wave of desperation that swept through him. He wrung his hands, went to the window, and surveyed the neighborhood. There were no blinking lights. No sirens. No policemen or newswomen. Some children skated on the pond in the middle of the common. A barricade had been set up around a manhole in the street.

"See anything?"

"No."

"Nobody?" Tewksbury rose and came to the window. "I thought the place would be crawling with police by now."

Slowly, like sunrise after a sleepless night, desperation gave birth to a desperate child.

"We still have time!" Albert said. "Help me with these." He stuffed the groceries into cupboards and the bags under the sink. "Get some of my clothes. There are stairs in back."

The snow behind the house was tramped flat and brown.

"Where are we going?"

"Back to the hospital," said Albert matter-of-factly. Tewksbury stopped in his tracks.

"What! To the hospital?"

Albert, directed by the idea that they should stay out of sight as much as possible, had hidden himself behind the dumpster.

"Come here."

"You're going to turn me in?"

"After all this?" said Albert. "Come on."

Tewksbury stood in Albert's too-small pants - his own had been torn during the escape - with a paper bag tucked under his arm and cocked his head like a dog. Finally, not without trepidation, he resigned himself to Albert's care. The ensuing game of shadow tag soon found them on the hospital grounds.

"What now?"

"The police are gone," Albert said.

"I repeat. What now?"

"I'll go in first, back to my room. Then you come in."

"And do what? Sign in and ask for a room with a view?"

"Just walk in," said Albert with uncustomary confidence. "There are so many people, no one will notice. Especially the ladies at the desk." It had been Albert's experience that people at desks never noticed. "They never notice."

"Where am I supposed to go?"

"Back up to your room."

Tewksbury looked heavenward, sighed deeply, and threw up his arms. "What I really need is a flashing neon sign I can hang around my neck, and someone marching in front of me - like a leper - shouting my presence to all and sundry." It was a moving gesture, but the theater was empty. Albert had struck off across the grounds leaving Tewksbury to founder or follow.

Chapter Nine

For several minutes Tewksbury stood there in Albert's overcoat, draping the air with puffs of steam like a derailed locomotive. He expected the authorities to descend upon him en masse at any moment. They didn't. "It can't be any worse than peanut-butter tacos," he resolved at last.

Albert was waiting in the second-floor lobby when Tewksbury stepped out of the elevator.

"That's incredible! Nobody stopped me! No one even noticed me?"

Albert wasn't surprised. He ushered Tewksbury quickly down the hall to his former room. "See?" he said, indicating the police ribbon. "No one will go in."

"No one except the police."

When Albert picked the lock, Tewksbury's confidence in him shot from tepid to lukewarm. A chill shivered through him when he saw the bed. The restraints were draped neatly across it like arms folded across a dead man's chest. Albert promised to bring food, closed the door, and returned to his room, leaving Tewksbury alone in the dark.

Jeremy Ash wasn't in his bed. Albert had dressed in his hospital gown and just gotten into bed when Miss Bjork tapped the door.

"May I come in?"

Albert nodded. He wondered if he'd remembered to tie the back of his gown.

Miss Bjork sat on the bedside chair. Albert looked at her and smiled without looking at her or smiling. He folded his hands in his lap.

"Where's our young friend?"

"I don't know. I've been out today," said Albert. "I just got back. He isn't here."

"Took my breath away."

"Hmm?"

"All that – yesterday." She nodded toward Jeremy's bed. "Oh. Yes."

"That's not all the excitement, though, so I hear." She was looking at him oddly. He remembered the red line on his face.

"Tewksbury, you mean," he said. He leaned his cheek on his hand with his elbow resting in midair. "He escaped."

Miss Bjork took off her coat and scarf. Albert felt suddenly uncomfortable. The lady at the bank came to mind. It was still Tuesday. No need to recheck the calendar.

"I'd never have figured him the escaping type," said Miss Bjork. The appraisal was flavored with a pinch of admiration. "I can picture him wandering around in the snow in hospital pajamas."

"A gown," Albert corrected.

"Mmm. Well, they'll have him before long, I'm afraid. They're everywhere."

"The police?"

She nodded. "He doesn't strike me as very resourceful."

Even if they did find him, Albert thought, he'd be right where they left him. What would they do? "He's very smart," he said.

"Well, it's all very exciting, but that's not why I'm here," said Miss Bjork, becoming more animated. "You remember I said I had something to tell you?"

Albert didn't remember. He nodded his circular nod.

"Well, it's about one of your colleagues. A professor . . . "

She took a notebook from her purse and flipped through the pages, "Alters?"

"Terry Alter."

"Right. Well, it seems Tewksbury wasn't the only one who might have wanted Glenly dead. Just last spring this . . . Professor Alter threatened to kill Glenly. Apparently he was a little drunk." She referred to her notes. " 'You're a dead man, Glenly. No matter how long it takes; I'll make you

114

sweat. I'll make you pay.' " She was reading the words in a courtroom monotone that belied their content. "He stood outside Glenly's house yelling one night last spring. Several of the neighbors heard it. This is a quote from one of them."

"What did Glenly do?"

"That's the ironic thing; apparently he wasn't even home."

They were both silent for a moment. Miss Bjork finally spoke. "Apparently this isn't typical behavior for Alter. They say he's quiet. Definitely not a drinker. What could've set him off?"

Albert was glad Miss Bjork was studying the floor as she spoke. It gave him a chance to study her, to try to figure what about her made his entire nervous system spongy. It brought to mind an experiment he'd done once involving a compass and a magnet. Miss Bjork made Albert's entire physiognomy point due north. He'd only begun to dwell on her salient points when something she said hit home.

"His daughter," Albert said almost involuntarily. "Glenly got her . . . made her . . . she was going to have a baby."

"Glenly's baby!"

Albert nodded. Miss Bjork rose and began pacing.

"Good Lord." Pace. Hesitate. Pace. Stop. "There's motive."

"She went away."

"His daughter?"

Albert nodded again.

"He'd've known about Glenly's reaction to sulfites. Motive, method . . . opportunity. There was plenty of that." She looked at Albert in a way that made his eyes water. "He could be the one."

Albert didn't want him to be the one. He wanted to prove Tewksbury innocent. That's all. Couldn't Glenly's death be attributed to Divine Retribution?

"Ah! There he is!" said Miss Bjork. Albert was shaken from his thoughts. Jeremy Ash was being rolled into the room on his stretcher. "Where have you been, young man?"

Jeremy Ash didn't look well. His face was a cold alabaster beaded in sweat. Albert saw Tewksbury in the boy's eyes. It occurred to him that no one ever visited Jeremy. He wondered why.

"How'd it go, Professor?" Jeremy said, brightening a little.

Albert gave him thumbs-up. The boy laughed as they put him on the bed. "Tell me later," he said, his words punctuated by sharp breaths of pain.

"You two have a secret?"

There was a sparkle in the boy's eyes. "Do we have a secret, Professor?"

"I guess we do," said Albert, warming to the notion of such a savvy confidant. "I guess so."

The boy laughed.

"Well, if you guys are going to be so mysterious, I'll just make like a tree, as they say," said Miss Bjork, getting her things together. "I've got work to do. But I'll be back tomorrow. Can I get either of you anything?"

Albert was carefully not watching Miss Bjork put her coat on and wondering what trees had to do with anything. "A small pepperoni pizza!" Jeremy Ash said without hesitation. "And a Frostie root beer!"

"You got it!" She tossed her Harvard scarf around her neck. "I'm going to meet with . . . the other gentleman," she said.

"You never know what might turn up."

"Secrets?" said Jeremy Ash with a smile.

"You're not the only one who can keep their mouth shut."

Jeremy Ash waited until her footsteps echoed down the hall. "What happened?"

"I went home."

"And?"

"Well, you know the . . . thing that was at my house?"

"Yeah."

"Well . . . it isn't there anymore."

"Where is it?"

Albert tossed his ball of twine into a nest of kittens. "You'd never guess."

Five minutes later the teenager had exhausted every possibility of his fertile imagination, including Buckingham Palace, the Taj Mahal, and the County Jail, but had failed to unearth Tewksbury.

Albert smiled. Tewksbury was supremely safe from detection.

"What's this, Twenty Questions?"

Detective Naples's sudden appearance, unheralded by so much as a shuffle, shook Albert to the core. How long had he been standing in the hall? Jeremy Ash turned on Gilligan's Island. Very loud.

"Well, Professor, better today?" Naples sat on the bed.

"Better," said Albert, who was anything but at the moment. The inspector was disappointed that Albert's friends had opted to send him flowers rather than chocolates. "This is for you." He handed a neatly folded paper to Albert who took it, opened it, and began to read, his expression growing more and more confused until he looked at the inspector over the top of the sheet. "What is this?"

"A search warrant," Naples said through horizontal lips.

Albert shuddered at the thought. "You want to search me?"

He handed the paper back to the inspector.

"Your house," Naples said, pushing Albert's hand aside.

"Why?"

"Because I think we'll find Tewksbury there, Professor. That's why."

"I don't think he's there," said Albert. "He doesn't have a key."

"And if he's not there," continued the Inspector, "maybe he has been. And . . . maybe he left his calling cards."

"Calling cards?"

Naples rubbed his fingertips. "Fingerprints, Professor."

"But . . . he was there," Albert stammered. "I mean, before. He visited. I told you."

"Fingerprints are like fruit, Professor. New ones are fresh, old ones are stale."

"Fresh?"

"As a morning in Paris," said the inspector. He stood up and began unbuttoning his overcoat. "By the way . . . I meant to ask you about the burn on your face and . . . "

The inspector's words froze on his tongue as Jeremy Ash screamed in pain, pushing himself up on his elbows, arching his torso and tossing his head back. Naples backed toward the door where he was temporarily stranded by the inrushing tide of nurses and orderlies. He mumbled something Albert didn't hear and left.

The screaming continued long after Naples had gone. Albert smiled. It was a masterful performance. But enough was enough.

More doctors and nurses came and went and there was a lot of noise and people yelling at each other. Finally one of the doctors said, "We're losing him!"

As the truth dawned on Albert, it tore the bottom out of his stomach. Something told him to pray. He did.

For the next two days the musical patient brought food to the historical prisoner at irregular intervals. Tewksbury was much improved. He'd removed his own stitches at the appropriate time and was full of praise for Albert's criminal ingenuity. Though the future was still bleak, he was over the despondency that had led to his suicide attempt and was ready to fight. He was much heartened, too, to hear that Miss Bjork doubted his guilt and had actively undertaken the job of proving his innocence.

Albert didn't say anything about Terry Alter. That wasn't good news.

On the morning of the third day after Tewksbury's escape, Albert had just finished his breakfast when Dr. Williams came in.

"Professor, glad to see you're awake." Albert's quizzical expression prompted him to continue. "I popped in last night . . . you were asleep."

"Oh."

"Well, today's the day, then!" Williams found some bacon between his teeth and was crunching at it thoughtlessly with his incisors. "Let's have a look."

The doctor removed Albert's bandages. "Ah," he said to himself over his glasses. He conducted all his business over his glasses. Albert wondered why he wore them. Without glasses Albert's world was a blur. "Beautiful seam. I should've been a tailor." He dropped the bandage in a pile on the table. A nurse appeared beside him in response to some telepathic communication only nurses understood.

The doctor held out his hand and the nurse slapped an odd-looking pair of scissors into it. "Let's just see if we can keep most of the gray matter in." He proceeded to pluck the tiny spiders of black thread from Albert's itching scalp. "Eighteen in, eighteen out!" he said, clapping his hands to his knees and rolling back on his haunches to survey his handiwork. "I'm getting better!"

"And hardly any leaks this time," said the nurse without cracking a smile. The possibility had never occurred to Albert. He was reassured. The nurse gathered up the remains of the operation and padded away in soft-soled white shoes.

"I expect you'll be wanting to go home today," said Williams.

Albert's mind suddenly began to race with the implications of the statement. What about Tewksbury? What about Jeremy Ash?

"What about Jeremy Ash?"

"Who? Oh, the boy." He lowered his eyes and shook his head. "He's in intensive care." Thoughtful pause. The eyebrows contract. "What he's been through, Professor, I don't know. He's got half a dozen ailments: hepatitis, kidney failure, not to mention the obvious." He slapped his knees. "God only knows what's going on inside." Pause. "Remarkable. I can't imagine where he gets the will to live."

"What happened?" Albert asked softly.

"Ah, so you're not a mind reader today?"

It was Albert's turn to lower his eyes.

"Sorry," Williams said. "His leg, you mean?"

Albert looked at the doctor.

"I'm talking out of school, I suppose, but," Williams stood up, pulled the chair within whispering distance, and sat down, "the boy's been abused most of his life. You see how small he is. How frail. As I understand, his mother and father were divorced. Mother had a drug problem, so the father got custody. This was some time ago. Jeremy would've been two or three.

"Anyway, his father remarried, and was killed in a car wreck – no motorcycle. Whatever. So, here's Jeremy left with a stepmother who'd've scared the bejeebers out of the Brothers Grimm. Kept him locked in his room, most of the time, according to the police report.

"Then a boyfriend moved in. So there he was with two stepparents . . . adoption by default and both of a mind in matters of childrearing.

"He'd watch TV. That was his only contact with the outside world. His only education. It's amazing he's not demented as well.

120

"Anyway, he took their abuse all those years . . . then it seems the stepparents took a long weekend in Atlantic City. Dead of winter. There was a power outage . . . the heat went off. Two days later neighbors heard the cries . . . his leg had been wounded, frostbite set in. To this day he won't talk about it."

Albert took off his glasses. He didn't want to see the picture that had just been etched on his brain. A solitary tear played hide-and-seek from whisker to whisker down his cheek. The doctor passed him a Kleenex and used one himself.

"That's how he lost it," Williams continued. "Worst case of gangrene I ever saw." There was a few seconds' silence. "He's been here for . . . fourteen, fifteen months now. One thing after another. A day at a time. Just when it seems he's over the worst . . . well, you saw."

Albert was speechless.

"You can see everyone here thinks the world of the boy. There's none of us couldn't learn a lot from him. When we get someone feeling oversorry for themselves, we bunk 'em with Jeremy a few nights." The doctor shook his head. "I'm not a religious man, Professor. Well . . . maybe I'm not as irreligious as I once was, but, I swear . . . if there's such a thing as angels, that boy's one of 'em."

For a few minutes the two men shared the sympathy of silence.

Albert spoke first. "There's a lot of pain out there."

"Speaking of which," the doctor replied, "did you ever get to see your lady friend the one who . . . " He tapped his temple.

"No. Jeremy Ash said she never came back after I was conscious. I've seen the other one, though. Miss Bjork."

"Miss Bjork? Oh. The lawyer? Yes. I've spoken to her . . . in the halls." The doctor stood up with his customary slap of the knees. "Much too pretty for a lawyer," he said. "If I were you . . . well, I'm not, am I? Good day, Maestro. P'raps I'll see you before you go." He was about to leave the room when, once again, Albert stopped him in the doorway.

Williams turned. Albert held out his hand, which the Doctor shook warmly, and left.

Albert wanted his piano.

Chapter Ten

"I didn't get to see Alter till yesterday afternoon," said Miss Bjork. The phone had rung just as Albert was stuffing the last of his possessions into a paper bag. He'd been wondering what to do with Tewksbury. The sudden beeping of the phone jolted his heart; there was something accusatory about it.

"How well do you know him?"

"Not very," said Albert. His hands were acting independent of his brain, loading the bag with the hospital jetsam that had washed up around his bed: a box of tissues, a glass, a washcloth.

"He teaches biology and . . . what I told you. That's all."

The bedpan wouldn't fit in the bag. He'd have to carry it in his free hand.

"He's a very nice man," said Miss Bjork. "I can't remember when I last said that about anyone, but . . . he's so nice. Quiet. Well mannered. A gentleman."

In the pause that followed, Albert caught himself cramming the phone base into the bag. What was he supposed to do with Tewksbury? Where was Jeremy Ash?

"I couldn't imagine him drunk in the streets, let alone . . . until I thought how a man like that would be affected by the news about his daughter." Miss Bjork sighed. "You never know."

"You never know." For some reason the words struck a chord in Albert, drawing him out of his worries for the moment, crystallizing a resounding, universal truth in their ringing simplicity.

He had found a credo: You Never Know. "You never know," echoed Albert, who never did.

"He knew who I was," Miss Bjork continued. "And he knew why I wanted to talk to him. He said he was surprised the police didn't question him after the murder. Then, well, it was as if somebody pulled a plug. He just spilled the whole story."

Albert stopped packing and sat on the bed. He didn't know what to do with the sheets.

"It turns out he'd been having a kind of affair with Mrs. Glenly." Albert sat bolt upright.

"Kind of affair?"

"Well, for lack of a better word. Apparently it was platonic. There was nothing physical."

Albert felt his cheeks flush.

"He was sorry for her. She was so much younger than Glenly, you know. Very morose most of the time. Depressed. She was Glenly's second wife. You know that, of course. She was just six or seven years older than his daughter. Anyway . . . Glenly treated her terribly, according to Alter. He didn't beat her or anything. But he was verbally abusive. Mentally and emotionally abusive."

Albert was reminded of what Miss Moodie and Professor Lane had said about the games Glenly would play. "I've heard that."

"Well," Miss Bjork continued, "a relationship developed between them . . . Alter and Mrs. Glenly, sort of a fellowship of sadness. Alter's wife had died about a year earlier. Maybe a year and a half. They consoled each other, you know? Then there was an academic conference of some kind."

Albert cringed. The school had made him attend a conference once. One of his recurring fears was that it would do so again.

The hospital was preferable. So was jail. Or outright execution.

"Glenly was drunk; monopolizing conversation, as usual." Beat. Breath. Sigh. "Mrs. Glenly had gone up to their room early. She couldn't go to sleep apparently. So she went down the hall in her dressing gown and knocked on Alter's door. Unfortunately he was there."

"Unfortunately?"

"They talked for a while and eventually she invited him back to her room for a drink. Glenly walked in on them. Aside from the obvious stupidity and impropriety, they hadn't done anything, according to Alter. He says they were just talking. But there they were, she in her pajamas . . . sitting on her bed . . . and Glenly was three sheets to the wind. He started yelling at the top of his lungs, calling his wife names. And Alter punched him in the mouth.

"Alter said Glenly just stood there for a minute, letting the blood run from his lip. Finally he held out his hand to Mrs. Glenly and pulled her to his side. Then he ordered Alter to leave the room. He wouldn't listen to any explanation. As Alter walked down the hall, Glenly yelled at him. Told him he'd get even."

There were traffic jams at the synapses in Albert's brain. Too many notes. He couldn't make out the music for the noise. Sometimes he thought he heard the faint strains of a melody . . . just enough to know it was there not enough to make it out.

"That's where Alter's daughter comes in."

All at once the noise resolved into a single, astounding crescendo of clarity.

"Glenly got her pregnant! That's how he paid Alter back."

"It makes sense," said Miss Bjork. "And that happened a long time after the threat. Says something about the kind of man Glenly was." Even over the phone Albert could hear her skin crawl. "So, it all comes together. That's what Alter was yelling about outside Glenly's house that night."

In the static-filled silence that followed, Albert could hear faint voices on the line. He wondered what they were saying. He wondered if it was important. "What did he do?"

"Nothing, he says," Miss Bjork replied. "And everything about him screams innocence. I mean, the guy's Father Theresa. Still, I've seen people driven to pretty desperate

extremes. You never know what someone's capable of until .
. ."

"You never know." There were those words again. They rushed through Albert's overheated brain like little lights. "You never know," he echoed, sotto voce.

"I take it they haven't found him yet," said Miss Bjork.

"What?"

"I take it they haven't found Tewksbury yet."

"No. They haven't found him, yet," Albert replied carefully. It was a good time to change the subject. "I'm going home today," he said. "The doctor said I could."

"Oh, good, Albert . . . Professor . . . I'm glad," she said. "I'm sure it'll be good to get back to a normal routine. I'll come by and visit when I get back to town."

"You're not in town?"

"No. I'm in Brattleboro, Vermont, didn't I say? This is where Joanne Alter lives. With her aunt. I had to do some research on another case so I thought I'd kill two birds . . . I'll be here for a couple of days."

Why was he upset by the knowledge that Miss Bjork was out of town? Why did the world suddenly seem to have the color sucked out of it? Before he could follow those thoughts - and their attendant emotions - any further, a desperate thought erupted in Albert's brain and, before he knew it, had formed on his lips. "Can I stay in your house . . . till you get back?"

If Miss Bjork had washed up on the beach, half drowned, Albert's question would have started her breathing again.

"I beg your pardon?"

"Something's not working in my apartment," said Albert.

"What's not working?"

Water? Gas? Light bulbs? The tape recorder? The clock? There was a selection. "The water," he said.

"Oh," said Miss Bjork. She began breathing on her own.

126

"Your pipes froze?" She didn't wait for an answer. "You probably forgot to leave the heat on. You should have them wrapped."

Albert was amazed. She was a plumber, too. "I guess you can stay at my place," she said. "I suppose," she added. "But it's a terrible mess." She gave him the address and told him where to find the key. "Just till I get back, though," she said referring to an experience in her past. "Then you'll have to go home."

Where else would he go? "Good-bye," he said. "Thank you,"

Just after dark that evening Tewksbury walked out of the hospital as casually as he'd walked in and, just as casually, he and Albert crossed town to Miss Bjork's apartment.

Once again Albert's concept of mess seemed at odds with the evidence. He anticipated having to force the door open. Miss Bjork's home looked like a furniture-store window without the price tags or the "sale" sign. The only thing missing was a salesperson.

Tewksbury was impressed.

"This is how the other half lives, Albert. Look at this stuff; numbered prints, lead crystal, Persian rugs. She doesn't pull in this kind of money defending people like me. This is old money; you can smell it."

Albert didn't know what old money smelled like. He was rooted to the doormat; this wasn't a residence, it was a temple, and he a ragged sinner, fouling the threshold.

This was a level of order he couldn't hope to attain.

"She collects first editions," Tewksbury droned on. "Look at this: Dombey and Son, The Pickwick Papers, the whole Dickens library! A Christmas Carol. Longfellow, Kipling, Alexander Pope, Samuel Johnson, The Pepys Diaries. Look at this stuff, Albert!"

Albert felt it would be disrespectful to speak out loud. He left Tewksbury rummaging through Miss Bjork's kitchen cabinets and went home.

The police who had searched his room had apparently operated on the principle of a cyclone. Not that it made much difference; such wanton destruction in a place like Miss Bjork's would have been devastating. At Albert's, it was redecorating. He left everything as it was, extracting things from various piles as he needed them.

He stared at the ceiling for a long time after he went to bed. Oddly enough, it wasn't thoughts of Tewksbury that kept him awake. Or Miss Bjork necessarily, it was Jeremy Ash. The boy's anguished cry replayed itself in his brain. Where had they taken him? What were they doing for him? Most haunting of all . . . what would happen to him after he was well?

Where would he go? His smiling face appeared vividly in Albert's imagination as he fell asleep in the company of tears.

First thing in the morning, he called to check on Tewksbury who had apparently discovered his element in the furniture commercial of Miss Bjork's home. His only complaint was the absence of beer in favor of wine coolers. Albert promised to deliver some cigarettes and hung up.

He hadn't seen himself in a mirror since his "accident." He was shocked. The burn mark on his cheek was bright pink and peeling against his see-through skin. A broad swath of hair had been shaved from his head to admit stitches and now with a week's growth, looked like a hillside cleared for power lines. His eyes were clear, though, bright jewels set in the rummage sale of his face.

After a shower and shave, he felt better. He ate some pork rinds and an Eskimo pie with his coffee. He preferred a cold breakfast. It was a good break from the routine of hospital food.

Somewhere in the course of his activities it occurred to him to go to the hospital and find out what happened to Jeremy Ash. He met Detective Naples coming out of the elevator. "Ah, Professor!" The inspector was always glad to see him.

"I've just been up to your room. They said you'd been released." Albert was standing halfway in the elevator and got blindsided by the door when it decided to close. "I was," he said. "I'm ... " he added. "I came ... I was going up to see ... " He'd suddenly forgotten the boy's name. It escaped him entirely. "The Teenager."

"Oh, yes," said the inspector. He pressed and held the "door open" button after it had slammed Albert a few more times.

"He's there ... had a hard time, I understand. Poor kid." Something in Albert responded to the note of compassion in Naple's voice.

"Dr. Williams told me all about him," the inspector continued. "Rough life. Makes you wonder about people."

Did it? Maybe so. Albert always wondered about people.

The inspector gently pulled Albert into the elevator and pressed the second-floor button. "I see your face is getting better," he said, stroking his own and prefacing the longest elevator ride of Albert's life.

"You know, Professor, I haven't been able to figure it out. I mean, I can't imagine how you could burn yourself like that. I really can't; especially since you were in bed the whole time, or the bathroom, was it? But, you know what? I like puzzles, Professor. I'll help you remember. You'll see."

Albert had pressed himself against the elevator doors in an effort to be as inconspicuous as possible. They opened, spilling him into the hallway. The inspector caught him by the arm. He turned his hands over, revealing the matching stripes on Albert's palms. "The hands are better, too. I wonder where else are you burned, Professor? Why won't you tell me how it happened?"

Albert pulled his hands free and started toward his old room. "I'd rather not," he said. "It's embarrassing."

Naples seized Albert by the shoulder and spun him against the wall. "Where's Tewksbury, Professor?" There was no smugness in his voice. No trace of playful conviviality in his glaring eyes.

Albert knew the look of frustration and anger.

"I don't have him," said Albert. His head was beginning to hurt. He'd been beat up often as a boy. He closed his eyes in anticipation of the blow.

Naples loosened his grip. "I know he's not at your place. We searched."

"I know."

"Of course, you could've called him. Warned him."

"Where would he go?" Albert slid free of Naples' hold. "Did you look at his house?"

Naples smiled with half his mouth. "I said he wasn't at your place. His fingerprints were."

"Maybe he went there after he escaped," said Albert. Did it sound as rehearsed to Naples as it did to him? "He knows where I keep the key." Thoughtful pause. "Maybe he thought you'd find him if he went home. So he went to my house," he concluded. "I was here."

"Then explain this," said Naples. He held up a grocery receipt. "Somebody bought groceries four days ago," he said.

"Who do you suppose it was, Professor?"

"Tewksbury?"

"I doubt it. A wanted man isn't likely to go shopping in broad daylight." Albert filed the possibility for future reference. "I checked, Professor. You signed yourself out that day. Why?"

"I bought the groceries," Albert confessed. "You gave me the idea."

"I did?"

"You said Tewksbury had escaped. I wondered where he'd go. He could go home, but you might find him there. He could go to the school . . . but the school would tell the police. He could go to Vermont, where his father lives, but they said there were roadblocks everywhere. He could go to my house," said Albert. "There was no food there."

"So, you bought some . . . just in case?"

"Is that against the law?" asked Albert, sure that it was.

Naples ignored the question. "Then you came back here and checked yourself in."

"Yes."

Detective Naples looked long and hard at Albert whose guilty puppy eyes avoided his gaze. "I'd be very careful if I was you, Professor," he said. "You're on thin ice as it is."

Albert looked down at his feet involuntarily. When he looked up, the inspector was walking down the hall.

"Inspector?"

Naples was drawn up like a junkyard dog at the end of his chain. "Professor?"

"Was the food eaten?"

The inspector's stare brought salty beads of sweat to the corners of Albert's eyes. When the stare finally broke, Albert collapsed against the wall.

Chapter Eleven

"Hey, Professor!" Jeremy Ash's face lit up when Albert stumbled into the room. "Lookit that haircut!"

An black women, somewhat beyond middle age, was sleeping in Albert's bed.

"Who's that?" he said softly.

"Mrs. Gibson," said Jeremy Ash. "They hadda put her in here 'cause there's no room. She's got gallstones." Albert was at the bedside. "You can talk normal. She's deaf as a brick when she don't have her hearing aid on."

"How are you?"

Jeremy Ash smiled. "Great!" he said. "Never better!"

Albert wished he'd brought something. "I forgot to bring something."

"Hey! Don't worry about it. The nurses give me more stuff . . . I think they clean out people's rooms when they leave, y'know? I get flowers, boxes of candy. Toys, too. Sometimes. Not many. I guess people are so glad to get out, you know, they just, forget." His smile slipped behind the clouds for a moment.

"I won't forget. When will you get out?" Albert asked. His thoughts had gone off chasing foxes in different directions; he was stumbling along to catch up.

The boy shrugged his whole body. "Who knows? I think they like me too much, y'know? I think when they go in to fix the carburetor, they grease the points. They want to keep me here."

"Where will you go . . . when you get out?" said Albert. "You can't go home."

The boy's demeanor changed. "I dunno. Foster home? I've got this social worker . . . " The remote control revolved in his slender fingers. "I never been to school."

They both stared at the darkened television screen. Albert didn't think he'd missed much. He didn't remember learning anything useful in school. "You know a lot," said Albert. "You knew about the lock."

"TV. I learned some stuff, I guess," said the boy. "There was a crack in the door of my room. TV was always on loud."

He looked at Albert; his eyes spoke volumes, and Albert didn't need a library card. "It ain't much of an education, I guess, but it's like a little of everything."

Albert hadn't had many notions. One occurred to him now, and he didn't know what to do with it. Experience hadn't taught him to take these rare gems of exiguous inspiration and store them away for closer examination at a later date . . . to hold them to the light and study them with a critical eye from every conceivable angle. Albert had nowhere to put a notion. So, like an unexpected burp, it was suddenly out in the open. "Why don't you come to my house?" he said.

Jeremy Ash was always in motion. Albert supposed the energy that would otherwise have been expended through his missing leg was redirected to his arms and fingers. For once, though, all activity ceased. The boy looked as if he'd been dowsed with ice water. Albert knew the feeling. "You could live there."

The boy finally worked his tongue free. "You mean, with you?"

That was just one of the many angles from which Albert hadn't looked at the proposal. He'd always lived alone, even growing up with his mother and sister. "With me?" he said. It was supposed to be a reply, but he couldn't keep the question mark out of it. "You never know," he added, not sure how it applied. But it had a hopeful ring.

"I'd like that, Professor." They shook hands to seal the bargain. "When I get out. Hey! Mrs. Gibson!"

Mrs. Gibson had awakened. The tiny hearing aid was lost in her pudgy, sleep-numbed fingers as she fumbled to insert it.

"Just a minute, I'll be right . . . dern thing," she declaimed. "Cussed thing's no bigger than Mr. Gibson's pride an' joy. There! There we go." She put on her silver-rimmed glasses and focused on Albert. "Have mercy. What happened to you?" she said as if the words were startled from her.

"That's the professor I told you 'bout, Mrs. G."

Mrs. Gibson was laboring to pull her substantial self to a sitting position. "Who?" She held out a hand to Albert. "Lemme hol' that pillow, young man," she said. "Who is he? My ears haven't woke up yet."

"The Professor!" Jeremy Ash shouted. "He was my roommate before you. I told you about him."

"Oh, yes . . . " said Mrs. Gibson. She wedged the pillow between the devil and the deep blue sea. "The Professor. Thank you, young man," she said in an aside, as if they'd been talking about somebody else. "Well, he looks like a road kill."

Mrs. Gibson spoke as if the rest of the world was as deaf as she was. It never occurred to her that anyone would hear her comments but the intended hearer. "He's skinnier than you, Jeremy. And bluer than a newborn white baby."

Jeremy Ash was too busy not laughing to respond.

"He takes fits sometimes." Mrs. Gibson confided. "Leave him be a minute. Here, you take some candy." She held out a box of Whitman's Samplers. Albert declined in sign language. "Take one!" she commanded. Albert took one.

"I'll have it later," Albert said. He forced his blue face into a lopsided smile that revealed too many teeth.

"What?" said Mrs. Gibson.

"I'll have it later." Albert said a little louder.

"You eat it now," Mrs. Gibson insisted. "You look more like a road kill than any man I ever seen. You eat that candy before you keel over and die on me. Look at you. A spring breeze would blow you into next week."

Albert swallowed the anchor whole.

Two candies, one apple, and a cookie later Albert—his head abuzz with sugar—was on his way to Miss Bjork's, sufficiently weighted against the wind. He stopped to buy a newspaper for Tewksbury and was on his way out of the store when he recognized Inspector Naples in a car across the street. He went out the back door.

"You should come back to my place," Albert suggested. A few days earlier "gaunt" was the only expression in Tewksbury's facial repertoire. Now he looked crestfallen. Aghast. Taken aback. He must be getting better. "Miss Bjork will be back soon." He looked around the room. Tewksbury's flotsam had washed up everywhere, indicating an erratic high-water mark.

"We'll have to clean up."

"Then what?" said Tewksbury. "Am I supposed to stay there the rest of my life?"

Tewksbury wouldn't get along with Jeremy Ash. Albert's head hurt for the first time in hours.

"It's no good, Albert. I can't go on like this forever. I'm innocent. Somebody out there's guilty, we've got to find him." He looked mournfully at Albert. "You've got to find him . . . you and Bjork."

Albert hung his head. He held a pair of Tewksbury's trousers in one hand, a newspaper and a glass in the other. This is where his concept of "picking up" always fell apart. If he had a big bag . . .

"How?"

"I don't know," said Tewksbury impatiently. "I can't do anything. You and Bjork . . . you can circulate. You can ask questions."

"We have," said Albert.

"And? Haven't you found anything?"

Albert mentioned the evidence incriminating Terry Alter.

"Alter's daughter!" Tewksbury exclaimed with a whistle.

As Albert detailed the evidence, Tewksbury punctuated the commentary with asides. Edges had formed on his face during imprisonment. His ready wink had become a nervous twitch. His eyes never settled, but seemed to be constantly searching for a way out.

Albert placed a pillow strategically over a beer stain in the middle of the sofa. He put the leg of an end table over a cigarette burn in the soft beige carpet. He'd never realized the importance of furniture placement in housekeeping.

Music and Archaeology stepped back to survey their handiwork.

Albert smiled.

"Looks like Troy after Schliemann," Tewksbury said.

Albert's face fell. That could be good or bad, depending on who Schliemann was and what he had done to Troy. It sounded bad.

They picked up their few wrinkled paper bags of possessions and leftovers.

Despite Albert's newly formed theory of conspicuous anonymity and the descending darkness, they took a circuitous route back to his apartment building. Once there, Albert deposited Tewksbury in the shadows while he went to see if the coast was clear.

The light was off on the landing outside Albert's door, but enough residual illumination oozed up from the first floor to reveal someone standing there in the shadows. Thinking it was Naples, Albert was overwhelmed by a compulsion to turn and run. Nevertheless his feet, like twin Judas goats, carried him one step at a time up the stairs.

"Inspector?" said Albert. The figure at the top of the stairs started and stepped back against the wall. It wasn't Inspector Naples. Instantly Albert was seized with an exquisite terror. This shadow matched the one in the school in every particular.

He stopped, anchored to inaction by his white-knuckled grip on the banister. His mouth went dry, its customary moisture apparently redirected to his eyes, which welled with tears of shock. His brain automatically played the first four bars of Beethoven's Ninth, full orchestra.

After a breathless silence, the figure made a hesitant step forward. Albert, correspondingly, took one step back. This process repeated four more times until Albert was back on the first floor and the figure was at the edge of the landing.

"Professor?"

It was a woman's voice;

"Professor?"

She took a step or two down the stairs, coming just enough into the light so that Albert could begin to make out her features. She wore a big black cape with the hood up over her long red hair. High black boots completed her visible wardrobe.

"Who are you?" Albert asked, as if he were talking to the Angel of Death. "What do you want?"

The girl retreated to the landing. "Come up here, Professor. I don't want him to see."

Albert hadn't finished deliberating before he was halfway up the stairs, one unsure step at a time, not once blinking or taking his eyes from the apparition. "Who?"

"Come up here," said the girl, stepping back to make room for him on the landing. "How are you? Your head ... it looks ... I'm so sorry."

Albert stood one step shy of the landing, once again unable to loosen his hold on the railing. "You're the one," he stammered. His hand went to his head.

There was a heavy silence upon which the woman's single word of reply fell like a penitent's confession on Christmas Eve.

"I'm so sorry."

Albert was close enough now, and his eyes enough accustomed to the dark, to see her clearly. She was crying. Or had been. He was close enough, too, to smell her unique perfume. The same, he remembered, from that night in the hallway at school. Sweet but musty. Old-fashioned.

"Who are you?"

"Daphne Knowlton."

Bells and whistles went off in Albert's head as the mental baggage handlers ransacked his brain for all recent information on Daphne Knowlton. First, though, they had to throw out his mental picture of her, foggy and unclear as it was. Her features were full, but she wasn't fat. She was like a woman in a painting. Her eyes perpetually downcast. Walter Lane's tragic story of her was intensified by what could only be described as her melancholy beauty.

"Why did you do it?"

The girl turned her face to the wall. "I didn't mean to hurt you. I . . . you weren't supposed to be there. I was, I . . . " Her words resolved in sobs. Albert was speechless, not so uncommon an occurrence that he was uncomfortable with it.

"Are you all right, now? Will you be?"

"I'm all right," said Albert reassuringly. He was perplexed by the inexplicable feeling of guilt that bubbled up in his conscience. Tewksbury would be getting hysterical about this time.

"I'm glad," said Daphne. "I just had to make sure you were all right. None of it was your fault." She started down the stairs. "You had nothing to do with it."

Most of the time when Albert didn't understand something it was his own fault. Not that he cared. This time, though, it wasn't. The woman suddenly wasn't making sense. A skip in the record!

As she brushed by him, he grabbed her arm. She collapsed to the steps like a punctured balloon. She buried her head in the encircling protection of her arms. "No, don't!"

The reaction was so unexpected that Albert let her go. She thought he was going to hit her. He was appalled. He sank beside her and instinctively put a hand on her shoulder. At first her body stiffened in resistance. Albert didn't pull or prod or make comforting noises. Finally she burst into tears and, sinking against him, let herself be comforted.

"You came to see me in the hospital," he said after a while.

She nodded against his chest. Her hood had fallen off and her hair was in his face. It smelled sweet and clean. He brushed his cheek lightly against it, almost reflexively. "You wanted to make sure I was all right?"

Daphne raised her tear-filled eyes and looked earnestly at Albert. His heart responded of its own accord and he held her a little tighter so it wouldn't knock her off the stairs.

"Oh, Professor!" she sobbed. "I felt so awful. I mean, I didn't know it was you . . . that night. But when I heard the next day and when they said how badly you were hurt, I didn't even . . . " She lowered her eyes again and Albert began to breathe. "I had the papers, so I couldn't tell anyone."

Suddenly she stood up and ran through the fire door toward the back stairs, leaving Albert with an armful of Daphne-scented shadows. "I'm sorry, Professor!" she cried. By the time Albert got to his feet she was gone. He followed, nevertheless.

"Albert? Albert!?" Tewksbury tore himself from the depthless patch of darkness behind the dumpster as Albert approached.

"Where in hell have you been? Was he there? Is he gone? What happened? It's freezing out here."

Albert had read something by F. Scott Fitzgerald once. Something about the South. Something about a war and women and men. He didn't remember the story. But he had noticed the language. Everyone talked so much, and everything was so well thought out. It made him feel deficient. Most things did. But people don't talk like that. They talked like Tewksbury just did. It was a wonder anybody made sense of anything at all.

They went up the back stairs. As they walked Albert told Tewksbury where he'd been, who was there, what she'd said, and how she had left.

"That's the strangest thing I've ever heard," said Tewksbury.

Albert unlocked the door and, once they were both inside with the door closed, clicked on the light. "Merciful . . . !"

The transition from Miss Bjork's apartment to Albert's had a profound effect on Tewksbury; culture shock.

"What happened here?"

"The police were looking for you."

Every cupboard, cabinet, and drawer had been opened and its contents tossed out.

"In the kitchen cabinets and sofa cushions?" Tewksbury started to take his gloves off.

"No! Keep them on," said Albert. "Fingerprints."

They cleared spaces to sit while waiting for the water to boil.

"Ah, hot!" said Tewksbury. He cradled his cup in both hands and sipped with his eyes closed, as if he were taking communion.

Albert shuddered to see coffee taken black. He lost count of the sugars he'd added to his own. He added one more. Better safe.

"She used to work here, at the school," Tewksbury said finally. "Daphne," he added in response to Albert's quizzical look. He studied the augury in his coffee cup. "I remember one night in the teacher's lounge . . . Glenly . . ."

"I know about it," Albert interrupted. He didn't want to hear it again. Nevertheless, Tewksbury elaborated in graphic detail.

Albert was embarrassed again. His heart broke for the girl. Quite other fires were stirred in Tewksbury's eyes.

"Poor kid," he said in summation, having poured the pox of his own memory into Albert's unwilling ears. He drained his cup.

"I saw her once after that. Where was it? . . . oh, I remember. She was talking to Strickland, downtown. She was walking down the sidewalk . . . by the village green . . . he pulled up in his fancy little car and called her. They talked a few seconds, then she got in and they drove away. Haven't seen her since."

What would Naples say now? Albert wondered. "Are you sure it was Strickland?" That sounded right.

"Oh, no doubt." Tewksbury held out his cup. Albert took it and went to the kitchen. "It was no surprise. That night at the school? . . . Strick was the one who rescued her in the end . . . put his coat over her, collected her clothes, took her home. It was him, all right. Besides, his car is pretty conspicuous."

Something troubled Albert. Something was glaringly out of tune. "But I thought she'd left town after . . . all that," he said. "Didn't someone say she went to New Hampshire. Home."

Tewksbury took a long, loud sip from the cup Albert handed him. "I hadn't thought of that. Now you mention it that's what I heard. I don't know." He got up and went to the kitchen.

"Maybe she came back . . . for some reason."

"What reason?"

"I don't know. To get something; see someone . . . Kill someone . . . " The words pushed their way into the open on the wings of a heartbeat.

Tewksbury had gotten up and gone to the refrigerator. The words froze him in mid-motion. Medusa would have been proud. A beat or two later he seized a St. Pauli Girl about the waist and liberated her from the yoke which bound her to her sisters. "You mean . . . " he stammered.

"When was it?"

"What?"

"When did you see her . . . with Strickland?"

Tewksbury sipped and thought, as if the acts were reciprocal.

Suddenly he stopped sipping. His face turned white and he lowered the can. "I'll be . . . "

"What?"

"It was that day . . . the day Glenly died!"

"Are you sure?" Albert was on the edge of his seat. He'd never been on the edge of his seat before.

"Positive." Tewksbury's eyes darted blindly around the room. "Positive. It was before I came to see you. Remember?" Albert remembered. "I was coming out of the town library. That's when I saw Strickland pull up across the green. At first I thought he'd seen me . . . that was why he . . . but then I saw her. They talked."

"And she got in," Albert concluded.

"Then I went somewhere. Probably the drugstore or the bookstore to get my paper. That's it! I rummaged around there for half an hour then I ran into Lane. That's when I found out about Glenly. Lane told me. Then I came to see you."

"You wanted a cigarette."

Tewksbury smiled and lit a cigarette. "You think there's any chance of it?" he said. "I mean, she had the motive, that's for sure. But . . . No. I can't believe it of her. She's not capable of it. "

"They say she was . . . " Albert tapped his temple.

142

"Crazy? Oh, no." Tewksbury thought a second. "I remember hearing something about her past emotional problems. Maybe she had a breakdown or something. Who knows? But that's not crazy. Not that I ever noticed."

"You knew her?"

"Well, no. Not really." The cigarette was dangling from the corner of Tewksbury's mouth. It reminded Albert that he'd left a saxophone at the repair shop. "I mean, we talked. 'Hello' in the halls, the weather, the Dean's haircut, you know. That type of thing.

"But, no. Not really. Still," he added, "she seemed pretty normal to me. Normal as anyone. Of course, those are the ones you have to worry about; the ones who seem normal."

No one had to worry about Albert.

"Did you ever see her with Walter Lane?"

"Lane?" said Tewksbury, leveraging his entire face with his eyebrows. "Now it's funny you should mention that. It just came to mind that instant. I didn't see them together, personally . . . but Strick said once that they'd well, nothing serious apparently, but Lane had an interest in the girl. I'd assumed it was just that father-daughter fondness, you know. I mean, considering her story and Lane's background man's a born social worker . . . well. Why did you mention her?"

"Just something I noticed. I wondered if he liked her," said Albert. "I don't know what it has to do with anything. It's like a puzzle." The analogy had just sprung to Albert's mind. He was surprised by its clarity. The Pure Force of Reason. "Like a puzzle where one piece may not seem to have anything to do with another, until they're all together." It didn't sound as profound as it felt, but it was still good.

Tewksbury belched long and hard. "What's for supper?"

Albert's first analogy; pearls before swine.

The phone rang.

"What on earth happened?" It was Miss Bjork. Albert didn't know what on earth happened. He said hello. "What did you do to my place!?"

She must have moved the furniture.

"Albert?" Pause. No response. "Professor!"

"I tried to put everything back . . . " said Albert. The words got slow and frail toward the end. Hollow as a political promise, "the best I could."

Albert reminded Tewksbury of Alfred E. Newman as he withstood the verbal blast that followed. His knees seemed to knock audibly. His stupid, dazed expression teetered on the brink between a smile and tears. Miss Bjork was a tornado, Albert was a trailer park.

"I'm sorry," Albert whispered softly at last. No buts. No excuses. No explanations. "I'll pay for all the damage. I have a lot of money in the bank." Hurricane Bjork dissipated inland, but damage to the shoreline was extensive.

However deserving of it, no one had ever spoken to Albert like that . . . ever. "I'm sorry," he said, almost in tears, and hung up the phone.

"Our Miss Bjork?" Tewksbury said in a way that was supposed to make Albert feel better. It didn't. "Not happy with our housekeeping, I take it."

"Women notice things," said Albert, who didn't. His tone was almost reverential. His knees settled down eventually. He could feel the color returning to his cheeks. "I guess it was a bad idea."

"Maybe so," said Tewksbury, whose brief, unjust incarceration had inured him to guilt. "I had to go somewhere. Seemed a good idea at the time. What's for supper?"

"I've got to go see her," said Albert.

"Bjork?! She'll have your head."

Albert threw on his coat and left.

Tewksbury listened as his protector's footsteps tripled down the stairs and out of the building. "Don't mind me," he said to the clutter. "I'll get my own supper."

Chapter Twelve

"Ah, Professor." Albert was arrested in his tracks by the greeting, which preceded the inspector from the darkness. "What a coincidence. I was just coming up to see you."

"I've got to go somewhere." said Albert with all the firmness he could muster. "It's important."

"This will only take a second," said the inspector. He blew into his gloved hands. "Why don't we go inside? It's cold out here."

Albert wondered how long Naples had been standing in the cold shadows.

"I can't," said Albert. His heart seemed, all of a sudden, to have given up and left his chest, leaving behind it an aching hollow that trembled with the echo of its beating. "Someone's expecting me." He struck off down the sidewalk. He couldn't resist the notion there was a gun pointed at his back.

"Professor!" The inspector fired. Albert stopped and turned.

"You left your light on." A near miss.

"I'll be back," said Albert. He struck off again, through the streetlight's halo, almost to the safety of darkness on the other side. Once again the verbal harpoon was leveled at his back and twanged through the silence. "I wonder what I'd find if I went up there."

Direct hit. Albert's knees buckled. He stopped, staring through the steam of his breath into the shadows that might have saved him. Something had to be done about the Inspector.

Albert spun defiantly on his heels and marched back to Naples, who stood in his aura, knee-deep in lamplight. "Here are the keys," he said. "I've got to go somewhere. You go ahead and look around and just leave the door unlocked. Put the keys . . . down somewhere I can find them."

The inspector stared deeply into each of Albert's eyes in turn, then smiled broadly. "I'll do that, Professor."

Albert's first bluff debuted with the same success as his first analogy. He had no choice but to play it out. His heart was back and beating furiously. He trudged off toward Miss Bjork's. He didn't turn to see the inspector enter the building. He walked blindly on with a quickened pace. He didn't turn when he heard the faint salute of the inspector's footsteps on the bare wood stair treads. The sight of a phone booth gave him a last, desperate hope. He got his number from directory assistance, (if this business kept up much longer, he'd have to remember it, or write it down somewhere), while he rifled his pockets for twenty cents. He deposited a quarter and dialed. The phone rang several times. Had it all happened so quickly? Was it over already?

The code! Albert hung up. The quarter dropped into the little metal tray. Having memorized the pattern of his number on the push-button pad, he dialed again, let it ring twice, hung up and repeated the process.

"Hello?" It was Tewksbury. "Albert?"

"The inspector's coming. He's got a key."

Albert heard a crash over the phone. "What was that? Is he breaking in?"

"No," Tewksbury whispered. "Something broke out on the landing."

"You've got to hide!"

"No! Wait."

In the breathless silence, Albert imagined more terrible possibilities than he thought himself capable of. "What?" he said at last.

There was no answer. "What is it?" Still no reply. "Tewksbury!"

"Shut up!" Tewksbury rasped harshly. He put the phone down and the tense bowstrings of silence shivered to stillness again.

Albert cradled the phone under his chin. His eyes watered and his hands shook in the pockets of his overcoat. Finally Tewksbury was back on the line.

"There was somebody out there."

"I know. Inspector Naples."

"Then he left."

"Left?" Instantly Albert imagined Naples sneaking up behind him, asking who he was talking to. Had he heard the phone ring?

Tewksbury continued. "There were footsteps ... just as the phone rang. Then this crack."

"I heard."

"Then there was some shuffling around. I couldn't tell what was happening from the sound that's when I told you to be quiet."

"To shut up," Albert corrected.

"Then these footsteps went down the stairs ... " Albert looked around quickly, fully expecting to see Naples staring him in the eye. "I'm going to see what happened."

"No!" Albert cried, but he heard the phone thud and rock on the table.

The series of sounds that followed painted a clear picture of Tewksbury crossing to the door, undoing the chain, turning the lock, and opening the door just a crack. A rush of footsteps followed.

"Caesar's ghost!" said Tewksbury, returning to the phone. "He's been knocked out cold!"

Who was knocked out cold? "Who!?"

"Naples!" said Tewksbury. "Wait a second!"

Again there was a thud and rock of the phone. Tewksbury closed and locked the door, came back and picked it up again.

"I heard some people on the stairs. Must've heard the noise."

"Inspector Naples?" said Albert in disbelief.

"Out cold," said Tewksbury. "Propped up against the wall on the first step of the next flight up."

"He's not ... "

"Not what? Dead? No, no. Just out cold. I felt his pulse. Somebody hit him with a flowerpot."

"A flowerpot?" Albert would have to find a new place to keep his keys.

"Must have. It's all over the place ... in a million pieces. I just heard some lady scream. They'll call the police, Albert. I've got to get out of here."

"Yes, you do," Albert agreed. "He was looking for you."

"For me? How do you know?" Tewksbury immediately sensed betrayal.

Albert explained. "It was all I could do."

Tewksbury saw that it was, but continued to nurse the threat of betrayal for the perverse comfort it offered. Suddenly he became aware of a sound in the distance, one that presented a real threat.

"Sirens."

Albert heard them, too. "You've got to go!"

"Where?"

Back to the hospital? Or Miss Bjork's? To school? To Crete? Albert's overburdened brain swam with possibilities. It was a big world. "Go out the back way. I'll meet you by the fountain."

Tewksbury hadn't unpacked. He gathered up his brown paper bag, shut the light off, unlocked the door and cracked it open for a peek at the landing. Four or five people were standing about in their pajamas with their arms crossed. A watchpost had been set up at the bottom of the stairs to monitor the progress of the police and all eyes were turned toward the watchman.

Tewksbury opened the door just enough to get out and closed it quietly. There was a tiny crowd huddled around the top step of the darkened landing. An older lady attended the inspector, mopping his oblivious brow with a cloth. No one was between Tewksbury and the back stairs.

"It's the ambulance!" cried the watchman. The strings of anticipation tightened to a fine pitch. Tewksbury darted across the landing and pushed the rear stair door open. It squeaked. He turned to see if anyone had noticed. One pair of eyes stared at him from among the knot of spectators; the woman attending Naples.

He looked at her pleadingly-the innocent supplication of all persecuted humanity evident in his dark eyes.

"Hey!" the woman said sharply. "Who are you?" The words were directed just as much at her fellow residents as at Tewksbury, who fled down the stairs. "Jim!" the woman cried. "He's getting away!" The words rang in Tewksbury's ears as he tossed himself into the night.

"We've had it now," said Tewksbury as he beckoned Albert into the shadow of the fountain. His choice of pronouns was not lost on Albert, but this wasn't the time or place to argue. He was probably right.

"Is Naples all right?"

"Naples?" Tewksbury puffed, lacing the air with chugs of steam. "I guess he'll be at our heels soon enough, if that's what you mean."

Albert started walking and Tewksbury followed. It had begun to snow. "Who did it?"

"Who knows? Who cares! We're the ones that'll get the blame. No fear. Where are we going?"

"To the bus station."

Tewksbury didn't resist. Albert's peculiar instincts had seen him this far. "Bus? To where?"

"Maine."

"What's in Maine?"

"My mother's place she's in Florida."

They walked across the common in silence.

"I've always liked Maine," said Tewksbury resignedly. "Where?"

"Near Sanford," said Albert. "It's out in the country. In the woods. Nobody goes near there except hunters in hunting season."

"When is that?"

Albert shrugged.

"I'll need money. You'll have to wire me some."

Albert liked it when problems and solutions were voiced in the same breath.

"We'll have to work out a code. And I'll need an alias. How about . . . Henry Rawlinson. He unearthed Ninevah."

"Henry Rawlins," said Albert with a distant-eyed finality that told Tewksbury it was Rawlins and not Rawlinson for ever and ever, amen.

"Rawlins, then," said Tewksbury.

By the time they reached the bus station they had formulated a simple code, and within forty minutes Tewksbury was safely on his way with twenty-six dollars and change, detailed directions to Albert's family homestead, the location of the key - if it was still where it always had been - and, just in case, a note from Albert giving Mr. Rawlins, nee Rawlinson, permission to use the house.

"There's no phone," said Albert.

"No phone!"

"My mother doesn't like a lot of . . . she goes there for the quiet. There's no TV, either."

"Great."

"Or radio."

"Almost Disneyland," said Tewksbury. "Does it have electricity?"

Albert thought a moment. "Yes." Pause. "It must."

Chapter Thirteen

It remained for Albert to confront the twin terrors of Bjork and Naples. He convinced himself it was too late to drop in on Miss Bjork. As for Naples, there was only one way to find out.

He turned his weary steps homeward.

There were no ambulances or police cars. That was a good sign. The house was dark and quiet. He tiptoed up the stairs, avoiding the creaking step, third from the bottom, and stumbling through the clumps of dirt and broken pottery which signified the earthly remains of what was once a flowerpot, opened his door. He winced but at the same time breathed a sigh of relief. Both terrors had been avoided. He collapsed on the bed and slept hard.

The phone woke him at seven in the morning, but had breathed its last by the time he found his glasses, focused his brain, and tracked it down. He dragged it out into the open and was halfway through his second cup of coffee and third cigarette when it rang again.

"Hello?"

"Albert?"

It was Miss Bjork. Her voice was calm. Even soft.

"Miss Bjork."

"I'm sorry I yelled at you last night," she said. "I was . . . the place was . . . "

"It's my fault," Albert interjected; something Albert never did. But it was true. He should never have stashed Tewksbury at Miss Bjork's. "There was a spill and a burn."

"Two burns."

Albert pictured his mother's house going up in flames. That was sure to attract attention. "It was my fault. I'll pay for it."

"Yes it was. And you will," Miss Bjork agreed. "I've already made up the bill and put it in the mail . . . I did it last night. But . . . I shouldn't have yelled at you."

Albert nodded.

"I met Joanne Alter," Miss Bjork resumed after an apologetic silence. Albert stopped nodding and waited. "She's a sweet kid. She decided to have the baby."

'Decided?' The word sat at the juncture of Albert's brows like a fat lady on a waterbed. "Decided?" Was there an option? Biology, witchcraft, alchemy, cosmetic surgery, as far as Albert was concerned they were all cut of the same cloth. Equally unfathomable.

"A beautiful baby girl. Joanne's aunt, sister of Alter's late wife, is helping out while Joanne finishes school at Amherst."

"Did you talk to her . . . about Glenly?"

The ensuing pause was deep with feminine emotions which Albert didn't rush. "Yes. Yes I did. She's an amazing girl, Albert. No bitterness. I mean, she was hurt; used. She realizes all that, and it still hurts, but she loves that kid so much. You should see them together. She's not the kind to let resentment fester. She knows that kind of nurtured hatred eats up peoples' lives. She said that herself. That from a nineteen-year-old."

Albert pulled on his pants. "And her father?"

"Well, something interesting did turn up there. Seems he was a Green Beret in Vietnam. There were pictures of him in uniform on the mantel. Hardly the past I would have imagined for such a meek fellow. He was decorated four times. You never know . . . still waters and all."

"You never know." Why hadn't somebody made a religion out of that? Or at least a song. It was so simple.

"He has no alibi for the day of the murder. He confessed that freely. Says he was at home, correcting papers." She paused to let her thoughts catch up. "I'd hate to think . . . "

So did Albert. Every time he did, things got more complicated. "I guess you haven't heard about Inspector Naples."

"Naples?"

Albert recapitulated the events of the preceding evening,
omitting only Tewksbury's part in them. He was not prepared for Miss Bjork's reply.

"Tewksbury did it."

"What?"

"He must have! He was prowling around your place;
maybe he was trying to contact you. That's it! I bet he was
trying to get in touch with you. What was Naples doing
there?"

"He thinks I know where Tewksbury is." True enough.

"Grasping at straws," Miss Bjork pronounced. "He's getting desperate. Still, he was there. He saw Tewksbury, or
Tewksbury saw him, or they saw each other, and Naples
ends up on the receiving end of a flowerpot. That must be
it."

Albert heard her take a deep, long breath. "Then he's still
in town. hiding out somewhere. I hate to say this, Professor,
Albert, but it doesn't make it look any better for him. I
mean, if he can smash a police detective over the head like
that . . . it doesn't make it difficult to suppose him capable of
a poisoning? Maybe your cigarette theory isn't holding up to
the light of day."

Albert wished he could tell her more, but felt things
would become infinitely more confusing if he did. She was a
lawyer, after all; one of those whose job was to complicate
things. He said nothing.

"But that woman that . . . "

"Daphne Knowlton," Albert volunteered.

"Daphne Knowlton. That's the strangest thing I ever
heard. I'll have to sleep on that one. Imagine," she imagined.
"She said she didn't want him to see?"

"What?"

"You said she told you to come to the top of the stairs into the shadows because she didn't want him to see. Him who?"

"Who?" Albert said, or thought. "I don't know. I mean," he shrugged.

"You think someone was following her?"

"I don't know. She's a very ... upset person," said Albert. "I don't know."

"If someone was following her, maybe they hit Naples. It must have been Tewksbury."

Albert was beginning to wonder what it was about Tewksbury that made him seem so guilty. It was dangerous to walk the streets with everyone jumping to conclusions.

"Well, at least that explains what happened to you," said Miss Bjork. "Poor thing." Whether this applied to Albert or to Daphne was not fully evident. "Do you know where I can find her?"

"No," said Albert. "We thought ... I thought she was in New Hampshire ... they said she went home after ... that night."

"I can't believe anyone could be so despicable." She lowered her voice. "Between us, Professor, whoever killed Glenly ... if it's Tewksbury or, whomever ... well, someone would've had to do it eventually." Pause. "I shouldn't've said that."

There was a knock at the door. Albert excused himself after agreeing to meet Miss Bjork that evening, hung up and answered the door.

A young man in a gray suit stood in the hall amid the earthy remains of the flowerpot. He identified himself as "Sergeant Lucci, Police."

Lucci shoveled Albert inside with businesslike alacrity and admitted himself to Albert's sanctum sanctorum.

As Albert cleared a place for Lucci to sit, he took the compass of him with a couple of glances. The officer was about Albert's height and similarly dark-haired. His full mustache was trimmed with military precision. He was built like a cornet, with no more ornamentation than necessary to the job. Probably in his late twenties. Married. His Italian name and the St. Christopher medal he wore around his neck combined to make him Catholic, probably had more than one child. His nails were stubbed but not bitten, traces of gray paint were evident between the cuticle and nail on one of his fingers. A Band-Aid on his thumb reminded Albert of the time he'd smashed his finger with a hammer. A handyman, perhaps? So much was gained in an unobtrusive glance or two. Albert found himself enjoying the exercise but, remembering Dr. Williams, kept the results to himself.

"Well, Professor," Sergeant Lucci began as he walked around the room with his eyes, "there was some excitement on your doorstep last night."

"Yes. Someone hit Detective Naples on the head with the flowerpot." He could put the key in the mailbox from now on, but that's the first place they looked, isn't it? "Is he all right?"

"Oh, yes, sir. As well as can be expected, I guess." His eyes lighted on Albert and rummaged through his face for a moment. "He's in and out of consciousness. No permanent damage, they say." A busy silence followed while the sergeant plumbed the depths of Albert's pupilless eyes. "What was he doing on your doorstep, Professor?"

Didn't he know? "He wanted to search my apartment again."

"For Tewksbury?"

Albert nodded. "He thinks I've put him somewhere."

If Albert had known how disarming he could be, his innocence would have worked against him.

"Then, you were home when it happened?"

"No," said Albert. "I had just gone out. I was on my way to Miss . . . to visit someone. I met the inspector outside and he said he wanted to search my apartment and he came up here."

"And you followed?"

"It's embarrassing when strangers go through your things," Albert said. "I kept walking . . . and stopped at a phone booth to call a friend." How closely could he skirt the truth without departing from it?

"Did you see anyone else?"

Albert thought of Daphne Knowlton. She'd had enough trouble. "After that?" The sergeant nodded, giving Albert permission to prevaricate. "No."

"How did you find out?"

"There were lights. And sirens."

"While you were on the phone?"

Albert nodded.

"So you went home?"

"I went to the bus station."

"The bus station?" The sergeant sounded like Albert, repeating things he didn't understand. "Why there?"

"Someone was hurt," said Albert. "At the apartment there was an ambulance." He looked the sergeant squarely in the eye. "I got sick once when I saw someone hurt. It just made things worse for everyone."

It was the sergeant's turn to nod, which he did, with a twitch.

"The bus station was open. So I went there," Albert explained. "They have cigarette machines. I needed cigarettes."

"You didn't go to your friends?"

Albert shook his head. "It was getting late," he said. "She doesn't smoke."

The sergeant hadn't written anything in his notebook yet, though he'd started to a couple of times. "Who were you talking to on the phone?"

"My friend."

"The one you were going to see?"

"I was going to see my friend," Albert said. "Yes."

"What was her name?"

There was no way out. "Miss Bjork."

"Bjork? The lawyer?" Lucci's eyebrows contracted sharply, then relaxed by degrees as a trail of conclusions occurred to him. "She handled Tewksbury, didn't she?"

Albert shuddered to think the depths Tewksbury's imagination would have plumbed had he heard the question. Albert was glad he wasn't there. "She lost."

Lucci was prompted to write something, but gave up. "What were you talking to her about?"

The conversation came vividly to mind. "Housekeeping?"

"Housekeeping?"

Albert explained the facts, carefully avoiding any archaeological inference, adding that he had stayed at Miss Bjork's while she was out of town because of what the police had done to his apartment. He hadn't planned to say it, but he liked it when it came out; while it wasn't the whole truth, it was wholly true. He'd have to remember that if ever he found himself in court again.

Albert didn't strike Lucci as the type to invent so many details, and he clearly wasn't thinking on his feet. From Lucci's point of view only one option remained. He folded his notebook and slipped it into his inside coat pocket. stood up, and held out his hand, which Albert shook. "Thank you for your time, Professor," he said, and turned to leave.

Albert habitually pushed his fingers through his thick rebellion of hair and the furrow of stubble that ran along the side of it. "Tell Inspector Naples I said . . . I hope he's better." Pause to let a thought catch up. "I know how he feels."

"I'll do that, Professor," said Lucci, and left. "Somebody should clean up the mess," he called back from the hall. Albert closed the door.

"Somebody should clean up this mess," he repeated, but he didn't have the flowerpot in mind.

Chapter Fourteen

Albert arrived at Miss Bjork's not long after the appointed time. Her hair was down around her shoulders. She wore a sweater of some soft-looking material which, though cut in a modest 'vee,' was sufficient to confound Albert's concentration for the remainder of the evening. She wore something else . . . pants or a skirt. She must have. But there was no trace of the lawyer. Nothing but a woman with all the fuzz on, and it confused Albert's heart and hormones to the core.

He was glad he'd shaved and brushed his teeth.

The night was like no other in Albert's life. Over a light dinner they summarized the events of the past few days, then the narrow trickle of conversation joined a wider flow of topics about which Miss Bjork did most of the talking. Albert nodded and smiled and, though he couldn't remember a word she said, sat in a stupefied expanse of awe so profound that he didn't recognize one of his own pieces playing on the stereo in the background.

Miss Bjork was comfortable and relaxed. But he wasn't in her company, he was in her presence, the warmth of which made sweat bead on his upper lip.

For the first time in his life, Albert was enchanted.

It was snowing as he walked home, but he didn't notice. The flakes evaporated in the warm glow of his thoughts long before they got to him. The dammed river of music within him overflowed in fits and starts - like an over-full cauldron being carried by a drunkard - sending frothy fragments of music sloshing into the depths of his subconscious.

It was Saturday night.

Sunday passed uneventfully. No one called. No one knocked. No one needed Albert. But Miss Bjork was everywhere, and Albert had only one place to put her.

Monday morning Albert went to school. Everyone had some word of welcome, and trusted he was recovered from his misadventure. He arrived late for his first class to find someone else teaching it. It was the right room, the one with the cracked window, they were the right students, as far as he could tell, but there was someone else teaching them. He was just about to leave, to go find another job, when one of the students rose and began clapping, then another, and another until all were on their feet.

Albert looked behind him; there was no one there. Even the teacher was clapping.

"Welcome back, Professor," she said as she stepped aside and gestured widely toward the lectern.

Albert hesitated. "Now, where was I?" he said. The tension dissolved in laughter. The Professor was back.

But something had changed for Albert. For the first time he found himself describing not just how sounds came together to make music but what the music expressed.

Someone had moved in to the vacancy in his heart.

Miss Moodie moved in early to renew her franchise. She hailed him on his way to the cafeteria.

"Professor!" She was at the far end of the hall, one arm loaded with books and a purse, the other swinging purposefully as a means of locomotion. Her huge breasts, insufficiently restrained, bounced out of synch in opposite directions. A lesser woman would have been thrown irredeemably off course at least, if not halved outright. Miss Moodie's lower regions, however, vigorous in the opposite extreme, provided a sort of gyroscopic counterbalance to keep her on course.

This was the hall in which Albert had collided with Daphne Knowlton. Miss Moodie burst through thick golden shafts of sunlight as if she was wading through fields of amber grain cut neatly in cubes prior to stacking. Albert was reminded of the rows of moonlight that marched up the wall with military precision that night.

Moodie nudged alongside Albert and drew him along in her slipstream toward the cafeteria.

"So grand to see you back among the living," she said. She remembered Albert's handicapped former roommate. "Oh, dear, I suppose I shouldn't've said that. Well, that's me all over. My good sense is always playing catch-up, 'ey, Professor? Of course, you know . . . Going to lunch?"

Albert knew he didn't have to answer.

"This is where it happened, isn't it? I mean, the . . . well. It's good to have you back, is all I can say," she said. But it wasn't. "Did you take class this morning? Oh, look, it's Lane! Walter! Look who's back!"

Albert wanted to talk to Lane, so he allowed himself to be drawn into the little social vortex into which Miss Moodie sucked all within earshot.

Throughout lunch Albert's greatest struggle, apart from cutting the barbecue beef with his plastic knife, was to keep his stories straight, a necessity that aggravated his digestion. He found it best to say as little as possible, at least until he could get Lane alone, which was another dilemma. He thought about Miss Bjork and later everyone agreed he seemed in remarkably high spirits.

It turned out, however, that he and Lane ended up alone at the table through natural attrition, thanks to the other demands upon the time of those present. Lane seemed unusually thoughtful. He wrung his hands constantly, fiddling with the large school ring on his left hand or the thick silver chain on his wrist.

"I suppose the police must have questioned you quite rigorously about that . . . about Naples getting smashed."

The incident was in the news and, because it involved a member of faculty, however remotely, was the topic around which most of the lunchtime conversation had turned.

"Sergeant Lucci came to my house."

Lane suddenly stopped fidgeting. "What did he do?"

"He asked questions."

"What kind of questions?" Lane asked, too eagerly. As if aware of the fact, he settled back in his seat to pick his teeth with the corner of a matchbook. "I mean, we don't often get excitement of this sort around here. Seems you've had more than your share of it."

"Excitement?" Dr. Strickland, lunch tray in hand, appeared beside Albert. "May I?"

Lane acquiesced reluctantly. Albert moved his book bag from the chair beside him. Strickland set his tray down and extended a warm hand of greeting. "Back among us for good this time, Professor, j'espare? Good. Now, what excitement are we talking about?"

"You must have heard what happened to Detective Naples? . . . on Albert's doorstep?"

Strickland had his mouth full. He nodded and swallowed. "Of course."

Albert wanted Strickland to leave. Lane was nervous; grasping for information. Albert wanted to know what and why.

"Strange."

"Well, that's what we were talking about," said Lane. Albert thought he was blushing. Did black people blush? "That's all."

He turned to Albert with something almost desperate in his eyes. "Well, how does it feel to be back? How does school food compare with that at the hospital? I imagine we should all get sick for our own good, eh?" He laughed nervously.

Strickland didn't want the subject to change. "According to the paper, Naples is . . . was . . . still investigating the Tewksbury business. Is that true, Maestro?"

Albert lit another cigarette, though he hadn't put out the first. He intentionally shepherded clouds of smoke toward

Strickland's face. He nodded. "He thinks I know where Tewksbury is."

"Let's talk about something else," Lane suggested pleadingly. "Poor man's been through enough without our reenacting the Inquisition. Right, Professor?"

Albert was watching Strickland who was smiling down at his cottage cheese with his eyes watering.

"And do you?" said Strickland, raising his head, but not his eyes.

"Of course he doesn't," said Lane. "How absurd."

Albert sipped contentedly at the dregs of his cold coffee. Strickland was eating cottage cheese and pineapple. A health nut. Why was he in the smoking section, allowing Albert to blow smoke in his face?

Strickland ignored Lane. "It's a natural assumption, I suppose," he said, "your being friends. And they've got to look somewhere." He cocked his head at an inquiring angle and regarded Albert closely. "'Were you very close?" The eagerness in his eyes was contradicted by the moderation of his tone. "As friends?"

Did he really want to know something? Or was he just curious, like Miss Moodie? She wanted to know everything. Albert blew another large, deliberate puff of smoke in his direction. He said nothing, this fanner of the air, this jogger, this ... eater of rice cakes. He blotted the corner of his eyes with his napkin, and smiled. Conclusive proof. He wanted information, too. But why?

Now it was Lane's turn to stick his oar in. "You'll be leaving soon, I expect? Back to Crete?"

Strickland looked at Lane without moving his head. "Crete, yes. Knossos. In two weeks."

"Two weeks," Lane echoed. "And now the dig will be under your supervision."

Strickland pivoted his head to center his eyeballs. "Yes. As head of the department ."

"Acting head," Lane corrected.

Strickland smiled from the nose down. "Acting head . . . at least for the season."

"So, Tewksbury's misfortunes haven't been tragic all 'round." Lane prodded at the insistence of some unspoken grudge.

"I'm happy to be head of the department, Lane, if that's what you're hinting at," Strickland said flatly. "But I'm no happier profiting from someone else's . . . bad luck . . . than you would be."

Here was Albert's chance to swing the conversation back to Tewksbury, but he wasn't quick enough.

"Still," Lane said. "Quite a promotion, leapfrogging from third to first like that."

Albert didn't want to go to Crete again. "You both know Daphne Knowlton, don't you?"

Lane reacted as if someone had dropped a basketball in his soup, though he recovered quickly. Albert was more interested in Strickland. He didn't flinch. Didn't blink, didn't miss a mouthful of cottage cheese, but the veins on his forehead stood out in exclamations. Daphne Knowlton was the flashpoint between these two.

"Yes," said Strickland into his cottage cheese. "Of course I remember. She had a tough time here, as I recall. The academic life isn't for everyone."

"Academic life," Lane huffed, his blood pressure rising audibly. "Her 'tough time', as you put it, was thanks to you and Glenly!" Albert had never sat on a geological fault at the very moment tectonic plates shifted, but thought this must be very much what it felt like. If only the situation could be contained long enough for some information to develop.

"Me!" Strickland retorted. The exclamation was genuine. "What did I have to do with it?"

Lane rose in accusation. "You took advantage of her!"

Albert sipped at his coffee cup, though it was empty.

"Sit down, Lane. You're making a fool of yourself. You seem to forget, I was the one who wrapped her up and took her home after."

"And what happened when you got to her place!" bellowed Lane, who hadn't sat down.

Strickland took a quick inventory of the room. Everyone had gone. There was no hiding the fact that he was caught completely off guard.

"What are you implying, Lane?" he said, the soul of self-control no more.

In the heat of his anger, Lane was saying more than he intended to. "She was half drunk, half naked, frightened, confused. She needed comfort."

"If you're insinuating that I . . . that I . . . " Strickland was standing now, struggling to get control of himself. "I don't have to listen to this to this. You're acting like a spurned lover, Lane." His eyes lit with the fire of his indignation. "Is that it, Old Man? Maybe you were planning to take her home that night, eh? Maybe you wanted to do the honors. Is that it?"

Lane lunged across the table with both arms outstretched.

Strickland had read the attack in his adversary's eyes and stepped out of the way.

To Albert, the action was as foreign as a cotillion. His his jaw dropped open, his thick eyebrows catapulted into perfect arches of astonishment. The force of Lane's impact on the table sent a bowl of cold soup sliding into his lap. He blinked once. Twice. Three times. The scene didn't go away. And the soup soaked into his pants.

Professor Walter Lane lay full-length across the table with his elbow in the residue of Strickland's cottage cheese and pineapple juice.

For his part, Strickland had grabbed a napkin and daubed his tie and lapel as he left the room, yelling over his shoulder, "Seems I touched an open nerve, 'eh, Old Fella? What would your wife say about that? It's no secret, you know? No secret." He was gone.

Lane's dignity was evenly dispersed in a radius of six or seven feet from the table. The kitchen staff stood frozen like very large, very surprised ice-cream toffees at the far end of the cafeteria. The air leaked out of Albert's eyebrows one at a time and they came to rest atop his horn-rimmed glasses.

Lane stood up slowly, leftovers hanging from various parts of his suit. "I'll kill that son of a . . . " He was looking at the door through which Strickland had departed. "I swear, I'll kill him."

Albert's gaze was riveted on Lane's eyes. If ever there was a man who could make good on such a threat . . . The timpani of Albert's heart beat strong, single strokes that telegraphed straight to his temples, making his glasses feel three sizes too small.

Lane looked at Albert, whose lap was strewn with the non-absorbable elements of vegetable beef soup. The cigarette dangling from his mouth had been extinguished by the tsunami. "Sorry, Professor," he said. "That's been a long time coming."

Not only was Albert speechless, he was almost motionless.

Lane brushed himself off, then applied the soggy napkin to Albert's glasses.

Finally Albert blinked again. "What happened?"

"I guess you deserve an explanation. Let's go for walk."

It was one of those rare, deceitful days misplaced from a previous spring that instantly takes root in the cabin-fevered brains of the populace, especially on a college campus. Everyone strips to the legal minimum and pretends it's not fifty-three degrees. The sun is out! The snow is melting! Every piece of litter is mistaken for a flower. It's spring delirium, mass hypnosis on a supernatural scale, a prodigious, almost spiritual turning of the other cheek ... which is soon to be backhanded by the careless hand of winter. Albert loosened his tie.

"That crack about my wife."

"Please, don't," said Albert, hoping he wouldn't. He did.

"We've had our ups and downs. We separated about a year ago."

Albert had never walked for recreation that he recalled. He only walked to get somewhere. As a result, he had developed a brisk stride which had to be reigned to keep in step with Lane who sauntered slowly. "Neither of us have had the heart to take it any further." He squinted into the distance, as if to bring something into focus. "All those years invested in each other. Hard to let go," he said. "Besides, I love her." He glanced abashedly at Albert. He hadn't meant to say that out loud." Anyway, Daphne," sigh, "she was a fish out of water around here. Remarkable girl, though. What do you know about her?"

"Nothing," said Albert.

"Neither did I, until much later."

"After?"

Lane nodded. "She was kidnaped ... when she was three years old."

Albert stopped walking. The cold soup on his legs was nothing to the cold world suddenly seeping into his being. "Kidnapped?"

"Mmm. She didn't tell me, I read it in old newspapers ... I happened to come across. Extortion. The kidnappers wanted money. I don't remember how much. Not from the parents, you understand. They were poor as church mice, but the maternal grandmother ... practically owned the town."

"In New Hampshire?"

Lane nodded. "Husband had owned the local factory, I guess. Something of the sort. He died left everything to her."

They resumed walking. "Apparently she'd taken a pretty dim view of her daughter's marriage in the first place. She'd never even seen her granddaughter. She simply refused to pay. Can you imagine that? Her own flesh and blood."

"Needless to say, Daphne's parents were frantic. They had nothing to lose by calling the police. I guess the kidnappers were frustrated, too. They kept extending the deadline, making threats. Terrible threats. Nothing moved the old lady. A couple of days went by, then the parents were tipped off by an anonymous phone call.

"They found Daphne in a little pit under the floorboards of an old barn. She'd been there over a week. Not much to eat. Out in the middle of nowhere. Probably the kidnappers thought she'd just be there a few hours. Out in the middle of nowhere," he repeated. "No one could have heard her cries."

There was a long silence, punctuated by the scuff of their shoes on the blacktopped path. Albert was struggling to keep the mental images of the story from etching themselves on his brain.

His efforts were in vain.

"They never found the kidnappers."

"How did you learn all this?"

Lane smiled and puffed a note of irony. "She talks in her sleep." Albert looked at him the way he knew he would. "That's what everyone else thought. It wasn't like that.

"Daphne and I are just . . . close friends. That's all. At first we both just needed someone to talk to. My marriage was falling apart, she was nervous about her first job. More than nervous, really; panicked. We were a mutual-aid society, I guess. Anyway, after the incident in the teacher's lounge, after that damned Glenly . . . she stayed with me for a few days, to pull herself together. I slept on the sofa . . . but that's when I heard her talking in her sleep. Night after night, the same thing. Just rambling and crying, mostly. Not much that was lucid, but there were clues that she was troubled by something in her past. One thing led to another, and I ended up getting the story from old newspapers."

"I thought Strickland took her home that night."

"He did, the son of a . . . and he took advantage of her, exactly as I said. That much she told me. Unfortunately she fell in love with him."

"Does anyone else know all this, about her past, I mean?"

"Not that I know of. She wouldn't even tell me, so I doubt she'd have told anyone else."

A noodle fell from the folds of Albert's shirt.

"Sorry about that," said Lane, who was. "It'll be all over campus by tomorrow." What would? The soup? "Not a smooth move, as the kids say."

"She fell in love with him," said Albert rhetorically. Suddenly the most obvious question of all leapt into his brain with both feet. "Where is she now?"

"Who knows?" said Lane. "She still has family in New Hampshire."

"You think she's there?"

Lane's stride had suddenly quickened. Albert tried to steal a glance at his eyes, but they were turned away. "Who knows?" Lane repeated into the wind.

Precisely what Albert was trying to find out. He thought he might tell Lane about his encounter with Daphne Knowlton. Then he thought he wouldn't, so they parted company without either being any the wiser.

Albert supposed he'd have to change his pants before the afternoon class.

Chapter Fifteen

That evening Albert went to visit Jeremy Ash. It began to rain just as he arrived at the hospital. He found the boy and Mrs. Gibson in a semi-darkened room, both transfixed like moths by the deathly blue light of the TV screen. He wouldn't have been surprised to find Inspector Naples laid out in a third bed. Fortunately he wasn't. But where had they put him?

The television was very loud, owing to Mrs. Gibson's hearing problem.

"Professor!" Jeremy shouted as Albert entered the room. "Hey! Mrs. Gibson! It's the Professor!"

Mrs. Gibson silenced Jeremy Ash with an empathic gesture.

Albert waited in the door until the next commercial.

"Turn it off, Jeremy," she said at last. "That's foolishness. You ain't interested in that trash, are you, Professor? You come sit down here." She patted the back of a chair between her and her roommate. Albert obeyed.

"Who's taking care of you, Professor?"

"Taking care of me?"

"Who cooks, cleans house, does your laundry?"

Albert looked from Jeremy Ash, who was smiling, to Mrs. Gibson, who was glowering. Was he supposed to have someone taking care of him? It would explain a lot. "No one," he said.

"Well, I'm glad to hear it." said Mrs. Gibson. "Otherwise they'd have to be shot for committing crimes against humanity. Look at you. You're nothing but a whisper with hair on. Don't you have a girlfriend?"

"No," said Albert, too quickly. He blushed. His whole face was a polygraph whose little red light was blinking: Lie! Lie! Lie!

Mrs. Gibson made an intuitive, knowing, ironic noise which has no spelling. She knew what Albert had not yet admitted to himself.

Jeremy Ash came once more to the rescue. "Mrs. Gibson!"

"Eh? What?"

"Me and the Professor want to talk private for a few minutes!"

The volume at which the request was delivered notified everyone on the hall that the Professor and Jeremy wished to have a private talk.

Mrs. Gibson looked from Jeremy Ash to Albert, to Jeremy Ash. She picked up a magazine and pretended to turn off her hearing aid. "Well, you don't need to hit me in the head with a blunt object."

Albert was about to speak when Jeremy held up his hand.

"You know what?" he said with a twinkle in his eyes. "Anytime you want everyone in the world to know something, just tell it to her and she'll have it all over the place before you close your mouth." He paused deliberately and, holding his fingers to his lips, gestured toward Mrs. Gibson.

It was immediately apparent that Jeremy Ash's redoubtable roomie had heard every word. Her entire face was compressed in a pucker of strained disinterest as she forced herself to remain quiet. Her eyes bugged out as she flipped aggressively through the magazine; something had to give, and they had nowhere else to go.

Jeremy Ash administered the coup de grace. "You should hear what the nurses said about her this morning."

"What did they say!" Mrs. Gibson didn't say, or remark, or inquire. She exploded, plastering her better judgment to the walls. "That skinny nurse with the Betty Boop lips! I know it is! Well, I could tell you something about . . . "

Jeremy Ash began to laugh. Albert tried not to. "Eaves-droppers never hear good about 'emselves," said Jeremy.

Mrs. Gibson flung a samurai glance at Jeremy that would have disemboweled most people, but her pride was no match for the boy's knowing smile. She laughed. "How did you know?"

"I'm not telling," said Jeremy. "I've gotta keep an eye on you."

Mrs. Gibson dissolved in teary-eyed laughter and turned off her hearing aid.

"It's all right now."

Albert studied the woman under cover of his eyebrows and spoke into his hand. "How do you know?"

"Hey, you ain't the only detective around here. See the volume knob on her hearing aid? It's got a little red dot on it. If that dot's up, she's tuned in. If it's down, she couldn't hear Jimi Hendrix."

They brought each other up to date on news of mutual interest.

"Are you going to see Naples?"

Albert's heart skipped a beat. "Inspector Naples?" His hand went automatically to his head. "I don't know. Is he conscious? I thought he was . . . "

"Nah. He's conscious, at least sometimes. He ain't exactly Solomon, I hear. But there's cops comin' and going all the time. He's in Tewksbury's old room."

Albert's heart almost skipped town. The images that came to mind were not comforting.

"How'd it happen, Professor?"

"What?" said Albert in every sense of the word. "Oh, a flowerpot."

The Hounds of Reason in Albert's weary brain were tired of jumping off hedges only to bash their heads against brick walls.

What had happened that night? Where did Daphne Knowlton come from? Where did she go? Who was following her? Strickland? Lane? Her imagination? Had anyone seen Tewksbury leave the apartment?

"Who hit him?"

Who indeed. The question fit so integrally with Albert's train of thought, he didn't realize it came from outside himself until it was repeated.

"Professor? Who hit him?" Jeremy's voice was low and conspiratorial.

"It wasn't . . . I mean . . . you didn't, like . . . it wasn't you, was it?"

"What?" said Albert. "Hit him?" The Hounds of Reason assembled in a line with their heads cocked waiting for a reply. "Of course not. I was in the phone booth." He suppressed an urge to add "Your Honor."

"Then it must have been Tewksbury!"

"No," Albert said quietly. What was it about Tewksbury? "He was the one I was talking to."

"Well, if it wasn't you, and it wasn't him, who was it?"

The boy's words reminded Albert of something he'd read somewhere: "once you've eliminated the impossible, what remains, however improbable, must be the truth." Where had he read that? A cereal box? On a men's-room wall?

The first job was to eliminate the impossible. It wasn't Tewksbury. It wasn't Albert. It wasn't Jeremy Ash. It wasn't Inspector Naples. It wasn't Miss Bjork, because he'd spoken to her just minutes before. It wasn't Professor Glenly, he was dead. It wasn't Daphne Knowlton, he'd seen her leave . . . but she might have come back. Hold Daphne Knowlton. Who else was involved? Miss Moodie? Very unlikely. She hadn't the motive or the dexterity. Motive. Motive. Legal people place a lot of emphasis on motive. Well, then, who would want to hit Inspector Naples on the head besides Tewksbury? No. Complete the list first. Who else? Strickland? Hold

Strickland on general principle, he smiled too much not to be guilty of something. Lane? Poor Lane. In the High School Yearbook of Life he'd be runner-up for Most Probably Guilty, after Tewksbury. The Alters? Joanne was in Vermont. Her father? Hold Professor Alter. That completed the list. But why would any of those people have been following Inspector Naples?

Suddenly a quick brown fox jumped over the groggy Hounds of Reason and the chase was on.

Who was it who had said they were being followed? Daphne Knowlton. And who would be following her? It had to be one of two from the list, Strickland or Lane. Whoever it was, they would have seen her enter Albert's building, but wouldn't have seen her leave. She went out the back way. Then? He would have seen Albert leave-meet Inspector Naples - who then went inside, where he would have found Daphne Knowlton, who had to be protected because because . . . The Hounds of Reason returned, winded and weary, but exhilarated by the knowledge that at least there was a fox in the forest. All Albert needed was a little more information.

Poor Lane.

"You okay, Professor?"

Jeremy Ash was shaking Albert's elbow. "What is it? You look like you swallowed something down the wrong way."

"I think I've got it!" Albert said. "I think I've almost got it figured out."

"You mean, who hit the inspector?"

"It was Professor Lane."

"Who's that?"

Albert explained.

"But why would he hit Naples? Unless . . . he's the one who killed Glenly!"

"Glenly?" Albert repeated. "No. He didn't kill Glenly. He hit the Inspector to protect someone else from something."

A thought occurred to him. "But why do you protect someone from the police?"

"Because they broke the law," said Jeremy. "Or, because they're not supposed to be somewhere, or because they're doing something wrong." The boy's mouth could barely keep pace with the possibilities.

The Hounds of Reason collapsed upon one another and went to sleep.

Albert asked Jeremy how he was doing, a question he never answered directly. Albert didn't press.

"She's leaving day after tomorrow," said Jeremy Ash, nodding at Mrs. Gibson. "She's been a good one."

"How many have you had?"

"Seven," Jeremy replied without thinking. "I wonder if she'll come visit me. She said she would."

"Then she will."

The boy's slim smile was knowing beyond his years. "They all say that. You're the first one that's done it."

Albert looked at Jeremy Ash. After a while he manufactured a feeble smile. Instinctively he put a reassuring hand where his leg should have been. There was nothing there.

Albert didn't want to visit Inspector Naples. As he walked to Tewksbury's old room, his conscience battled the hope that the inspector was still in a coma.

"Professor!" It was the Familiar Policeman, guarding the Inspector's door. "Hey, your hair's growing back."

Albert ran his fingers through his hair. He nodded toward the door. "Inspector Naples?"

"Detective," said the policeman.

"I know," said Albert.

The policeman nodded. "Happened at your place, didn't it?" he said. "Boy, what a crack!"

"A flowerpot," Albert explained. He could imagine how it felt. He winced. "Is he going to be all right?"

"So I hear. It was touch and go for a while there." The policeman wanted to be asked what he thought about it. "I don't know, though . . . "

"Hmm?"

That was good enough. "If he's really all right, you know?" He tapped his temple. Albert had never realized what a handy gesture that was, or to how many people it applied.

"Why?"

"Well, when he's conscious, he rambles on mumbling, you know? Like a bag lady. Nothing that makes any sense. Names. sometimes. I've heard him say your name once or twice, Professor. And Tewksbury's. Then he goes on talking about Belgian waffles, ceiling tiles, and the 1964 World's Fair. You know what I mean? That flowerpot knocked the plaster loose, if you ask me," which Albert didn't. "Lettin' a little too much sunshine in,"

"Is he awake?"

"No. Oh, no." said the policeman. He looked at his watch. "He's been out over an hour now. He usually comes to during the night shift. I'll be off duty then."

"Then, I can't see him?"

"'fraid not, Professor. I mean, I don't care you understand. But rules are rules, you know how it is."

God bless rules.

"Who do you think did it, Professor?"

Albert shrugged. "Who knows?"

"Ceiling tiles." If Naples had gotten that far, Albert had to work fast. Something had to break somewhere . . . before the Inspector came to his senses.

Albert didn't sleep alone that night, he was haunted by Miss Bjork. So were Tewksbury and Jeremy Ash, Professors Lane and Alter, Mrs. Gibson, Miss Moodie, Dr. Strickland, Inspector Naples . . . on and on. And they all kept him awake until three in the morning. He half expected the neighbors to complain about the noise.

His train of thought, however, traveled on a circular track and always brought him back to the same station; the same inescapable conclusion: Professor Lane had hit Inspector Naples on the head with a flowerpot to protect Daphne Knowlton from something.

Something.

Suddenly a spur opened up on the circular railway just as Albert's train of thought was passing and he rushed down it; what if Lane hadn't been protecting Daphne Knowlton, but himself? What if she knew something that he didn't want her to tell the police?

Only one clear thought had presented itself for inspection by the time Albert went to sleep, one shabby, silly possibility in clothes that didn't fit; could Lane have killed Glenly? Lane the would-be social worker . . . with murder in his heart? and if Daphne knew; but where was she?

All the little question marks melted into one huge interrogative club and beat Albert into a fitful semi-consciousness.

It was late in the morning when Albert finally awoke. He'd missed his class, but apparently there were others to take his place. He wondered who. Was someone always there, waiting in some kind of musical limbo, for the chance to take his place?

He shaved his chalky face and brushed his yellow teeth, put on some clean underwear and his wrinkled suit, and went to the bank to wire Tewksbury some money. Whatever a wire was. It promised to be an interesting morning.

Albert hadn't slept well. His brain was still foggy, still full of half-formed thoughts as he crossed the common and walked up the steps of the bank. It was this state of mind that excused his running squarely into Dr. Strickland as the latter emerged from the bank. The impact sent Strickland's briefcase to the ground, and the leather camera bag on his shoulder dropped to the crook in his arm, knocking him briefly off balance.

"I'm sorry," said Albert. "I wasn't looking. I was . . . "

"Don't mention it, Professor," Strickland replied. He seemed uncharacteristically nervous; resituating his belongings and fiddling with the zipper on the bag. "I was in too much of a hurry, as usual." He noticed Albert noticing the bag. Had he seen the camera? "I'm afraid I came off the pompous idiot with you and Lane."

Albert looked at Strickland. He felt embarrassed for him . . . even though he was the one who'd ended up with the soup in his lap.

"Lane and I have just never . . . he was in love with the girl . . . Daphne. Imagines he's Prince Charming riding to her rescue or something." The bag and briefcase switched sides. "Anyway, she's a grown woman, right? She can take care of herself."

The assumption was unsettling. The Daphne Knowlton Albert knew could not take care of herself. His inquiring gaze must have intensified. Strickland turned away.

"Well, good running in to you," he said, laughing weakly. He pretended to glance at his watch. "I'm late for class. Gotta run."

Albert watched after him as he ran across the street to his little red sports car. He dropped his bundles through the rear window and got in. He smiled and waved.

"I'm sorry about your camera!" Albert called. "I hope it's all right."

The smile evaporated like a liberal at a tax reduction rally. The wave wrapped itself around the wheel and the little red sports car crushed an empty beer bottle to dust as it squealed away.

Albert recognized the bag. It was the same one Strickland had carried the first time they met in the bank. Was there a camera in it then, too?

"May I help you, sir?" The voice belonged to a young teller with last night in her eyes.

"I'd like a wire to send, please," Albert ventured.

There was a bustling commotion in the region behind the counter as Mrs. Bridges breezed out of her glass-walled office.

"Brenda!" she called as she came. "Brenda, dear. Miss Domba . . . I'll take care of this gentleman."

"Fine," said Miss Domba, whose heart was set on four o'-clock.

"Well, Professor," said Miss Bridges. "Good to see you again. Did you get the papers I sent you?"

"Papers?"

"The Keogh application ." She waited for a dawn that never came. "The Keogh account we talked about? I sent it in the mail . . . all filled out. You just had to sign it."

Albert didn't know what she was talking about. "Oh, yes. Yes," he said. "I haven't checked the mail in a few days. I will, though."

"I understand, Professor. Life has a way of interfering with the best-laid plans, doesn't it?"

How did she know?

"Well, what can I do for you today?"

"I'd like a wire . . . I want to send money to someone."

"You'd like to wire some money."

"Yes!" Albert could see why Mrs. Bridges was the manager. Nevertheless, she demanded specifics; to whom was the money going?

"To whom?" Not Tewksbury . . . it began with an "R" . . . or a "W." Robbins? Riggles? Riglins? "Rawlins!" Albert yelped. "Harold Rawlins!" That wasn't quite right. "Mr.

Harold Rawlins." Neither was that. "Henry," he said softly. That was it. "Henry Rawlins."

Mrs. Bridges was very patient and, with diligence and quiet persistence, the form was completed, with one exception.

"Now, Professor. How much money are we going to send?" Was she going to send some, too? The confusion that surfaced from the depths of Albert's field-mouse eyes was more than Mrs. Bridges could bear. "A hundred?" she prompted. If they'd been classmates she would have let him copy her test answers.

Cigarettes were so expensive. Who knew how much they were in Maine.

"Five hundred?" she suggested.

And groceries. And clothes! Tewksbury needed new clothes. How much was a shirt? Ten dollars? Nine hundred?

"Perhaps you could tell me what the money is for, Professor. I could . . . "

It was too late. Albert had thought of a figure. "Ten thousand dollars," he said.

"Oh," said Mrs. Bridges on the inhale. "Ten thousand? I see. Well, we'll need to fill out another form."

An hour later Albert had writer's cramp but the money was on its way and Tewksbury would have beer and cigarettes enough to last, with probably enough left over for a shirt, a pair of pants, and a haircut.

"There, Professor. That wasn't so bad, was it?" Albert thought it was hell. "Is there anything else?"

"Yes." There was one thing. "Could you tell me . . . what is a safety posit box?"

"A safe deposit box? Surely, Professor," Mrs. Bridges said, and she did.

Chapter Sixteen

A safe-deposit box was an awesome concept for Albert. A place for valuables. A little box in a bank that was almost sacrosanct; holy. And mysterious. It had two keys, and no one could touch it. Albert had felt that way about his apartment once.

But what valuables? Sheet music? A piano? Cigarettes? Miss Bjork? Beer? (Miss Bjork had moved up in Albert's subconscious estimation.) These formed Albert's scope of things of value. And all were much too precious to be kept so far out of reach especially someplace that didn't open until 9:00 and closed at 3:00.

Albert stopped at the Redi-Mart to get cigarettes. Some kids were playing the pinball machine, and he stopped to watch. He'd always enjoyed the lights and balls, they reminded him of music struggling toward birth, but he had never attempted to understand the game.

It was all so clear now. The shiny metal ball was trying to find the straightest route home, while the boys joyfully, almost maniacally, pushed the buttons that flipped the flippers that sent the ball spinning back to the beginning, to attempt its perilous journey all over again.

Often the players waited until the last millisecond to push the buttons.

The analogy formed all by itself; the ball was Albert, bouncing from possibility to speculation, doubt to confusion on his way to the truth. Without direction, or pattern, and just when things seemed clearest, just when the end was in sight, he'd be blind sided by a fact that didn't fit. A new possibility. Some unexpected evidence that sent him spiraling back to the beginning.

It would continue that way as long as Albert had no plan. So far, he'd just bumped and bounced from one thing to another. He needed to do something on purpose. He resolved to prove or disprove that which was closest at hand; had Professor Lane hit Inspector Naples on the head with the flowerpot? If so, why? If not, who did?

"Professor Lane!"

The Professor emerged from a classroom at the far end of the hall just as Albert entered the building. Albert's voice, resounding from the cinder-block walls, arrested everyone in their tracks, including Lane, who waited until Albert caught up. They walked on together.

"You look better without the soup."

Albert had been plotting a way to delicately broach the subject he had in mind. "You hit Inspector Naples with the flowerpot."

It was supposed to have been a question, but its effect as a statement was immediate and imperative. Lane grabbed Albert by the arm and pulled him into the men's room.

"Who told you that?" His eyes flashed neon signs of guilt. He pressed Albert against the wall and spoke directly into his nose, as if it were a microphone. Maybe he was going to blow into his nostrils. 'Testing. 1-2-3. Testing.' He'd probably get feedback.

"Who told you? Why did you say that?"

"My arms hurts," Albert said. His voice sounded calm and soft, but that was only because he'd had the breath knocked out of him.

Lane immediately released his grip and took a step back. "I'm sorry, Professor . . . Albert," he said. "You startled me." Sweat broke out on his brow and his eyes looked like a leopard on the cover of National Geographic. Albert felt like the aged wildebeest on page six hundred and eighty-four.

"Who've you been listening to?" Lane said with a forced grin.

A smiling leopard was no comfort. He paced quickly up and down in front of the stalls, checking under each one.

"Nobody," said Albert. "I just figured it out."

Lane spun on his heel and glanced at Albert who had compressed himself against the wall involuntarily. "You did?" he said. He took Albert by the arm and squeezed hard.

At that moment one of Albert's graduate students entered. Albert recognized him, Peterson . . . or Ginsberg.

"Professor," Peterson or Ginsberg acknowledged. Lane nodded and tightened his grip on Albert's arm. "Professor." The student looked sidelong at Albert as he passed. Albert closed his eyes, broke out in a sweat, and nodded.

"Is everything all right?" the boy asked.

"Fine," said Lane. Squeeze. "Fine."

The following silence was broken only by the gentle flow of nature, which did nothing to relieve the tension. The student left.

"Let go of my arm," Albert said quite commandingly. Again, Lane complied.

"I'm sorry, Albert . . . but . . . what you're saying. Why did you say that?"

"You did it," said Albert. "You were following Daphne Knowlton when she came to see me."

Lane forgot to prevaricate. "Why did she go to see you?" Lane demanded. "You don't even know her, do you?"

"No," Albert replied. Lane had hit Inspector Naples. Mission accomplished. Another plan would have to be made if Albert got out of the men's room alive. He peeled himself off the wall. "She came to apologize." Now that was something, wasn't it? Did Lane know it was Daphne Knowlton who had put Albert in the hospital?

"Apologize for what?"

"She's the one who knocked me down that night . . . in the hall."

Albert had recently seen a young man hit in the groin with a snowball. Lane wore a similar expression. He hadn't known.

"What are you talking about? Daphne? Knock you down? You're crazy." Lane leaned against the opposite wall. "She wasn't even in town."

"She was," said Albert. "She said so."

"She doesn't know what she's saying," Lane replied with enough spark to straw the fire that was smoldering just below the surface. "She's not well."

"Maybe so," said Albert cautiously. He took a step toward the door. "But she was in town that night. She was here. She knocked me down."

Lane nudged himself away from the wall. "Why was she here? It was after hours. What would she have been doing here at that time of night?"

The answer jumped feet first into Albert's brain, though he hadn't given it a thought since he'd heard it.

"She was after some papers."

"Papers? What papers?"

"I don't know. I just remembered, she said something about getting papers. That's why she was here."

"From where?"

"I don't know," said Albert. "It was . . . she was outside Tewksbury's office when when she . . . "

"Tewksbury's office," said Lane aloud to himself. "Papers from Tewksbury's office?" He looked at Albert. The leopard was gone. A bewildered kitten had taken its place. "What papers? Why?"

Albert shrugged. What papers would Tewksbury have had in his office? "Archaeological papers?"

"What?"

"That's what Tewksbury would have in his office. Archaeology. Archaeological papers," said Albert. "He's an archaeologist."

"Archaeology?" Lane echoed. "What's that got to do with anything? What archaeological papers? Daphne doesn't know anything about archaeology."

"I don't know," said Albert, just as the light of his inner eye fell on a vague possibility. There was only one connection between Daphne and archaeology. At least, only one that was apparent.

"Unless ... " His eyes came to rest on Lane. "Strickland . . . "

The flame was passed. Albert watched it catch fire in Lane's eyes. "Strickland," he said. "Strickland." He strained the word through clenched teeth. "You mean, she was getting something for him? From Tewksbury's office?"

Yes, that is what Albert would have meant if he'd had time to think about it. "Would she have done that for him?"

Lane slowly lowered his head. "She'd've done anything for that manipulating son of a sodomite."

"But what was it?" said Albert, formulating the next step of his plan simultaneously.

Lane shrugged. "Assuming there's anything to what you say ... I can't imagine what it was." He glanced at his watch. "I'm late for class."

As they were about to leave the men's room, Lane placed his heavy hand on Albert's shoulder. "Albert ... about the inspector ... "

"He's going to be all right," Albert said. "They're pretty sure."

'What papers would Tewksbury have had that Strickland would have wanted?' The question had been revolving in Albert's consciousness all the way to Miss Bjork's. He was surprised not to find her home. He was even more surprised when, after reviewing his conversation with Lane, he realized he still didn't know why Inspector Naples had been hit with the flowerpot.

He didn't know if Lane had done it to protect Daphne Knowlton or himself. He did know that he would not wish to be on Lane's wrong side ... and if Glenly had been...

Miss Bjork arrived in her lawyer suit and three-piece demeanor.

She greeted him as she would the custodian, opened her apartment door and invited him in. Maybe she expected him to fix something. He should have brought some tools. He'd have to buy some.

"Have a seat, Professor," she said as she breezed down the hallway toward her bedroom, doffing the lawyer in bits and pieces along the way. "I'll be out in a minute, then you and I are going shopping."

A minute later, Albert heard the water running in the shower.

He tried to think of some music with a raindrop motif but he couldn't. Involuntarily he pictured Venus de Milo in the rain. He paced the room.

Within thirty minutes Miss Bjork emerged from her cocoon.

The transformation from lawyer to woman was complete. She hadn't showered; she'd been sandblasted. All the jagged edges had been smoothed to whole notes.

"How's that?" she said, spinning in a circle, holding the hem of her skirt out like Shirley Temple. Albert noticed the dress this time. It was black, or navy blue, and very . . . floaty. With little polka dots, or squares, and some kind of trim. Or the other way around.

He beamed, and blushed, and nodded like an arctic fowl. Before he could clear the steam off his glasses they were at the mall. Albert hadn't even known there was a mall. It was a different world. The most uninspiring place he'd ever been. It was art by committee, music by a newspaper critic. Hollywood in a concrete box.

For two hours Miss Bjork fussed over him like he'd never been fussed over. She bought him two suits, two shirts, two pairs of shoes, a pair of sneakers, two ties. It was like Noah's ark, everything came in two's: two belts. She tried to buy colored underwear but Albert's dignity forbade. He also drew the line at having his hair cropped a uniform length. His head was not socialist.

Nevertheless, it was a new Albert who strode self-consciously into the light of day, chaffing from neck to ankle, but as Miss Bjork slid her arm through the crook of his elbow he decided it was a pain he could endure. He stood a little straighter, carried his chin a little higher as they walked to the car. For the first time in his life, Albert wanted to be noticed. He wanted the world to see the woman on his arm.

Albert had never felt like the center of the universe before. He'd hardly felt connected to the universe. He was simply a comet that raced about in opposition to accepted laws. But now he had fallen into orbit around a heavenly body; Miss Bjork.

She knew everything. She knew about prices, designers, and advertising. She even talked about the lives of dead composers. He'd never thought about them as people; living beings with egos and imperfections. The more she told him, the less he felt he had in common with them.

"Now we're going out to dinner," she declared.

"At a restaurant?"

"The best in town."

Albert hated restaurants, except Dunkin' Donuts, especially since they had started serving soup and sandwiches. He hated menus. He hated words in French like soup du jour, and a la carte. He never had those. His mother had said the French will eat anything. You never know.

Most of all, Albert hated headwaiters. They represented the uppermost branches of that family tree that had City Hall bureaucrats among its lower members.

"Do you like Chinese?"

None came to mind except Professor Ping at the business school. He seemed nice enough. "I don't know many," Albert said.

Miss Bjork laughed as if he'd made a joke. She looked at him and saw that he hadn't, so she stopped laughing and almost hurt herself. "I'm sorry, Albert." He loved it when she called him that. "I mean, Chinese food. I should have said."

Albert hadn't had rice in years. "Yes," he said. "With butter and salt."

Over dinner Albert acquired a new understanding of Chinese cuisine. Meanwhile, he brought Miss Bjork up to date on Lane, and Naples, and Jeremy Ash, and Dr. Strickland and safety-posit boxes.

"Do you have one?" he asked.

"A safe-deposit box? Hardly. I don't have anything worth putting in one."

Tewksbury would have disagreed.

Albert smiled and rearranged chicken bones in a little pile on his plate. "Neither do I," he said. "What would you keep in one . . . if you did?"

"Oh, they're very good for important papers, wills, stock certificates, that kind of thing. Anything one considered precious or valuable. Some women keep their jewelry in them."

"What if they wanted to wear it?"

"They'd go get it."

"To the bank?"

Miss Bjork nodded over her teacup. "That's not the important thing, though, Albert. The important thing is Lane. Somebody like that would have to be pretty desperate to hit a policeman over the head. And you're right, he must have done it to keep the Inspector from finding out something; something Daphne Knowlton knows. Now, we've got to do one of two things."

"Find Daphne Knowlton," said Albert.

"Or get the truth from Lane . . . if he killed Glenly." Albert looked surprised "Don't look surprised. Albert. You've thought as much yourself. If he killed Glenly and Daphne Knowlton knows about it, she could be in deep trouble . . . if she's not already."

Such a scenario, common in Miss Bjork's profession, was completely alien to Albert. He couldn't reconcile the manner in which she proposed them, matter-of-factly, almost callously, with the way he felt about her.

"Where could she be?"

"Who knows?"

'Who knows?' He'd heard that before recently. 'Who knows?' Lane had said it, when he turned away. That made him realize something. "She's all right."

"How do you know?"

Albert remembered the look in Lane's eyes when he'd told the story of the kidnapping. The sound of his voice. She was safe with him, safe as a leopard cub. "I know where she is."

"Where?"

"I'll show you," said Albert, who wanted proof himself.

Miss Bjork paid the bill while Albert looked up Lane's address in the phone book. Within minutes they were parked in the shadows across the street from Lane's two-story duplex. His car was in the driveway.

"We wait?" said Miss Bjork, both the question and its answer. Albert nodded.

Lane's shades were drawn. A few lights were on. Now and then a window shade would blink with his unmistakable silhouette. There was no Daphne-shaped shadow.

Two hours later Albert had stepped out of the car for another cigarette. He was leaning on the roof of the car, watching the house, trying to trace his thoughts among the threads of smoke that wisped up in the still spring air. Suddenly Lane's door squeaked loudly open. Albert dropped his cigarette through Miss Bjork's open sunroof.

By the time they'd found the smoldering ash, Lane had driven away. The smell of burnt Corinthian leather filled the air. Miss Bjork's eyes were closed. She seemed to be praying.

"I'm sorry," said Albert in his new clothes. He crossed the street and walked up to the front door of Frank's house.

"Albert!" Miss Bjork cried as she scrambled out of the car. She tripped over the lead suspended between a man and his dog, who had taken one another out for a stroll. The man helped her off the grass. The dog licked her ankles. "Excuse me. I'm sorry, I didn't see you."

The man and his dog had nonspeaking parts in Miss Bjork's life, and went about their business with a tear and a smile.

"Albert!" she whispered sharply. "What are you doing?"

But he'd already done it. The gentle rap echoed up and down the street. There was no reply from within.

"If she's in there, you're going to scare her off."

"I'll go to the back door. You stay here and keep knocking."

At the rear of the house, Albert climbed the few steps to the kitchen door. The light was on. The kitchen was very clean. The dishes had been done and stood in the drainer. The floor was shining and a little basket of fruit stood on the table. On one side of the refrigerator a doorway led to a small darkened room and then the living room beyond. On the other side was an open door revealing a narrow stairway and, at the place where the steps made a sharp turn up and out of sight, all curled up in a wide-eyed ball, was Daphne Knowlton.

Albert tapped softly on the window. The girl started, the fear in her eyes sent shockwaves through Albert. He wanted to take her in his arms and soothe her. He smiled and waved.

Like a frightened bird, Daphne Knowlton was grounded by her fear, halfway between flight and fainting. Albert waved again, smiled a little broader, and mouthed the words, "It's me."

The recognition showed on her face. She got up slowly, upsetting the wellspring of tears that overflowed her eyes. She descended the last two of three steps and tentatively began to cross the kitchen. "You see anything?" said Miss Bjork, as she rounded the corner. "I don't think she's here."

Albert had no time to react. He was taken off guard, as was Miss Bjork, at the sight of Daphne Knowlton frozen in suspended animation halfway across the kitchen.

The paralyzing effect of Miss Bjork's appearance in the window next to the smiling, waving music teacher, wore off almost instantly and Daphne bolted up the darkened stairs.

Miss Bjork tried the screen door. It opened, compressing Albert against the railing.

"Sorry," she said as she tried the interior door. It swung inward.

Suddenly, there was a series of dull, heavy thuds, and Daphne Knowlton reappeared at the bottom of the staris in a tangle of arms, legs, and red hair.

"She's fallen!" Miss Bjork screamed. She raced to the girl's side with Albert at her heels.

"Is she . . . ?"

"Call the hospital!"

Albert jumped up and, taking a quick inventory of the room, located the phone over the microwave. As he reached for it, he heard the heavy squeak of the front door.

"That must be Lane!"

Miss Bjork cradled Daphne's head in her arms.

Albert dialed "0," throwing caution to the wind. The operator was helpful. She didn't scold him, but she did ask a lot of questions.

Fortunately Miss Bjork was there to help with the answers.

Momentarily the ambulance was on its way.

"Albert!" Miss Bjork whispered as soon as he'd hung up the phone. "She's saying something! I can't make it out, can you?"

Daphne Knowlton's eyes were closed. Her lips moved slightly, trying to form words from whispers. Albert put his ear close to her mouth.

The sounds had a pattern. She was repeating the same thing over and over. One word at a time. Albert pieced most of the refrain together.

"'I killed him. I killed him'," he repeated. "That's what it sounds like."

Chapter Seventeen

Her lips moved in the same pattern as the attendants lifted her onto the stretcher and rolled her into the ambulance, but there were lights, and sirens, and radios. No one could hear her.

Lane's car screeched into the driveway just as the ambulance drove away, wailing like a banshee. He jumped out of the car clutching a bag of groceries. He glanced from the ambulance to Albert and Miss Bjork.

"What's happened!?" he said. "What are you people doing here?"

Albert nodded in the direction of the receding ambulance.

"Daphne Knowlton . . . is in there."

"What!?" Lane took a step in the direction of the ambulance, then stopped. "What?"

"They say she'll be all right," Miss Bjork added quickly. "She just had a mild concussion, and probably a broken collarbone."

"A concussion?"

For the second time Lane had that snowball-in-the-groin look. "I just left twenty minutes ago. She was fine. What happened?" He rounded the car, clutching the groceries reflexively. "How did you know?"

"I knew if she was still in town someone would have to be taking care of her," said Albert.

"We knew that if Albert was right . . . if Miss Knowlton was here . . . you'd never admit it, much less let us speak to her," said Miss Bjork. "So we waited for you to leave."

"I knocked on the door," Albert explained. "But she didn't answer."

"So he went around back to the kitchen door and saw her sitting on the stairs."

"She recognized me," said Albert. "She was going to let me in . . . then . . . "

"Then she saw me, and bolted up the stairs," said Miss Bjork. "She must have tripped."

Lane hadn't blinked. His knees gave out beneath him, and Albert and Miss Bjork helped him to the front steps. "I thought I was being so clever," he said. "And you read me like a cheap magazine."

The piano player and Miss Bjork bookended him on the step.

"Why don't you tell us everything, Professor Lane," said Miss Bjork. Albert detected a hint of courtroom coolness in her voice.

The ambulance had gone, but Lane's tear-filled eyes followed. "I've got to go with her. She'll need me."

Miss Bjork put her hand on his shoulder. "Tell us, first, Professor. Why?"

"Why what? Why did I keep her here? Why didn't I tell anyone?"

"That'll do for starters."

Lane still stared into the hollow of the tree-lined road as if he could see them taking her away. "Poor kid," he said. "Poor, poor kid."

"Do you love her?" Miss Bjork said in church tones.

He looked at her from the bottom of dark pools of sadness. "Not in the way you think . . . the way they all think."

Lane sighed long and deep. "My wife . . . " Sigh. "My wife and I had a daughter . . . Debbie. She was only sixteen when she . . . " His dignity gave way beneath the weight of his grief, he dropped his head to his hands and sobbed. "It was six years ago," he continued. "Before we came here."

"I'm so sorry," said Miss Bjork quietly, laying her hand on his elbow. "I didn't know."

Know what? thought Albert. What did she say? What did he say? He'd missed something; again.

"No one knows," said Lane. "We moved here to forget. Ran away, I guess. Away from the pain of it. She was all we had."

He raised his eyes to the merciful night. "It didn't help. We hung on for six years. Six long years. But it finally ate away at the foundations of the marriage. The sorrow. Emptiness. We finally just . . . well, I got this place and just stopped going home."

Tears slid silently down his cheeks.

Albert didn't look up.

"What happened?" said Miss Bjork.

"Drunk driver." The weight of the words was more than Lane could support in a sitting position. He sprang to his feet and paced the yard in a small semicircle. "Drunk driver." He laughed at a private irony. "Got off with a fine and a suspended sentence . . . for killing my daughter. Debbie! My baby girl!"

The truth hit Albert like a stone.

With supreme effort, Lane finally got himself together enough to continue. "It left a hole in me the size of . . . "

"Daphne Knowlton," said Albert.

Lane stopped in front of Albert and stared at him. Albert looked up.

"Daphne Knowlton," Lane said. "Just the size of Daphne Knowlton. She needed me. I needed her. It just happened that way. I had a daughter again."

"Everyone thought she went home, back to New Hampshire," said Miss Bjork. "Why is she here?"

"Like I told Albert, she stayed with me a few days after that night in the lounge after Strickland took her home. She needed time. That's when it all began.

"I'd just moved out on my own. I thought I was comforting her, but I guess I needed her just as much as she did me. I didn't rush her to go.

"She did, though. After a week or so. I was relieved in a way. All she talked about the whole time was how ashamed she was. How she hated Glenly. How she wanted to ... "

"Kill him?" said Miss Bjork.

Lane hesitated, then nodded. "Not in so many words but . . . and how wonderful she thought Strickland was. I could see she was falling in love with him. Mind you, Strickland was supposed to have been dating Glenly's daughter at the time, but ...

"She finally went home, though. Like I said. There was nothing else she could do. She couldn't show her face on campus. She'd already resigned. I thought that was the end of it." Lane fell silent.

"But she showed up again?" Miss Bjork prompted.

"Three times. The first time about a week before Glenly died. The second time, about three weeks ago. Then again a few days ago. Each time she stayed about a week. Didn't say much of anything, just that she wanted my company. Didn't even mention Strickland. Still, I was curious about her feelings for him, so I mentioned him. She acted as if she'd forgotten who he was. At first I was relieved, then I got suspicious.

"This last time, she went out at night. She often did. I was sure she was going to meet him. so I followed. I wanted to have it out with him. I wanted her to see him for the snake he is."

"But she came to my house," said Albert.

"I couldn't understand it," said Lane. "I didn't even know it was your house, then I saw you come out. You met Naples, talked with him, then you went away and he went inside."

"You thought he was after Daphne?" said Albert.

"I guess so. I don't know, really. I didn't know what was going on. I just wanted everything to stop until I could figure it out, before Daphne before she said something foolish." He paused. "I told you about her, Albert. She's not well. She doesn't know what she's saying half the time." He paused again.

Albert let him collect his thoughts. "I don't think she knows what she's doing."

"What did you do?" Albert asked gently. He knew, but he had to hear it from Lane.

Lane looked at Albert as if he was unable to form the words. Miss Bjork was still some steps behind.

"Did Daphne kill Glenly?" said Albert.

Those were the words that breached Lane's tottering wall of reserve. He fell against the side of the house, massaging his temples distractedly in an effort to stem the tears. Finally he nodded.

Miss Bjork was stunned. "Daphne?!"

"I'm sorry," said Albert.

"You're sure of this?" said Miss Bjork.

Lane nodded. "It all adds up."

Daphne Knowlton's last words rung clearly in Miss Bjork's memory. She clambered over a fence and fell into the same pasture. "That's why you hit Naples!"

"I figured she was in the apartment your place, Albert. I went up the stairs, Naples had knocked on the door already. The phone rang inside, there was some kind of commotion, so he didn't pay any attention to me.

"I pretended to start up the second flight. I didn't know what to do. Then I saw the flowerpot." Lane hung his head. "All I could think was . . . what if they locked her away? After all she's been through?"

Mentally, Miss Bjork dragged herself to a sitting position and brushed herself off. "Of course! The hatred that must have been building up inside her all that time. The resentment and hurt. She had plenty of time to think about it . . . to plan." She was already orchestrating the defense; it couldn't be justifiable homicide, or temporary insanity, too premeditated, too much time. But when Albert told Lane to fill her in on Daphne Knowlton's background, the case solidified. Insanity. Plain and simple.

Why hadn't Daphne Knowlton mentioned Strickland? Albert thought. He knew she had met him the day of Glenly's murder. They'd driven away together in the little red sports car; Tewksbury saw them.

"Tewksbury!" Albert blurted involuntarily.

It hit Miss Bjork at the same time. "He really is innocent."

That thought had another snapping at its heels. Albert turned to Lane. "You knew."

"Not at first. I thought he was guilty." Lane sat down again. "Everybody did. I still hadn't put the pieces together . . . with Daphne, I mean. The case against Tewks seemed cut and dried."

"Yes. It did," said Miss Bjork in her own defense. She wished she hadn't.

Lane's words had made a hole in the road of reason. He stepped to the edge and looked in. "Then, a piece at a time, everything came together. It couldn't be anything else. But Tewksbury'd been tried and convicted by that time.

"I didn't know what to do. Then I read somewhere that he could get out, pardoned, in seven years, maybe less. Seven years." He looked from one to the other of his bookends. "He didn't have any family to speak of. No wife or kids. He could start over again." He paused. "That's the first time I've said that out loud. It sounds pretty heartless, doesn't it?" He folded his hands and rested his forehead against them. "But, Daphne . . . she'd just wither away and die if she was put away.

"I liked Tewks."

They left Lane on his front step, a middle-aged man living out of boxes, clutching his bag of groceries like a lifeline.

"You did it, Albert!" Miss Bjork proclaimed once they were in the car. "You did it!"

Albert didn't say anything.

"You proved Tewksbury innocent."

"No, I didn't," said Albert. "I proved Daphne Knowlton guilty."

"Same thing."

Albert didn't think so.

"Anyway once she's ready to talk, we'll get a confession from her and Tewksbury's home free."

"What about the escape?"

"Oh, he'll still have to answer for that, but . . . in light of the evidence, compared to murder? It'll be a slap on the wrist. Suspended sentence, if that."

Albert wanted to ask what would happen to someone who had helped Tewksbury escape, but he decided not to. Miss Bjork wanted to ask if Albert knew where Tewksbury was. She did, but retracted the question before he had a chance to answer.

"No, never mind. We'll find him once we have the confession. Once he's cleared. That's safer," she said. "For everyone."

"How long will that take?" asked Albert. He wondered if it took as long to find a man innocent as it did to find him guilty.

"Not long. Not long." Miss Bjork was on an adrenaline high, her entire persona radiated an enthusiasm, an excitement that Albert would have found contagious if not for Daphne Knowlton; if not for the aching intuition that something still wasn't quite right. That is, things seemed even more wrong than usual.

No sooner had Daphne Knowlton recovered from her fall than she began confessing to the murder of Justin Glenly. "I killed Professor Glenly. I poisoned him because I hated him. I hated him." She repeated the refrain over and over, to anyone who would listen. Nothing added. Nothing amended. In fact. she said nothing else.

Miss Moodie's theory of gender tactics was borne out. 'If it's poison, you may be sure a woman done the deed. Read your Christie.'

Nobody questioned the girl's motive. Nor could anyone truly silence the angel of their conscience that whispered there was justice in the act.

Miss Bjork relied heavily on the details of Daphne Knowlton's past to argue innocence by reason of insanity. The jury agreed, committing her to Bridgewater State Mental Hospital, there to remain until such time as her doctors were assured that her madness did not exceed that of the public in general.

Tewksbury was exonerated in absentia, and Miss Bjork argued the remaining charges against him down to thirty days, applicable retroactively, and a five-hundred-dollar fine, waived.

"What are you thinking?" Miss Bjork hadn't said much for the first hour of the drive. What was he thinking?

"Everything," Albert said. "Glenly, Daphne Knowlton. Tewksbury. None of it had to happen."

"Seldom does," said Miss Bjork. She should know. "When are you going to tell me where we're going?"

"North," said Albert with an impish smile.

"Maine?"

Albert gestured north through the windshield.

"I love Maine."

Miss Bjork couldn't follow where Albert's thoughts were heading him, so she drove in silence. It was enough like spring so she let the window down a crack and made believe the tingle-ridden wind was just a brisk breeze. Besides, she had thoughts enough of her own. Thoughts that were kindled and rekindled by stolen glances at Albert in his worlds away. Thoughts that had nothing to do with the life she'd set in order like alphabet blocks.

Albert had no use for the alphabet beyond "G."

They drove over the bridge that staples Maine to the rest of the country. It was mid-afternoon when they turned off 95 on 29 West.

It was past mid-afternoon when they passed through Sanford and Alfred in quick succession without having to apply the brakes. It was late mid-afternoon when they turned up a narrow dirt road through thick woods, bordered on either side by bright-orange-on-black No Hunting signs.

"Where are you taking me?"

He was taking her to his childhood. "My mother's."

Miss Bjork was genuinely surprised; she hadn't imagined Albert having a mother; of course it was an absurd notion, still . . . .

"She's not here."

They rounded a bend in the road and the thick woods instantly broke away on either side, reaching out with aged arms to embrace a huge field that rose in orderly swells to a small hill placed at the foot of an unpretentious mountain. On the hill, like a thoughtful offering, was a graceful white farmhouse that had grown there.

The car slowed reverently. "Albert! This is beautiful."

He was hoping she'd say that. He still didn't know why, for sure, but he needed her to say things like that. Especially about this place.

Between the hill and the mountain was a small hollow where nature had put a perfect red barn for contrast. Obviously the place had once been a working farm, but had long since given itself over to perfection. It was the kind of place only a calendar photographer finds; the earthly remains of a place and time that was no more. They stopped beside the house.

Miss Bjork did what all people do when something tugs at the spirit, she breathed deeply and didn't exhale for a long time. Albert's mystique was at once complete and comprehensible; he hadn't been raised in the real world.

Albert had unloaded the suitcases and tucked them under his arms. He lowered his head to window level. "Do you want to come inside?"

She got out and walked beside him. "I feel like I've died and gone to heaven." She slipped her arm in among the suitcases.

Suddenly the porch door burst open and Tewksbury issued forth.

Miss Bjork's descent to reality was abrupt and profound. "Tewksbury!" Her mind told her body to react somehow, but it didn't.

"Albert, are you crazy? Why did you bring her here?"

Albert calmly handed a suitcase to Tewksbury and climbed the porch steps. "You're innocent. It's all right," he said, holding the screen door open for Miss Bjork, who negotiated the steps without bending her knees. Her eyes were fastened on Tewksbury like staples.

"Innocent? What do you mean?" Tewksbury's silly-putty eyebrows vaulted as if propped by exclamation points.

"Somebody else killed Professor Glenly. She confessed. They had another trial and . . . somebody else did it. Miss Bjork got them to drop the charges against you."

Tewksbury looked from Albert, who was smiling, to Miss Bjork, who still hadn't blinked. "Is it true?" he said, almost fearful to hear the answer.

With a sudden, violent effort Miss Bjork shook herself loose from the suitcases and took an involuntary step backward, as if to get a better footing in reality. "You've been here all this time?" She didn't say the words. Didn't shout them. They escaped her. But she never got an answer. A muffled explosion suddenly rent the peace of the valley and applauded itself through the trees. Miss Bjork fell toward Albert, her eyes fixed wide in terror.

"She's been shot!" Tewksbury cried.

Albert dropped the suitcases and tried to grab her listless body as it slid down his own. She ran through his fingers like water, drawing him down with her.

"She's been shot. My God!" Tewksbury cried again. His eyes ransacked the nearby woods for signs of a gunman.

Silence closed in once more, like water around a pebble.

"Albert?" said Miss Bjork. She grabbed at his collar and held fast. "What happened? Albert?"

"I'll get the doctor!" said Tewksbury. "Where are the keys? Never mind, they're in the car. You stay here. You stay with her. I'll get the doctor . . . and the police. She'll be all right, Albert. She'll be okay. You should have a phone up here, Albert."

"Have I been shot, really?"

Albert couldn't see for the tears in his eyes. He wiped at them furiously. He wanted to see her clearly.

"Did Tewksbury do it?"

"No," he said softly. "No. He's gone to get a doctor."

"Then who . . . ?" Suddenly her muscles spasmed and she winced in pain. Blood was pooling on the porch, running down through the cracks between the boards. Albert's tears fell on her face. "I'm going to die," she said.

"No!" said Albert. But it was all he could say for some time without crying outright. He scanned the forest from where the shot had seemed to come. The thick woods, though leafless, consisted mostly of evergreens and revealed nothing. His mother had always warned him of the hunters—armed drunks who roamed the Maine woods driven by the lust for blood.

Miss Bjork seemed to be asleep. She was breathing; the pained expression had left her face. Albert didn't know what to do. He held her closely and gently cradled her head in his lap.

Finally she opened her eyes. "I love you."

An inexpressible fire swept through every atom of Albert's being. "I love you!" he cried, clutching at her as if he was a drowning man.

"I thought so," she said. She turned her head and looked out over the fields. "I'm going to die."

It was true. There was too much blood. Albert knew it. He nodded.

"I wonder who did it," she said. She fell silent once more. "Albert! Albert, are you there?" She clutched at him.

He squeezed her. "I'm here," he whispered. He couldn't say anything else without bursting into tears. That's not what she needed now.

"I had a dream about us," she said. "We were married. Did you ever think about getting married?" she said. She sounded sleepy.

He hadn't dared think such a thing. "Yes."

There was another spasm and a long silence during which he stared at her, as if to fix every particle of her expression in his memory.

Her breathing settled down. She opened her eyes again. "Albert?"

"Yes?"

She smiled. "I feel like ... I've got so much to do. I can't die now. I've got to do my will. Everything's a mess." She coughed.

"Albert?"

"What?"

"I'd like to be buried here."

Albert broke down and cried, for the second time in his life. He clung to her all the harder. She didn't mind the pain as he squeezed; something in it reached through her flesh and caressed her soul.

"There's more to me than this, Albert," she said. Suddenly the muscles on her face relaxed. She sighed as if the pain had stopped. "Somebody shot the baggage, that's all. I'll go on."

Albert had never thought about death in the first person.

"I wonder what comes next?" said Miss Bjork weakly.

There was only one response. "You never know." Maybe he said it aloud. Maybe not. He never knew.

By the time the ambulance arrived it was dark. Miss Bjork had been dead in Albert's arms half an hour. She was becoming cold and rigid.

Her eyelids didn't flinch when his tears landed on them.

Tewksbury read the story in Albert's eyes and actions as the paramedics put Miss Bjork in the ambulance. Finally he had something beyond himself to worry about. Suddenly he realized all Albert had done for him; sacrifices for which no amount of thanks could compensate.

Chapter Eighteen

The revolving red-and-white lights chased each other through the trees in circles of alarm as the ambulance drove quietly away, crunching gravel under its tires. They didn't use the siren. There was no need.

When Albert nearly fell asleep in a living-room chair, Tewksbury assisted him to his old bedroom, put him in his pajamas, and there Albert awoke early next morning to the worst day of his life.

For a moment, it might all have been a dream. His whole adult life might have been one interminable, dull dream. The wallpaper was the same familiar wallpaper he'd awakened to every morning throughout that eternal youth. There were two places where the seams never matched; time hadn't brought them together.

The curtains were the same. The breeze that came in through the propped-open window might even be the same breeze. His solitary trophy stood on the same doily in the middle of the bureau, beside a bronze Statue of Liberty and a Coke-bottle image of Abraham Lincoln he'd made in the fifth grade.

He might be a child still.

Suddenly pale blotches of blue light arched across the walls. Everything came back, clear, hard, and cold. He stepped to the window. In the surreal light of dawn, two police cars stood at the edge of the woods opposite the house.

Tewksbury was still asleep in his chair. Albert went out in his bare feet, haunting the morning with his chalk-white face.

He stopped halfway down the hill. There were four or five policemen in uniform crisscrossing the forest edge with flash lights. He could hear their voices, but he couldn't make out what they were saying.

Another man sat on the hood of the car with a map spread across his knees. His pot belly had filled the promise it had shown in earlier years. His rusty hair had gone white and he'd grown a mustache, but there was no mistaking Charlie Gault. He'd been one of those kids who seemed born for middle age. He wore it well.

Charlie felt the eyes on him and looked up. At first he furrowed his brow and squinted. He took a couple of serious pulls at his pipe as he reconstructed an old acquaintance from the specter before him.

"Albert?" he said. "Good Lord in Heaven, Albert?"

He rolled off the car and propelled himself up the hill like an overweight garden gnome. It was head-down work and he didn't raise his eyes until Albert's feet hove into view. Even accounting for the passage of time, he was stunned.

"Well, I was gonna say you ain't changed a bit. But you look like hell." He held out his hand which Albert shook lethargically, not that Charlie expected more of a piano player. "How long's it been, Albert?" he said. "I ain't seen you since, what? Musta been fifteen years or more now."

Albert wondered how he'd feel in another fifteen years. He wondered if he'd forget; if the pain would stop or just become a part of him.

"I heard you was up last year, wasn't you?" said Charlie. Albert made no reply. He was watching the policemen. "One of 'em found this." He held up a spent shell casing. ".410 slug."

There was a silence. Some morning birds had started to sing. A rooster crowed somewhere. The sun was coming up, sifting gold onto the steel blue. "What'n hell happened here, Albert?"

Albert turned and faced the house. Charlie turned, too. "Miss Bjork died."

"That her name? Bjork? B-j-o-r-k?"

Albert had never spelled it. "I don't know."

"I know a Bjork runs a lumberyard over to Sabbath Day Lake. You 'member Kitty Hopkins? She married him. He spelt his name B-J-O-R-K. Had one a them personal license plates with it on there."

Albert was looking at the house as the first rays of light ignited the second-story windows and painted the clapboards golden yellow.

"Your mother's down to Florida, ain't she? With your sister?"

Albert nodded. There was another silence. Charlie relit his pipe. "It was hunters done it," he declared. "Somebody out shootin' rabbit. Happens all the time. Every year some fool hunter . . . She your girlfriend, Albert?"

Girlfriend? Albert had never had a girlfriend. How did he want people to think of his relationship with Miss Bjork? "She was my friend," he said. "We were friends." Pause. "Why would a hunter shoot her?"

"They see somethin' move and they just blast away, then they go find out what it is . . . wasn't no one 'round here done it, though," said Charlie. "They know better'n to cross your ma's fence."

"Fence?"

"She had some barbed wire strung up round the whole property some years ago. Had all them signs put up down by the drive. You know how she hated gunfire ever since they shot that old dog she had. You remember that old dog?"

"Midas."

"Midas! That was him. Big ol' Great Dane."

"Saint Bernard."

"Saint Bernard, was it? I always get them two mixed up. I knew it was one a them big ones, though." He relit his pipe.

"That's the kind you see carry's that little barrel've brandy 'round their neck in the mountains over to Switzerland and around there." Draw. Puff. Puff. "Explains why ski-in' caught on so, I guess. Yup. Midas. I remember."

Albert was beginning to feel the cold. Midas had survived the shooting, but it would have been better if he hadn't.

"Nossir, whoever was hunting up here knew they wasn't s'posed to be here. They had to climb the fence, or either come up the drive. More'n likely somebody from Mass'chusetts or somewhere outta state." One of the uniformed policemen emerged from the woods and walked up the hill toward them. "People up here got more sense; least they're sneakier."

"Charlie," said the uniformed policeman as he joined them. "I think we've found where they parked. Down in that little turn-off just past the driveway."

"Find anything special?"

The policeman shrugged. "Nothin' special."

Charlie turned to Albert. "Mr. Rawlins was here when it happened?"

"Rawlins?" Albert echoed. "Oh, you mean . . . Rawlins. Yes. He was right there."

"Could you show me exactly . . . you know . . . where everyone was standing. How it happened?"

Albert restaged the scene using the uniformed officer - whose name, according to a little sign over his pocket, was LaPointe - as Rawlins, and Charlie Gault as Miss Bjork. He fought consciously to keep the horrifying images of the preceding night from replaying as he reenacted the event. When he had finished, Charlie Gault lay on the porch in Albert's arms. There was something grotesque, almost irreverent, in the act.

"What do you make of it, Tommy?" said Gault as he puffed and grunted to his feet. Albert got up, too.

Tommy thought. Charlie relit his pipe. Albert struggled in vain to keep his eyes off the rust-colored stain on the porch.

"If she was standing here, like he says, and Rawlins was standin' where I am and the bullet was fired from over there where we found the casing . . . hit her on the right side, here," he held out his hand to indicate the approximate trajectory and drew it slowly toward himself in a straight line. "Speakin' as Rawlins, I'm lucky to be alive."

"Meaning?"

"Meanin' if she'd stepped outta the way at the last second, this'd be Rawlins's blood."

Albert tried hard not to ask why she didn't move, why it couldn't have been Rawlins's blood that stained the porch forever. Then he remembered. She had moved at the last possible second. Not out of the path . . . but into it.

The police went to rouse Rawlins. Albert trudged off barefoot in no particular direction, the dew-soaked hems of his pajama legs slobbered at his ankles like a toothless dog. He kept trying to put his hands into pockets that weren't there. Habitually he frisked himself for a cigarette.

Perpetual frustration at a subconscious level has a warming effect on a cool morning.

Albert found the shallow turn-off that Officer LaPointe had mentioned. He looked blankly at the perfectly imprinted tire tracks; it might as well have been modern art. Why did tires have treads anyway? He stared at them nevertheless. Perhaps he could assimilate some clue through osmosis.

A pickup truck drove by. The driver leaned out the window and offered a terse critique of Albert's habiliment for the benefit of a companion in the cab.

Albert didn't hear what they said. His attention was drawn to the truck's tires. Fat. Far apart. He compared them to the imprints at his feet. The tires that made them were narrow and relatively close together.

A pickup truck had not made these tracks. At least not a big one. Neither had an eighteen wheeler, or a camper, or a train.

But what had?

Albert sank to his knees, cleaned his glasses on the hem of his pajama top, and bent to inspect the treads. They reminded him of garden rows, or a huge zipper. Parallel grooves that zigged and zagged but never met, except in one place where some large imperfection in the tire spanned two of the outside channels.

The pattern repeated itself at regular intervals for the length of the track. Even Holmes couldn't have made much of that. There was nothing else.

"They just asked me what happened," said Tewksbury over his coffee cup. "I told them."

"Did you tell them who you are?"

"Things are complicated enough, aren't they?" Tewksbury was suddenly conscious of the sharpness of his words. He softened the edges. "No, I didn't."

Albert looked out the window for a long time. Tewksbury could almost eavesdrop on the memories.

"I'm going to take a shower," said Albert at last. He stood and walked toward the stairs.

"Albert?"

Albert turned. He didn't want to hear it.

"What're you going to do about her?"

Albert sighed. "She asked me to . . . to, bury her out there." He tossed a nod through the window, almost choking on the impossibility of the words as he spoke them. Tewksbury's eyes followed to see where it landed.

"It's pretty up here."

They were quiet. Albert started up the stairs.

"Albert?" Tewksbury felt something much bigger than he'd ever put into words, feelings that distilled themselves into the only thing his tongue could handle. "I'm sorry."

The end of the world was in Albert's eyes as he turned and trudged up the stairs.

It was snowing as they drove back to school four days later. Tewksbury was at the wheel of Miss Bjork's car, just as he'd been at the wheel of Albert's life for the past ninety-six hours. Albert wasn't surprised that everything got done without him. It always had. It always would. It never occurred to him to wonder how Tewksbury managed to do whatever had to be done to get Miss Bjork buried on his mother's property.

He wasn't surprised when Miss Bjork's parents showed up at the funeral. Of course they would; she was their daughter. He wasn't surprised that other people were there. Miss Bjork knew people. She enjoyed their company.

Albert cried through the service. He tried to listen to the minister, but he couldn't hear over his own sobs. What was he saying about her? Where was she going? Why had she died? Why had she lived? What if he was missing all the answers? The only thing that surprised him was that Miss Bjork had a younger sister. They met afterward, when everyone had gone inside to mourn over lunch.

She looked like Miss Bjork, had the same tilt of the head, the same eyes, except they were red with weeping. She even had the same name: Miss Bjork. She was much younger, though. Less worldly. Less knowing. Less guarded. She hugged him when they were introduced. Miss Bjork had never hugged him.

"I know how much you meant to Melissa," she said.

Who? Melissa? He remembered. It was the name on the gravestone.

"She loved you."

"She told me," said Albert.

"She told me, too."

"Did she?" Albert asked with his eyebrows. How long had she known?

Miss Bjork nodded and pressed his arm gently. There was something hopeful in that which Albert couldn't understand.

"She wrote about you in her letters. I'll send you copies, if you like."

"No," said Albert. "Please don't do that."

They walked along the ridge toward the house.

"She loved your music."

Music. It seemed like a foreign language. Did anybody speak it anymore?

"She had your records." Albert never knew what to say when people told him that. He didn't say it now.

"May I write you?"

Chapter Nineteen

"You all right?" said Tewksbury.

They turned off 95 onto 495 west. The snow was thick and wet. Large flakes flung themselves against the windshield, turned into tears, and were swept away by the mechanical click and thud of the wipers.

Albert didn't answer. The question got sillier as it hung in the air.

"Seems strange, being free," said Tewksbury. "I can't shake the fugitive mind-set. I want to hide my face, afraid somebody might recognize me. But free . . . !"

Albert didn't say anything.

Tewksbury droned on while Albert withdrew into a single disturbing thought that had plagued him for four days; had Miss Bjork . . . Melissa . . . not moved into the line of fire at the last second, Tewksbury would be dead and she would be driving.

Something Tewksbury was saying burned through the fog.

"What?"

"I said I'll be glad to get back to Crete. Not just miles away from all this . . . light years away. Thousands of years."

"Dr. Strickland is going to Crete."

"He always does."

"I mean, he's the Director now."

Someone might have removed the windshield and let the large, wet flakes hit Tewksbury in the face at sixty miles an hour. "What do you mean? Well, yes . . . of course . . . he filled in. Someone had to. With Glenly gone; me gone . . . "

'Leapfrogged both of them.' Who had said that? Moodie? Lane? It was Lane.

"It would be Stricks, of course," Tewksbury concluded. "But now, well, I'm back, aren't I? I'll be reinstated. They'll have to reinstate me. I've got tenure. Stricks will probably be bumped up to Glenly's post. That would make sense."

"But he would have taken yours. That's what he did. It's what he wanted."

"Who wouldn't?" said Tewksbury, trying on his academic demeanor for the first time in months. It felt funny. Not as comfortable and important as it once had. "But now I'm back."

You wouldn't be if Miss Bjork hadn't moved, thought Albert. He almost said it.

"After all, I'm innocent! You proved that, God bless you!"

Albert thought his contribution was negligible.

"Of course, Miss Bjork, I'll always be grateful to her, too. Always." Heartfelt sigh. "But you were the one who believed in me. The only one."

"Your dad."

"Dad. Yes. Him, too. Poor guy. I don't think he understands what's happened. But it's all over now. The whole nightmare. He'll be glad of that. I'll call him tonight."

The nightmare wasn't over for Albert; it had just reached a higher level of absurdity. If only he had taken a step toward Miss Bjork . . . it would be she and Tewksbury driving home in the snow. Not a comfortable notion. Albert wrestled a bizarre, totally irrational twinge of jealousy. What if he had stepped into the path of the bullet? What if he had died in Miss Bjork's arms?

Would she still have said the things she said? The thought was almost musical. Romantic. He didn't want to think it and had tried to block it when he saw it coming.

These and other thoughts wandered the dark, lifeless canyons of Albert's brain in no particular order until, just as they drove into town, two random quarks of information came flying around a corner in opposite direction, collided, creating an alarming possibility: the tire tread with that bothersome little blemish repeating itself at regular intervals. Something was embedded in the tire. What became embedded in tires? Glass. Like when Strickland's car drove over the beer bottle.

The way Albert was thinking there was no direct route from one thought to the next. Each was an individual entity that traveled in its own erratic orbit and ran headlong into a goodly number of other ideas on the way, each time gathering itself up, somewhat stunned, brushing off and moving on. It was next to impossible to keep up.

Strickland's little red sports car ... the wheels would be compact. Close together.

"Do you know where Strickland lives?"

"Yes. The other side of town, Arundel Woods."

"Go there."

"But ... "

"Go there," said Albert. Concentrate. So many little info-neutrons were wearing the same uniform; if only they could only be sorted out and put in a line ... like a parade. Think like Sousa.

Suddenly, magically, the band assembled, with one or two exceptions who were probably still in the ladies' room or whose mothers hadn't dropped them off yet. "I know who killed Miss Bjork," he said.

"What?"

Albert was busy trying to grab the tail of each idea as it raced by, to bring it to ground and shake the sense out of it. Only one person had been in the direct line of fire. Tewksbury. If the gunshot was intentional ... if it was ... he had been the intended target. "Never mind."

"What do you mean 'never mind'? You said you know who killed her. Why? You think someone killed her on purpose?"

"No. That was an accident."

"Then what did you mean?"

"They were trying to kill you."

"Me?!" Tewksbury looked at Albert in alarm. "Someone was trying to shoot me?"

"And she stepped in the way," Albert said softly. Tewksbury focused his dazed eyes on the road just as a squirrel darted in front of the car. He swerved to one side, plowed through a row of plastic garbage bags, and narrowly missed a fire hydrant before coming to a stop half on the sidewalk, half on the road.

"You're crazy. Who'd want to kill me?"

Albert shook his head slightly, bit his lip and massaged the bulging vein in his forehead. "I have to make sure," he said. "Go on."

"To Strickland's? You think Strickland did it?"

"I need to check some things," said Albert.

Tewksbury eased the car back into the road. "Why do you think Stricks would want to kill me?"

"I didn't say he did."

"You said you know who killed Melissa Bjork, then you said they were trying to kill me. Now you tell me to take you to Strickland's to check something. You must think . . . that's absurd. What would Strickland want to kill me for?"

Now was as good a time as any to see if the balloon held water.

"He wanted your position."

"My position!" Tewksbury was speaking exclusively in exclamations. "Ancient History? You mean . . . he wanted my job?"

"Well?"

"Albert," said Tewksbury, weatherproofing his tone with a sort of paternal patina. "You don't kill someone for a directorship. Leastwise not a temporary one."

Albert ran his fingers around the outside of the balloon to see where the leak was. "Temporary?"

"Of course temporary. Stricks doesn't have the creden-tials to fill the slot. Nobody knows that better than he does. He's just filling in ... in the interim."

"But he's directing the project ... in Crete," said Albert, applying makeshift patches to the shrinking balloon.

"The dig. He was directing it, yes. Too late to get some-one else. Thank heavens. He'd've got one season out of it. Good experience and he'd do a good job, no doubt. He's a smart kid, even if he is an egotistical pain in the peduncle. Still, come fall it'd be all over. One summer in Crete is not something you kill somebody for, Albert. Especially since he was going as my assistant anyway. Besides, all he has to do is bide his time. He'll be head of the department someday. Here we are."

Miss Bjork's car turned up a hillside drive.

The trial balloon was little more than a damp rag by this time.

Albert sat in the car staring blankly at the neat two-story colonial with dark-green shutters, the carefully manicured lawn. On the red-brick doorstep was a newspaper wrapped in plastic to keep the moisture in. But there was no car in the driveway.

"There's no car," Albert observed.

"It's school hours," Tewksbury said. "He's at school." He suppressed the urge to add, "You remember school?"

Albert hadn't thought of that.

The motor grazed quietly on the asphalt. "Well?" said Tewksbury. "What now? Is that what you wanted? His car? Why?"

Why? Thank you, Tewksbury! Of course Albert didn't need the car to check the treads! He got out and marched to the narrow strip of road salt and sand the tides of winter had deposited at the foot of the driveway. He was down on his knees inspecting the tire tracks when Tewksbury am-bled up beside him.

"What on earth are you doing, Albert? What're you looking for?"

Albert found it. "This!" he said, pointing to a small bar-like imperfection in the otherwise symmetrical tread marks.

"What is it?"

"It's proof that Strickland was parked beside the road at my mother's house the morning you were . . . Miss Bjork was . . . It's the same mark!"

"Could be coincidence."

"It's not," said Albert. He began walking toward the house. "It goes from G to D."

"Goes where?"

"From G to D," Albert said over his shoulder. "There are five grooves in the tread . . . four spaces between them. Just like a staff. The mark made by the broken glass goes from G to D."

Tewksbury stooped to verify. "He's right," he said to himself. "You're right! G to D. But you said glass. How do you know it's glass?"

"A beer bottle," said Albert. "Do you think it's open?"

"What? The house? Now wait a second, Albert," Tewksbury protested. "This is only my fifth day as a free man. I'm not going to do anything to jeopardize . . . "

"Wait here, then." Albert walked around to the back of the house. Tewksbury followed. The snow, meantime, had metamorphosed into a fine, bitter drizzle that approached the world at an angle like the Eldil, and congregated on the necks of passersby.

"What do you want to go in there for? I'm sure it's locked." Tewksbury took a burglar's-eye-view of the neighborhood.

"Come on, Albert. What are you looking for? What do you expect to find?"

The storm door was open.

"Listen, Albert, you've done a lot for me, I owe you, but if I get caught breaking into someone's house . . . "

Albert tried the door; it swung open noiselessly.

"We don't have to break anything."

"I'm waiting in the car," said Tewksbury. The desperation throw to first went sailing harmlessly into the dugout; Albert was already inside. Tewksbury followed.

"As long as we're both going to jail for the rest of our lives - assuming they don't hang us outright - do you mind telling me what we're looking for?"

"A gun," said Albert. "Where do people keep guns?" He opened the refrigerator and some cupboards.

"What kind of gun?"

"A .410."

"A rifle rack. Strickland hunts sometimes."

Tewksbury led the way to the front hall and into the study. "Here it is. 12-gauge, 24-gauge, couple've .22's. Look at this flintlock!

"Is that a .410?"

"No," said Tewksbury. "He told me about it once. He keeps it loaded, for self-defense. Makes his own bullets. It would give him some kind of perverse satisfaction to shoot a burglar with a two-hundred-year-old weapon. Poetic justice, I suppose. All the slots in the rack are filled. Nothing seems to be missing. No .410."

"Michael?"

The woman's voice came from the top of the stairs. The tenured intruders raced down the hall, through the kitchen, and out the back door like freshmen caught in the girls' dorm. Both had the presence of mind to pull their coats over their heads as they dashed for the car.

"Our Miss Glenly," said Tewksbury as the car bottomed out at the foot of the driveway, the muffler striking a brief trail of sparks as they squealed from the concrete onto the pavement. "I forgot about her. What if she sees the license plate?"

What if she did? thought Albert, to whom license plates were just something that came with the car, like the trunk or the ashtray. What if she saw those?

Tewksbury dropped Albert at his apartment and, with thanks, drove off in Miss Bjork's car to begin constructing something habitable from the ruins of his life.

Albert opened the door and stood there. A small mound of junk mail had sprouted from the floor. Spring had a powerful effect.

The room seemed smaller than before. Dirtier. Messier. Not big enough to contain the emptiness he felt. He closed the door and walked the serpentine pathways through the clutter. The air was draped with shades of stale blues and grays that smelled of old cigarettes, congealed coffee, and spilled beer. Homey.

The piano slouched in the corner; the discarded lover no longer caring for her appearance, hoping in her pathos to rekindle his affection.

He touched a high D#. It flew across the room on crystal wings and died against the wall. The quiet that followed was more profound than any Albert had known and gave birth to the sick-making loneliness he'd been trying to keep at bay, that chewed slowly through his soul in small bites with now and then a brutal kick to the heart to assure breathing. Beyond this, sorrow, like love, deserves privacy.

When the sun retrieved its last thin veil from the corners of the room, Albert was still alive. Surprising. The sadness hadn't killed him, after all. He hadn't fallen into the hollow of his heart. He still clung to its edge by his fingernails. The effort was halfhearted, though. If he fell, he fell.

The tears collected around his eyes and made his cheek sticky. He couldn't help feeling it would all make perfect sense to someone more familiar with the world; someone who shaved without thinking. Someone with a selection of suits and a driver's license.

Where was the .410?

Chapter Twenty

A sharp rap at the door resounded in synch with a gun-shot in Albert's dream. He awoke with a start, springing from the couch involuntarily. It was morning. Fairly late by the look of it. He'd needed the sleep.

"Who is it?"

"Sergeant Lucci, Professor," said Sergeant Lucci. "I spoke to you before, remember?"

Albert remembered. "Yes."

There was a pause during which nothing happened.

"May I come in?"

Albert went to the door and opened it.

"So, you're finally home."

Albert didn't answer.

The sergeant started to cross the threshold then stopped and took a step backward. Dogs do the same thing at a drunkard's grave. There must be some anti-policeman agent in the air.

"Detective Naples would like to see you."

"Inspector Naples?" said Albert. He'd almost forgotten. "Is he still in the hospital?"

"Yes, sir. He is. But he's much better," said the sergeant. "He's been in and out. But he's almost himself again. He wants to see you."

Albert went quietly along with the young sergeant who smelled of Aqua Velva. Albert had always liked that smell. He wondered why some people had it and others didn't.

"Inspector," Lucci said as he opened the door. "I have the Professor here."

"The Professor! Send him in!"

Albert seemed to recall a fairy tale that began the same way. The notion made him hesitate on the threshold before entering.

The room was dark except for an anemic halo of light cast by the headboard lamp. The inspector could have been Tewksbury. Except he didn't look pathetic and scared, and he wasn't tied to the bed, and his wrists weren't bandaged. The more Albert's eyes became accustomed to the dark, the less like Tewksbury the inspector seemed; they'd both been more or less horizontal, that was the only similarity.

"Well, Professor. This is a pleasure." Albert didn't think so.

"Come, sit." Naples cleared some newspapers off his bed-side. chair. "I was just thinking about you."

Albert didn't like being thought about. The room was littered with flowers and boxes of candy.

"I didn't bring anything," Albert apologized.

"Sure you did," said Naples. My, what big eyes he had. "How are you feeling these days, Professor? You look better."

Then why did he feel so much worse? He could feel the inspector inspecting him.

"I see the burn on your cheek is almost gone."

Albert's hand started toward his cheek, but stopped mid-way and fell back into his lap.

"Another day or two and you'd never know it was there."

They were in the room where it happened. Albert felt his face flush. He was seized with an almost uncontrollable urge to look up at the ceiling. He had the feeling the tile had been taken out, exposing his hiding place. He was glad the room was dark. "Tewksbury didn't kill Glenly," he said.

"That's what I hear. Some crazy broad did it."

"Daphne Knowlton did it," Albert corrected.

"You know her, too?"

Albert didn't really know anyone, but that's not what the inspector meant. He nodded.

"They're keeping her here for observation. Downstairs, somewhere. I understand Tewksbury's back in town." Was

225

he looking past Albert . . . at the ceiling? "He was out of town for a while, wasn't he, Professor?"

"Was he?" Albert knew he was saying just what the inspector wanted him to say. The conversation was being orchestrated, but he could only play his part.

"Under the name of Henry Rawlinson."

Rawlinson? The Inspector's Prodigious Detecting Brain wasn't infallible, but it was inescapable, at least. Frightening to think what he'd know if he hadn't been semi-conscious all that time.

"I'm sorry about the girl. Bjork."

Albert jerked his eyes toward the inspector.

"She was a bright kid. Had a future."

Did she? What if she'd been meant to die all along? Albert searched Naples's face for meaning.

The inspector was uncomfortable beneath his unabashed gaze. "Hunters," he said, effectively breaking the spell.

It wasn't hunters. Albert wanted to say so. He wanted to pour the puzzle out on the sheets and ask the inspector to help him put it together. But too many pieces were missing.

"How's your head?" said Albert after a silence.

"Better." said the inspector. "Probably the best thing that could've happened, in the long run. I needed the rest, you know?" He paused a moment. "Not often I get the chance to laze in bed . . . and stare at the ceiling."

Albert's eyes closed slowly in supplication. Not this ceiling. Not this room. Not now.

"It's a drop ceiling, Professor. Did you know that?" Pause. "I'm sure you do. Must have had the same thing in your room down the hall. Wonderful innovation, drop ceilings, don't you think? They make these big, drafty old rooms cozy, easier to heat; don't you think? They're much lower than the original ceiling, you know. Probably a good three feet or so."

Naples tried to guide Albert's eyes to the ceiling, but they were fixed firmly on the floor.

"It's made of tiles, see? You can pop 'em in and out. It'd be a good storage space, except the panels are too weak to hold anything." Albert wanted to evaporate, simply cease to exist. "Unless you strapped it to the plumbing. You can see the water pipes over in the corner how they disappear up there. Now they'd hold something, all right. They'd be awfully hot, though. You wouldn't want to put anything up there that might burn."

The strain of tension produced wells of tears in Albert's eyes. He looked away and wiped them with trembling hands.

"People underestimate you, don't they, Professor?"

Albert doubted that was possible.

"If I didn't know better," the inspector continued, his hands going to his head, ". . . but it wasn't you behind me on the stairs, was it?"

Albert cast a startled glance at the inspector. "You saw who it was?"

"Not really. No. But I saw who it wasn't. And it wasn't you."

"No. It wasn't."

"And it wasn't Tewksbury."

Albert must have looked surprised. "Why do you look surprised, Professor? He was inside your apartment, wasn't he?"

Albert cleared his throat. "He knows where the key is."

"He knows who his friends are," said the inspector. "One of your neighbors saw him leave your apartment, and I know whoever hit me bolted down the back stairs. That much I saw before I blacked out."

"So, you don't know who it was?"

"Do you?"

Albert almost said, 'I asked you first.' "Is that why you wanted me here?"

"No, no." Naples straightened out the sheets and brushed some crumbs onto the floor. Albert wondered what his apartment looked like. "I just wanted to see how you were doing. A lot's happened in your life while I've been . . . away . . . I thought, you know, we could talk. There's plenty to talk about; architecture, for instance. Ceilings and stairways and houses in Maine. Just catch up, really. Tying up loose ends." Long uncomfortable pause. "Do you know who hit me, Professor?"

Albert thought of Lane sitting on his doorstep, clutching his groceries and crying. He fixed his eyes on the Inspector's. "I won't tell you, Inspector. You can put me in prison or whatever you do . . . but I won't tell you. He didn't mean to hit you. He was trying to protect someone. It won't happen again. He's not the kind of person who would . . . do that again."

The inspector was quiet for a minute. "He almost killed me, Professor."

"Someone almost killed me, too."

"Mm."

Albert folded his hands. "You're all right. You'll be okay."

Albert was dying for a cigarette. He fidgeted while the inspector studied him. "So, Daphne Knowlton killed Glenly because of what he did to her that night at the school?"

Albert shrugged.

"And Tewksbury's free."

"And Miss Bjork is dead," said Albert. And Lane, and Glenly, and Daphne Knowlton and music. They were all dead in varying degrees. Who could say how many of the walking were mortally wounded?

"What now? Will you arrest me?"

"You?" said the inspector with a snort of irony. "Hardly." He deliberated. "You're not just another Tewksbury, Professor. I don't need an international incident on my hands. No . . . it wouldn't be worth it."

Albert didn't know what he was talking about.

"Not that I don't think you deserve it," Naples added.

There was another prolonged silence that crept to the corners of the room and settled down like hand-knit draft dogs.

"Lane hit me," said the inspector softly.

How did he know? Albert had heard of mind readers. He'd probably been thinking too loud. "How do you know?"

It had been a desperate attempt on the inspector's part. A last cast with a baitless line. He never expected a bite.

"I didn't." He watched as the weight of his words seeped slowly into Albert's consciousness. He wasn't satisfied. A minor riddle had been solved, but the enigma was complete. No one as clever and calculating as he supposed Albert to be would have . . . still. There he sat, stupefied in the darkness. For the first time, Naples caught a glimpse of Albert as he really was. But it was a glimpse clouded by skepticism. Experience had hardened him to the possibility of innocence.

"That's another reason I knew it wasn't you or Tewksbury that hit me. It was a black man. Daphne Knowlton had been staying with Professor Lane who's black. Simple enough. Still, it was just a guess. One thing leads to another."

"One thing leads to another." Albert was amazed how people dispensed these nuggets of wisdom like multi-colored spheres from broken gumball machines. "One thing leads to another."

That's how they did it.

"But there wasn't any motive that I could see. No proof . . . until now," said the inspector. "I could subpoena you to appear in court."

"One thing leads to another!" thought Albert. It's what Holmes and the Hardy Boys were all about. Albert had been looking for one thing that explained it all. He ran from the room.

The inspector let him go without comment.

Of course, Albert had been following a trail of sorts, but he'd always been expecting to find the truth, the whole truth and nothing but the truth, around every corner. He'd expected the whole puzzle to fall suddenly into place. But ... one piece at a time. One thing leading to another.

Every question answered was another piece in place.

If he only someone would tell him the questions.

Chapter Twenty-One

Jeremy Ash and Mrs. Gibson were watching cartoons. They shut the TV off when Albert came in; a high compliment.

"Professor!" said Mrs. Gibson. "You should be in this bed. I've seen leftovers looked healthier. Come sit here. When was the last time you ate?"

"We read about that lady . . . the lawyer," said Jeremy Ash soberly. "She was nice." He looked at Mrs. Gibson. "He liked her."

Mrs. Gibson shook her head in sweeping disgust. "Them hunters should be shot," she decreed. "Give the bears guns, and show 'em how to shoot, then there'll be some good sport in the woods."

The conversation ricocheted from one subject to another for the next half hour, though Albert didn't have much part in it, since Mrs. Gibson made it her job to see that his mouth was full most of the time.

"The boy says he's coming to live with you when he gets out."

What had made him say that? Where among the trash would he put Jeremy Ash? Albert smiled with half his mouth. "Mmm."

"Didn't you say you were going to live with the Professor, Jeremy?" said Mrs. Gibson.

"He said it," said Jeremy, in whose ears Albert's "mmm" echoed like another betrayal.

Of course, the mess could be cleaned up. And Albert had another room or two; there were doors he'd never opened. There might be rooms he didn't know about. He'd have to find out.

"I'm just wondering . . . I have to get everything clean first," said Albert. "There's an awful lot of cleaning to do."

Jeremy sighed. Mrs. Gibson picked up the hint that wasn't there and spun it into a nice flannel housecoat that fit her perfectly. "They say he can go in the next two or three months, if they can stop the leaks," she said. "Since I get out in three days, that leaves a few months. I could clean up Hiroshima in that time."

She hadn't seen Albert's rooms.

Nevertheless, the contract was sealed with nods and winks for which she took Albert's nods and winks to be reciprocal. Albert always nodded and winked when his ears couldn't handle the overflow. It was a natural distilling process.

Jeremy Ash sensed there was something on Albert's mind. "Professor, take me for a walk, will you?" In an instant there appeared to Albert's overworked brain a series of possibilities as to how this might be accomplished, most of them grotesque, some comical, to someone with a distorted sense of humor. Albert had no sense of humor. He was relieved when Jeremy Ash nodded toward the wheelchair across the room.

For a long time neither of them spoke. Jeremy stuck the flap of his plastic ID bracelet in the spokes and let it putter rhythmically as they went up and down the halls.

"You don't have to take me to your place."

"What?"

"There's this place in Boston. Not a hospital. A kind've home . . . for kids like me."

It hadn't occurred to Albert there might be other children like Jeremy Ash. How many? How many would fit in his apartment? Another thought shelved these speculations for a moment.

"Why would a man take a camera into a bank?"

Jeremy absorbed the question as though it followed the flow of conversation perfectly.

"To take pictures."

"Of what?"

"I dunno. Money?"

Albert didn't think Strickland had been taking pictures of money. "I don't think so."

"I dunno."

The walk continued in silence except for the tickety-thick of the ID bracelet. Everyone said hello to Jeremy Ash and smiled at Albert.

"He'd take it into his safety-posit box."

"Who would?" Albert didn't answer so, after a moment, Jeremy said the next thing that occurred to him. "He wanted to take pictures of what was in it."

One thing was leading to another. "Why?"

"Cause he wanted to look at it."

Albert wondered what was the point of anything you just looked at, but he'd come to accept the fact that there was just no accounting for human behavior. "Why wouldn't he just take it home and look at it?"

" 'Cause . . . it was too valuable." The boy was a possibility machine; endless permutations of logic popped out of him like sheet music sliding off a wooden stool. " . . . . or fragile."

"Fragile?"

"Or secret."

"Secret?" said Albert. His mind was spinning. "Secret?" he repeated.

"I dunno," Jeremy said and shrugged. "Who are we talking about?"

"Professor Strickland," Albert replied. The name meant nothing to Jeremy Ash. "Twice."

"I don't know who that is."

"He's in archaeology."

"Bones and stuff?"

Albert wasn't clear on where anthropology ended and archaeology began. "Minoans, and Etruscans," he said. "Old things. Ruins."

"He digs 'em up, right?"

"I guess so. He goes with Tewksbury in the summer. I guess that's what they do. Dig things up." In less complicated times Tewksbury had talked endlessly about archaeology. Albert almost wished he'd listened.

"Then they bring stuff back?"

Albert hadn't thought of that. "Do they?"

"Sure. They put it in museums, don't they?"

"They do?"

"I dunno," said Jeremy Ash. "I think that's what they do."

"But not safety-posit boxes," said Albert.

"No," said Jeremy, but before his lips had closed around the vowel, his possibility mechanism had produced another. "Unless it was gold."

"Gold?"

"Or diamonds."

"Diamonds?" echoed Albert Canyon, conversing by rote.

"Something like that," said Jeremy Ash. "I dunno. There must be a list."

Albert was reminded of a quote from Shakespeare, but he couldn't remember it. "Would they?"

"What?"

"Would they keep a list? What kind of list?"

"Wouldn't they? I dunno," said Jeremy, then proceeded to demonstrate the contrary. "A list of all the things they dug up and brought home, I guess."

"You mean the manifest?" said Tewksbury. He held a beer and cigarette in one hand as he opened a cardboard box labeled Prf. Tewks.-Misc. Papers-#1 which was followed by a long number, a date, and someone's initials. "Bloody thing's in here somewhere. I guess." Sigh, swear, sip, puff. "I need it, too. Every season we have to go over the previous year's manifest and account for everything - artifacts, tools, supplies. Have to satisfy both the Greek and Turkish governments. Very jot and tittle, you know, those folks. Especially when it comes to provenance. We get to find it, catalog it, clean it, and tell them what it is . . . do all the bloody work . . . and they get to keep it." Sip, puff, sip.

"You mean, you have to take all the bones and things back to Crete?"

"Bones?" Tewksbury made a sound that might have been a laugh. "That's what you think, isn't it Albert? You picture me walking around Crete digging up bones, tossing them over my shoulder and slogging them back to the States."

Not really, thought Albert. A big canvas bag figured into his imaginings somewhere.

"Don't answer that," said Tewksbury, unnecessarily. "Most of what we find, we have to return. Yes. We get the glory, they get the gain."

Neither struck a chord with Albert.

"Administration, I hate it. Looks like they packed these boxes with a back-hoe. How am I supposed to know what's in Prof. Tbwks.-Misc. Papers-#1? f'r pity sakes?" Sigh. Puff. Puff. Sigh. "They just tossed things in after they got through tearing it all to pieces. Looking for evidence, I suppose."

Tewksbury continued his halfhearted one-handed sift search through the partially opened box. Albert had seen part of a documentary showing a grizzly bear that, having gorged to its satisfaction, pawed disinterestedly at the internal organs of a half-eaten salmon. He didn't remember the bear having a can of beer and a cigarette in the other, but otherwise the comparison was uncanny.

"This is just one carload. I'll be making weekend trips to New Hampshire for three months after I get back in the fall." Sigh. Stare. "Look at all this junk."

Albert looked at all the junk.

"Well, at least Good Mother Nuesbaum didn't lease my rooms. You can bet she would have if there'd been any takers. Tough time of year, I guess. Mind you, she still hasn't had them fix the radiators. Waiting to see if they come drag me away again before she makes the investment, I should imagine.

"I'm having to use those little electric heaters . . . glorified toasters. Dangerous contraptions . . . Wait a second!" He snapped the cardboard lid closed. "It's not here. It's at school!"

"The list?" Albert ventured.

"Manifest. It's in my desk . . . with some other papers my journal."

"Can I see it?"

"I don't understand. What do you want it for? It's just a list."

"It might be important," said Albert, fighting to suppress the conviction that he wouldn't know what was important if it bit him. A label would be nice.

Tewksbury looked at Albert the way he looked at his simple-minded Uncle Edgar on his mother's side. He swilled the remainder of his beer and embedded the can in a boxtop. "May as well, Uncle Edgar. I'm not getting anything done here anyway."

Within fifteen minutes they were at the school. Tewksbury stopped and drew a deep breath as the door closed behind them. "I love the smell of these halls. I didn't realize how much I miss it. Like the ocean." He opened the door to his office. "Surprise! They didn't change the locks."

Albert stayed in the hall. He looked up and down the corridor. Sunlight flooded the corner where Daphne Knowlton had stood that fateful night. He remembered the smell of her perfume, and the pain in his head.

"It's gone!" Tewksbury was trashing his desk.

"The manifest?" said Albert. He wanted to be sure.

"Yes, the manifest. It's not here." Tewksbury leaned on the desk with one hand and reopened the top drawer with the other. "I don't understand. I put it right here, under my journal. I know I did."

"But it's gone?"

Tewksbury looked at Albert as if to say, "Yes, the manifest is gone, stupid."

"And the journal is still there?"

Tewksbury held up a blue-covered notebook. "Here."

Albert would be the first to admit he was no detective. He couldn't deduce. In fact, repeated blows about the head and temples with weighty clods of evidence most often failed to strike a spark. Instead, things just sometimes occurred to him. Something occurred to him now.

"Daphne Knowlton took it."

Tewksbury stopped his search and looked at Albert. "What do you mean Daphne Knowlton took it?"

"That night," said Albert, rubbing his head. "That's why she was here. She said so . . . "

"Said what?" said Tewksbury.

"She had some papers."

"My manifest?"

Albert shrugged. "Papers. She said papers. If that's what's missing."

"But . . . what would she want with my manifest?" Tewksbury was now in the doorway, his eyebrows wedged in the crags at the summit of his forehead.

"For Strickland," said Albert.

The eyebrows fell. Such a fall for lesser brows would have been fatal. "Stricks? What is this thing you've got about Strickland? Granted, he's no prince among men . . . he's got his own copy."

"Of the list?"

"The manifest. Of course."

"I want to see it," Albert demanded flatly. Tewksbury glared at Albert. Even Uncle Edgar had never been glared at like this. "I've never seen you like this, Albert," he said when his glare had returned to him void. "What's so important about that list?"

"Manifest," Albert amended. "Yours was stolen. There must be something."

Tewksbury slammed the drawers. "Maybe you're forgetting she was crazy. She killed Glenly." Tewksbury stepped into the hall and locked the door behind him. "She wasn't behaving rationally." They started down the hall.

"For a reason," Albert added.

"What?"

"She killed him for a reason."

"So?"

"If she stole the papers, the manifest, it was for a reason."

"What reason does a crazy person need? I mean, what seems perfectly logical to her may make no sense whatever to the rational mind. Here's Strickland's office."

And there was Strickland, with his feet up on his desk, engrossed in the study of a piece of paper with a magnifying glass. He started when they entered.

"Hello, Stricks," said Tewksbury.

"Tewks!" Strickland stood abruptly and placed the paper facedown on the table with the magnifying glass on top of it. "Professor," he said, rounding the desk and extending his hand to each of his visitors in turn. The shock had worn off, the mask through which sharp eyes stared too long at everything, except Albert, was securely in place. "Am I glad to see you, old fella," he continued on tiptoe. "I hear you'll soon be back in harness, what next week? Not a minute too soon, either, believe me." He was working his way back behind his desk.

Tewksbury had picked up a recent copy of Biblical Archaeology Review and was warming himself in the glow of its pages. Albert watched.

"I could handle the classes pretty well. Lectures, too, but . . . all that and prepping for the dig, well. My waters are a little too shallow. You're a sight for sore eyes."

Tewksbury hadn't heard from Strickland while he was in jail, or the hospital. He hadn't heard from anyone. He wanted them all to twist slowly, slowly in the wind a while—suspended at awkward angles on the threads of their threadbare words of welcome. When he spoke, he didn't look up from the magazine. "Can you lay hands on your copy of the manifest?"

Albert watched keenly as the mask dissolved briefly, then reformed itself, a little tighter at the lips, a little sharper at the eyes. He began leafing through the papers on his desk.

"The manifest? Pause. Smile nervously. "Sure. I mean . . . I'm sure it's here somewhere, old man." Albert half expected to see Tewksbury age before his eyes. "I had it out last week, went to the warehouse Ah, here it is!" He handed the stapled pages to Tewksbury who didn't see the smile that came with it. Albert did. "Be good to be back in Crete, won't it?" 'Old man' wasn't spoken, but Albert heard it anyway. "Safe in the past. away from everything."

Tewksbury scanned the pages. "Where's the original?"

"What?"

"This isn't the copy I gave you. Mine was done in the field, on a typewriter. This was printed on a dot matrix printer."

"Oh," said Strickland. Albert wondered if it was possible for a mask to blush. "Of course. I forgot. I spilled coffee on it, so I keyed it into my word processor." Something like a laugh issued almost involuntarily. "I'd forgotten. Happened months ago." He flashed a quick smile at Albert, then back at Tewksbury. "It's all there, though." Smile. "I don't think I missed anything."

"There'll be hell to pay when we get to Crete," said Tewksbury, handing the manifest to Albert. Strickland's eyes followed with question marks in them. "The customs seal was on that copy, and my original's missing."

"Really?" said Strickland. "Well, so much has happened. Easy for people to misplace things, I should imagine."

"I didn't misplace anything." Tewksbury said sharply. "I know exactly where I left it, and it's gone!"

Albert was pretending to read the manifest but was, in fact, watching the little drama through the narrow space between the top of his glasses and the overgrowth of his eyebrows. He saw Strickland, when Tewksbury had returned to a cold study of the journal, take the paper from beneath the magnifying glass and tuck it quietly among some other papers. In that split second Albert saw it was a photograph.

"Anyway," said Strickland. "As you can see," he nodded toward Albert, "I've already checked everything; had help from some of the kids. It all checks out, except for a couple of hammers, chisels. The usual." He sat down again. It seemed to Albert that he was much more relaxed since he'd shuffled the photo out of sight. "I think the native help take them. Things always go missing, don't they, Tewks. We even budget for it."

"Mmm," said Tewksbury, vastly overestimating the chill factor of his cold shoulder. He looked at Albert. "Ready?"

"What did you do with the first copy?" Albert inquired softly.

"Do with it? I guess I threw it away." Strickland was unable to comprehend Albert's presence in his office or why Tewksbury had handed him the manifest, or why he was asking questions about it. "I really don't remember, Professor. Why?" He turned to Tewksbury. "I can give you all the copies you need, Tewks. But, as I said, I've already checked. I know just where everything is."

Holmes would have said, "I've no doubt you do, Professor Strickland." Albert didn't say anything, but he thought it.

"I'll leave one on your desk, first of the week," Strickland continued. "Now, I've got to go home and grade these papers."

He picked up the papers among which he'd shuffled the photograph. Tewksbury turned to go.

"Good to have you back, Andrew," said Strickland. The voice was hollow and distant, coming, as it did, from behind a mask. But the eyes were bright as ever.

Chapter Twenty-Two

The academic duo kept silence as they walked across the common, until they got to the parking lot.

"Stickland's car!" Albert cried on the downbeat. An instant later he was on his hands and knees inspecting the tires and tread marks on the little red sports car.

"What on earth do you think you're doing?" Tewksbury said. He ran a furtive glance around the campus, as if he had some objection to being seen with Albert at the moment. "Stand up, will you!"

Albert appeared opposite him, holding a two inch-long piece of green glass. "From G to D."

"Oh, come on, Albert. Strickland didn't kill anybody. That's just a coincidence. You're getting carried away by this theory of yours," said Tewksbury. "Whatever it is."

"What about the safety-posit box?"

"What safe-deposit box?" Albert told him about Strickland's visits to the bank, the safe-deposit box, and the camera. The telling had the dual effect of putting things in order for Albert while striking a tiny spark of disquiet in the comfortable miasma of Tewksbury's brain.

Some people feel silly when the obvious takes a while to crystallize. Not Albert. He was freshly amazed - triumphant - every time two or more pieces of information collided, purely by chance, in a bright, shiny Rockefeller's dime of reason. "That's what he was looking at in his office . . . with the magnifying glass! A picture he'd taken in the bank!"

"A picture of the . . . thing in his safe-deposit box?"

"Yes," said Albert, not stopping to breathe for fear the gusher of thoughts would collapse in dust before they made their way into the open, where he could make sense of them. "The thing that was on the original manifest . . . but not on the new one. Something Strickland wants for himself. He had Daphne Knowlton steal the original manifest from your desk ... so no one would know what was missing! She would have done something like that ... for him. Lane said so."

"You mean, he smuggled something out of Crete the legitimate artifacts, and tools?"

"That's what Jeremy Ash would say."

"Who?"

Albert ignore the question.

"Why take pictures of it?" said Tewksbury. "I mean, money has it's attractions, gold, jewels, what have you, but you don't take pictures of it."

"He wasn't just looking at that picture, he was studying it ... with a magnifying glass."

Tewksbury's floundering reason blubbered to the surface for one last grab at the tree limb. "You're mad. How do you know it was a picture?"

"I saw it."

"You did?" The branch broke, the only thing left to grasp was the chalky white hand of the music teacher. "What could it be?"

"There's only one way to find out." Albert was thinking like Jeremy; simply and pragmatically. It was exhilarating.

"What?"

"We have to look at it."

"And how do you propose to do that? If what you say is true, which, I have no doubt, it is not, Strickland is hardly going to invite us to have a look at the whatever-it-is." He read the response in Albert's eyes. "Break into his office?! What's the matter with you, Albert? You think just because you've learned to pick a lock the world is yours to plunder? There are laws against that type of thing."

"It's not in his office," said Albert at last. "It's in with the papers he took home to correct."

Tewksbury broke in. "Oh, so all we have to do is break into his house again. Wonderful! And Miss bloody Glenly will scream and call the police, and Strickland can shoot us with his two hundred-year-old musket."

"We've got to make a plan," Pooh-Bear conceded.

"I don't believe this," said Tewksbury. He knelt to inspect the mark in the tire tread. "G to D," he said to himself.

"He's coming!" Albert was alarmed.

They hunkered in scholarly little balls and hastened toward the hedges at hood-top height and watched as Strickland approached.

His movements were quick and sure; he knew exactly which pocket his keys were in and which key fit the door. And, although his restless eyes intimated an uncustomary nervous tension, he was impeccably dressed. He must have someone taking care of him; Mrs. Gibson would know. He wedged his black leather valise between the bucket seats and contorted himself into the car.

"So, what's the plan, for lack of a better word?" said Tewksbury. He pulled Miss Bjork's car to the curb half a block from Strickland's house where the early shoots of a maple tree tried to conceal them from the glare of a streetlight. Strickland's sports car was in the driveway.

"We have to go in and get the photograph."

"That's not a plan, Albert. That's the objective. How do we get in? How do we find out where he put the picture? How do we get out without getting shot? Answer those few trifles and you've got a plan."

"I don't know," Albert said. He got out of the car and closed the door.

Tewksbury got out halfway. "What are you doing?"

"I'm going to look in the windows to find where he put the papers."

"You think they're lying on the coffee table?" Tewksbury got out the rest of the way. The sarcastic tone in which the statement had been delivered was meant to bring Albert to his senses; at least give him pause. It didn't. "What if some-body sees us? You see that sign over there?"

"Where?"

"On that telephone pole by the driveway. That's a neigh-borhood watch sign. It means people take turns sitting by their windows . . . watching for people like us . . . " said Tewksbury, immediately amending: "like you. Probably all card-carrying members of the NRA."

Albert cast a weary eye over the neighborhood. In most houses one, in some cases two, windows were illuminated by the ubiquitous bright blue light. "They're all watching TV."

In defiance of all the watching neighbors, he plunged into the pool of streetlight at its deepest point and waded across the street. Tewksbury kept to its banks, so by the time he reached the lawn, Albert already had his nose pressed against a large picture window. The blinds were im-perfectly drawn leaving slots of elongated triangles through which they could see without being seen.

Strickland was standing at the bottom of the stairs yelling something that couldn't be heard at someone who couldn't be seen. He was angry, gesturing imperiously with one hand while the other rested at an indignant angle on his hip.

"What's he saying?" Tewksbury whispered as his face joined Albert's in the sliver.

"I can't hear."

Tewksbury cast a wary eye up and down the street. He wouldn't have been surprised to see a torch-bearing horde of armed citizens descending upon them from all directions in righteous wrath. He was a little surprised they weren't. "Trouble in Paradise, you suppose?"

"He's yelling at Miss Glenly?"

"No doubt. Not unusual, from what I hear. They belong to the Virginia Woolf school of lovemaking."

Strickland, still yelling, suddenly turned and stomped across the room to a desk which sat directly in front of the window. He threw together a stack of papers and stuffed them in his briefcase, which he then locked in a drawer. He dropped the key in his vest pocket.

"Were those the papers?" Tewksbury whispered.

"They must be."

Strickland left Tewksbury's line of sight. "What's he doing? Can you see?"

"He's putting his coat on."

"He's coming out!" Tewksbury was half way across the street by the time Albert turned around.

"Where are you going?"

"Shh!" said Tewksbury. "He's coming!" He fell into something dry and leafy in the shadows on the other side of the street. Albert stood at the corner of the house and watched as Strickland stormed out, slamming the door behind him, got in his car, and drove noisily away. He returned to the window to see what Miss Glenly would do.

After a minute or two, when she didn't appear, he went to the back of the house. The door, having so recently been slammed, was unlocked.

Tewksbury had extricated himself from whatever he'd fallen into and was crabbing sideways up the driveway. Albert wondered if he thought it made him harder to see. Or maybe he figured if somebody saw him they'd say "Yes, Officer. And he walked like this . . . " effectively throwing suspicion elsewhere.

Albert went in, leaving the doors open behind him. The kitchen light was off.

"I'm not coming in," Tewksbury whispered sharply from the top step.

Albert felt his way toward the hallway that led to the den. Tewksbury propped the door open and followed. "Is she still upstairs?" Tewksbury hissed from halfway across the kitchen.

The lights were on in the den. A wide double door opened into the living room, where other lights were on, and Albert could see clearly to the top of the stairway. If anyone came, he'd see their shadow. He stepped carefully from the carpeted hallway to the large braided rug in the den.

"I'm not coming in there," whispered Tewksbury from halfway down the hall.

Albert tried the drawer. He was sure it was locked, but you never know.

It was locked.

He began rummaging through the cubbyholes and pencil holders. "What are you doing?" Tewksbury hissed from midway across the dining room. "That's not where he put it. It's in that big drawer on the bottom."

There wasn't a bobby pin in sight. Albert was dismayed but undaunted. A paper clip would have to do. He bent it into a more convenient shape. "Watch the landing for shadows," he said, adopting Tewksbury's conspiratorial whisper

"Do what?"

"Watch the landing," said Albert. "The top of the stairs. Tell me if you see any shadows, anyone coming." He slid the paper clip into the lock and gently turned it to feel the configuration of the mechanism. The L-shaped end of the clip dropped neatly in the slot behind the lift lever. Pull slightly. Turn a quarter to the left. Nothing. A half. Nothing. Three--quarters. Click. Full turn, down, pull back, double click. The drawer popped silently open.

"Open sesame," said Tewksbury, not without a touch of awe. He'd have been only slightly more amazed if Albert had levitated before his eyes.

"Watch the stairs," said Albert. He took the briefcase out, placed it on the table, and began going through the papers.

"See it?" said Tewksbury.

"Watch the stairs!"

"I am. I am," said Tewksbury, who wasn't. "D'you see it?"

Albert leafed through the stack of papers. It wasn't there. "It's not here."

"What do you mean it's not there?"

"It's not here."

"Maybe you missed it."

"Maybe."

"Try again."

"Okay," said Albert. He tried again. What if Strickland had already taken it out? What if he'd put it in his safety-posit box? Or burned it? What if he'd been mistaken? Wasn't he always? What if there never was a photograph after all? It may have been a drawing; or a smudge of Ding-Dong filling on Albert's glasses.

The third time through he found it. "Here it is!"

"You found it?"

"Here." He glanced at it as he passed it to Tewksbury. It was a picture of something round, clay or a stone, with a spiral pattern on it and odd little figures. Albert's heart fell. It wasn't gold or, jewels, or cigarettes or beer. Nothing valuable. Tewksbury didn't seem to realize this. As he stared at it, his eyes grew wider and wider and his hands began to shake.

"Good Lord."

"What?"

"I don't believe this."

"What?" said Albert. Even he was getting excited, or at least confused. When Tewksbury raised his eyes from the photo it seemed to Albert they had glazed over with a kind of euphoric madness. "What is it?"

"It's a Rosetta stone." Albert wished it was something else.

"Oh."

"A Rosetta stone for the Phaistos Disc." Things were not getting clearer. "It's in Mycenean and Greek."

It would be Greek, thought Albert. "Is it important?"

Something suddenly dawned on Tewksbury. "That slimy little son-of-a ... he found this in Crete last season!"

"The stone?"

"He smuggled it home!"

"How?"

Tewksbury had forgotten there was someone else in the room. "What? Oh. Oh . . . I don't know. There are ways. He could have . . . I don't know. There are ways. That's why he destroyed the original manifest."

"That's what Jeremy Ash said."

"Who is this person you keep referring to?"

"He said that there was something on the original list . . . manifest . . . that wasn't on the new one."

"Who is Jeremy Ash?"

"Strickland smuggled this stone into the country in a box marked 'tools' or something. Then, when all the stuff was on campus, he snuck it out and took it to the bank."

" . . . and put it in the safe-deposit box."

" . . . safety-posit box." Albert said at the same time. "Why?"

"Nobody would ever find it. He took a picture of it, so he could decipher it at his leisure. It'd be the archaeological coup of the decade . . . the half-century."

"Why?"

"Prestige, Albert. The kind of notoriety that would come with this kind of discovery would mean . . . Troy. A Nobel Prize,"

"Oh," said Albert. He couldn't understand awards, or why administration kept dressing him up and sending him out to receive them. He shuddered. "Troy." He fell silent. He hoped if he thought for a minute about what had been said, it would make sense.

Tewksbury had returned to devouring the photograph with his eyes.

The minute was up. "I don't understand."

"What?" said Tewksbury, focusing his eyes on Albert across a span of a few thousand years. "Understand what?"

"About Troy," said Albert. It had always been his custom to ignore things he didn't understand. He'd survived. But this time, he needed to know. "What's Troy got to do with it? Why didn't Strickland tell you about the stone last year, when he found it?"

"Recognition, like I said. It's the dig director . . . that gets the recognition for whatever turns up during a dig. And the school, of course, as the sponsoring organization."

"But if he found it . . . "

"Oh, he'd get a mention. A footnote . . . like the French lieutenant who found the Rosetta Stone . . . what's-his-name? But I'd've gotten the lion's share of the credit . . . like Napoleon."

Albert wondered if that was fair. Of course, nothing was. "You would?"

"That's the way it is," said Tewksbury. "The director organizes . . . orchestrates . . . that's it! Think of the director of an archaeological dig as the conductor of an orchestra. He puts the whole show together. Gets the job, auditions the musicians, decides what selections are to be played . . . and who gets the credit when the curtain comes down, or whatever it does. Not the musicians. Not the people who made the horns or the violins, or the tailor who made the tuxedos . . . it's the conductor. You see?

"It's the same in archaeology. I'm the director of that project. The conductor. I'm the one who developed a hypothesis that might be archaeologically demonstrable, which got the funding, which got the school backing, whose imprimatur attracted volunteers, all of which validated the project in the eyes of the government officials - both here and abroad - whose cooperation I need. Then I hired the staff, made the arrangements. So, I get the credit."

Albert tamped the papers together and slipped them back in the briefcase. "And that's important," he said, without adding the question mark he was thinking.

"Men have killed for less."

Albert glanced at the stairway. No shadows. "What are you going to do with the picture?"

Tewksbury grasped the photograph by the edges with both hands. "Take it back to my place. Study it. That's the most important thing. Then, in a day or two, I'll confront that feculent little cephalopod."

"But he'll see it's missing."

"That's the beauty of it! What can he say? Thieves can't report it when things they've stolen are stolen."

"Put that down!"

Miss Glenly stood in the door of the hallway, staggering under the weight of the musket that she had pointed at them. Albert glanced reflexively at the top of the stairs. She wasn't where she was supposed to be.

"Put it down now, Professor."

She'd been crying.

"But ... "

"Now!" she commanded, pulling back the hammer on the musket's firing pan. "I know how to shoot this." She choked back some tears.

Tewksbury placed the photograph gently on the edge of the table. "He stole it ... Strickland. It belongs to the school."

"Where did you get it?"

"What do you mean?"

"Where was it, just now?" Her words wrapped themselves around sobs.

"Well ... in the desk, but ... "

"Whose desk?"

"Whose? This desk, here. Strickland's," said Tewksbury nervously. "But . . . "

"And you took it. That makes you the thief. And you," she swung the gun barrel in Albert's direction. It passed him by a good six or seven inches before she could stop it. She didn't have her finger on the trigger. If there was a comfort in that, it was negligible. "Now, you leave, or I'll call the police."

"Go ahead."

"What?" said Miss Glenly.

"What?" Albert said contrapuntally.

"Call the police . . . if you want to see Strickland in jail." Miss Glenly was not in a mood to be confounded. Her face reddened, her eyes flashed a danger even Albert could read. She put her finger on the trigger. "If anyone's going to jail, it's you!" Albert wondered if it took longer to die when you were shot with an old bullet.

Tewksbury picked up the photo. "Strickland's up to his eyes in trouble, Catherine. This proves it. He smuggled a rare artifact into the country; concealed it from me."

The offenses chronicled by Tewksbury scarcely figured in Albert's suspicions of Strickland's crimes.

"His entire career could be in jeopardy." He waved the photo in the air. "Go ahead," he challenged. "I'm sure the police would find this very interesting."

"And there are worse things," Albert said softly. "The police will find out."

The woman lowered the gun somewhat. She stared at Albert. Her eyes widened and brimmed with burning tears. Tewksbury took the opportunity to sneak the photo behind his back and tuck it into his overcoat pocket. "What things?"

Albert was able to take his eyes off the musket for the first time. He looked steadily at her. "You know."

What she found in the depths of his eyes as she searched them for answers unlocked her tears. As her resolve gave way, her knees buckled and, clinging to the ancient weapon like a shepherd's staff, she sank to the floor. "Get out of here," she said softly. "Go away. Leave me alone."

Albert's heart was breaking. He knelt in front of her, and gently brushed the hair from her forehead. She flinched and shot him a glance filled with a confusing tangle of feelings he couldn't begin to unravel. He stood up abruptly and backed away.

"Let's go!" said Tewksbury, tapping his pocket and pulling Albert by the coat sleeve. "I've got it."

Albert shuffled slowly toward the door, unable to take his eyes off Miss Glenly. She looked like a wounded animal. The emptiness in the eyes with which she followed him to the door rattled him to the core. He wondered how many other people were out in the night, clinging to muskets and grocery bags with the end of the world in their eyes.

Chapter Twenty-Three

"She won't call the police?"

"I doubt it," said Tewksbury. He downshifted through the gears again. He was getting very attached to Miss Bjork's car. "She knows better than that."

"Did you see her eyes?" Albert said. He hadn't blinked since they left Miss Glenly. He blinked. "I've never seen a look in somebody's eyes . . . like that."

"I didn't notice," said Tewksbury. He shifted up through the gears on a straightaway. There was a primal gratification in the response of the engine, the stiffness of the steering wheel. He'd never have bought a car like this; he wasn't that kind of academic; but he'd always nursed the secret desire. He was that kind of academic. He downshifted as they rounded the curve. "She won't call the police."

Albert's mind was busy trying to hear itself over the fevered whine of the engine. "Why did he wait?" he said at last.

"Who?" said Tewksbury. "Strickland? You mean . . . why did he keep it to himself?"

"Yes."

"Why not? All he had to do was hold on another few months. Remember he figured he'd be directing the dig this summer? He'd produce it then."

"How did he know he'd be the director of the dig?"

Tewksbury smiled his condescending smile. "'Cause like I said, with me in jail . . . "

"But how did he know you were going to be in jail?"

"What are you talking about?"

Albert shepherded his words into a straight line. "Well, he had this . . . thing, this stone, last fall, right? When you came home from Crete?"

"Right. So?"

"I still don't see why he didn't tell you," Albert complained. "As far as he knew at the time, you were still going to be the director this year. And next year. And the year after that. He'd never get the credit."

Tewksbury didn't say anything for a change. He stopped shifting.

"So, why didn't he show it to you last year? Wouldn't it be better to get a little credit than none, if that's what he wanted? Why did he bring it back and try to figure it out?"

"Decipher it," said Tewksbury from a distance.

"Would that give him prestige, figuring out what it said?"

"Anyone could figure out what it said," said Tewksbury, "if they had that disc."

"Then I don't understand." They stopped in front of Albert's house. Albert stared at Tewksbury. Tewksbury stared straight ahead, as far into the night as the headlights would allow. The engine underscored the scene with rhythmic tension. "Strickland knew he was going to be director this year," Albert said.

The river was beginning to flow at a perilous rate, and the bank where Tewksbury was standing was slippery, beginning to give way under foot. "But Daphne Knowlton killed Glenly ... " he said. His words were barely audible.

"She'd do anything for him. Lane said so. She stole the papers; she nearly killed me."

"That was an accident."

"Strickland made her kill Glenly."

"Don't say that!" Tewksbury yelled suddenly. "No one would do such a thing?!"

"You said people have killed for less."

"I wasn't ... I was speaking figuratively. I didn't mean kill as in ... kill. Strickland may be an ambitious, lying, conniving SOB ... but he's a scholar." The words were weak as watercolor. "A colleague."

Suddenly Albert understood. Everything. As he sorted it out in his mind, he watched the same realization overwhelm Tewksbury's objections. "He made Daphne Knowlton kill Glenly," he repeated flatly.

" . . . to get me out of the way," Tewksbury whispered. He realized the notion had been in his subconscious for some time, but he'd battled it back as too ignominious to consider.

"But you were found innocent."

"Thanks to you and . . . " The final, chess piece fell squarely on Tewksbury's forehead, knocking the wind out of him. "Miss Bjork!"

Albert lowered his eyes to the shadows at his feet. "She got in the way."

Tewksbury's head wagged slightly from side to side while his eyes remained fixed on the dashboard. Finally he raised his stupefied, silly-putty face to Albert. "It was Strickland . . . shooting at me." He turned off the engine.

"It was supposed to be a hunting accident," Albert summarized. "That's why he didn't shoot again. It wouldn't have looked like an accident."

Tewksbury took the photograph from his pocket and held it in both hands, resting his arms on the steering wheel. "Glenly was killed . . . just to get me out of the way?"

"If he'd killed you, then took your place as Director and discovered the stone . . . I don't know. Maybe he thought people would be suspicious."

"Then he distanced himself from the crime . . . by convincing poor Daphne Knowlton . . . " His voice fell off in a whisper. Albert wondered if her name appeared that way on her birth certificate; 'born this day, Poor Daphne Knowlton.'

"If things fell apart . . . he knew he could get her to confess," said Albert. "Just like she did."

"Which put him back at square one."

Albert nodded. "That's when he tried to shoot you . . . in Maine."

"And got Melissa Bjork instead. Two people who had nothing to do with anything, dead."

Dead. Albert's lips formed the word, but nothing came out. Somehow it seemed there had been more than two deaths.

"All for this." Tewksbury rattled the photograph in his hands.

Albert got out and stepped in a puddle halfway up to his ankles. He lit a cigarette and leaned on the open door. The sky was low and starless, the night close and still. Raindrops gathered at the ends of budding branches like laughing children and jumped to the rivulets below. Otherwise it was perfectly quiet.

"What do we do now?" Tewksbury said finally.

"We should tell Inspector Naples."

"Tell him what? What proof is there? He's already got Daphne Knowlton; signed, sealed, and delivered. The only way he could associate Strickland with Glenly's murder is if she's willing to talk and that seems unlikely, given all she's done for Strickland this far. That kind of woman expresses her love through martyrdom. The more worthless the object of their affection, the greater the sacrifice; the greater the love. At least, that's how the love-benighted idiot would view it."

"What about the tire tracks? The glass? G to D."

Tewksbury tossed the photograph on the dashboard and, wearily, rubbed his face with both hands. "That's not evidence, Albert. Those tire tracks are long gone by now. There's only your word they were there in the first place. Nobody else saw them."

"The police did."

"Well, that may be. But they didn't notice that G to D business. Apparently they weren't impressed enough to take pictures. Anyway there's no murder weapon. Strickland doesn't even own a .410." He peeked out from between his fingers. "Sorry, Albert. Convincing me— and I'm not saying you have, not a hundred percent—and convincing a court of law ... are two different things."

Courts of law were strange things, able to find Tewksbury guilty when he wasn't, probably equally unable to find Strickland guilty when he was. Somebody should do something about that.

"What about the stone in the safety-posit box? What about that picture?"

"He'll have the devil to pay for that, all right. His career is over. At this school, at least. Thank God he didn't have tenure. But ... that doesn't make him guilty of murder, not by a long chalk."

"But, he'd have to say why he held on to it; why he waited."

"He could say he intended to sell it, he was just waiting to find the right buyer ... the right price. Wouldn't do his reputation any good, perhaps, but it'd be preferable to a murder charge." He breathed the familiar note of irony. "What can we do beyond that?" he asked rhetorically. "If your suspicions are true, then we're up against someone who seems to have planned for every contingency."

Albert was exhausted. He couldn't think anymore. Finally, he understood everything, but could prove nothing. He shut the door, waded ashore, and went inside. When he looked out the window, the car was gone. He went to bed.

Miss Bjork was in his dream. She had been flying in and out of the windows of his mother's house in Maine, laughing, teasing the curtains and the treetops with her toes. She settled in the garden and began weeding tires and beer bottles from among the rows of heads that grew from the ground. Some heads he knew, some he didn't. But they were all very happy, singing a beautiful chorale, very baroque and flowery. Appropriate for a garden.

A phone rang in the house, but no one would answer it. Miss Bjork didn't seem to hear it. When Albert tried to move he discovered he was planted up to his waist in the garden. Besides, he had to direct the singers.

The phone kept ringing, working its way into Albert's subconscious and laying waste the dream. He groped from the abyss of sleep with Minoan stones hanging from his eyelids and tied around his feet. He said "Hello" twice before he found the phone. He knew he was still half asleep. Maybe he was only dreaming he hadn't found the phone yet.

"Hello?"

"Albert! Did I wake you up?" Albert had the phone upside down. He turned it over a few times. "Hello?"

"It's Tewksbury," said Tewksbury. "You'll never guess who just left."

Albert didn't doubt it. "Tewksbury?"

"Strickland!"

"Tewksbury?" Albert turned the phone over again.

"Did you hear what I said? Albert? Strickland was just here."

"Strickland?"

"He just left."

"Dr. Strickland?" said Albert. He found his glasses and put them on, but it didn't help; he still couldn't open his eyes. His fingers found a cigarette and matches. He lit it. "At your house?"

"He just left."

Something about the thought of Strickland visiting Tewksbury had a resuscitating effect on Albert. "What was he doing there?"

"Seems Miss Glenly told him about our visit."

Albert wedged his right eye open with his fingers. There was a small fire in the vicinity of his mouth, he'd lit the filter.

He dropped the cigarette into a cup where it hissed and died and sent a stinking soul up to scratch at the doors of heaven. He lit another.

"He just laughed it off."

"He admitted he smuggled the . . . disc?"

"What else could he do? I had the picture, I have you as a witness . . . Catherine Glenly, too, if it comes to that."

"What did he say? Why didn't he tell you about it?"

"He was going to, at first, so he says. Then he decided there wasn't any rush. He'd bring it home, decipher it . . . there was a chance what it said is more important than what it is."

"So, he brought it back . . . like I said?"

"Just like you said. Put it in the safe-deposit box . . . out of sight. Took pictures of it so he could translate at leisure. If it presented some startling revelation, he could advance it as a theory . . . smuggle the disc back among the finds at some future date; mislabel one of the equipment boxes and suggest it had been misplaced, arrange for somebody else to find it. Somebody like me. Affirmation of his theory would overshadow the discovery itself.

"Of course, it was all the remotest speculation on his part, and very risky, as far as his career is concerned. But a risk he was willing to take apparently."

"Did he figure out what it says?"

"That's the amazing thing! It seems to shed some pretty shattering light on the history of Crete after all."

Albert waited.

"First you need a little background, or you won't appreciate what's happened. No one had much luck deciphering the Phaistos disc . . . for years. I mean, the usual crackpot attempts, 'predatory birds flying over the threshing floor' type of things. Generally about as far from the mark as you could get. Why would anyone go to all that trouble to write about birds flying over a frigging threshing floor, predatory or otherwise? Then someone discovered that certain of the symbols stand for constellations. Well, that's all it took. All of a sudden the disc is a calendar, a celestial calculator, a pocket-sized Stonehenge.

"Well, I haven't had time to verify it yet, of course, but if Strickland's translation is accurate . . . and whether or not he's a weasel . . . he's a decent scholar, everything changes; it's none of the above."

"Then what is it?"

"A history."

"Oh," said Albert, easily concealing his enthusiasm.

"Apparently Crete's earliest god-kings were thought to be descended from the stars, so they were named after constellations. The disc is their hereditary history a validation of their presumptive royalty.

"And that's just the beginning. According to Strickland, the disc seems to suggest that the island's founding race was from Sumer."

"Sumer?"

"Refugees from the Chaldean invasion of the Sumerian Peninsula." Tewksbury was breathless. "Just think of it, Albert!"

Albert didn't want to think of it. "What about Miss Bjork . . . and Glenly?"

"What? Oh, well . . . I think that's where your theory falls apart. I mean, Strickland was right up front about his little sleight-of-hand. Right off the bat. 'So, you caught me red-handed, old man,' he said. 'Can't blame a fellow for wanted to get ahead. I saw a chance and took it.' I'm paraphrasing, but that's the gist of it. Then he explained what I told you . . . said he was blinded by his own ambition and all that. He said he was willing to take the consequences, hoped there were no hard feelings. Mind you, sounds as if he's got his defense all thought out; insanity by reason of greed, or ambition. Who knows? Granted, he's beneath contempt. But I must say, I can understand why he did it." Tewksbury sniffed. "Something stinks. Must be the soup I spilled down around the gas ring on the stove. Thought I got it all up. Phew! Where was I?"

"Greed."

"Oh. Right. Anyway . . . nothing in his plans seemed to call for anybody's dying. Glenly was killed by the Knowlton girl, just like she confessed. Bjork was shot by a hunter . . . accidentally."

"What about the glass?"

"Oh, man! Don't start that business again! It was just co-incidence! Who knows how many cars there are going around with some kind of . . . blemish or imperfection? Might be a company that makes them that way, for all we know. Coincidence, Albert. That's all. Just like everything else. Coincidence; and not very convincing ones at that, when you think about it. And like I said, Strickland doesn't own a .410.

"Don't get me wrong. You were on the money about the disc . . . the safe-deposit box, the manifest, and for that I'll hug you, and kiss you, and call you George. But the rest . . . just coincidence. Tragic, but . . . " He sniffed again. "I swear the smell is getting worse, hold on a second."

He put the phone down and Albert heard him banging around in the background. What if he was wrong? Tewks-bury was right, there was still no evidence of the kind that would impress Inspector Naples. Only the tire tread, which was gone, and Albert's suspicions which were . . . just a pi-ano player's suspicions. What did he know, anyway? Until a few weeks ago his idea of Chinese food was rice.

Come to think of it, who was he, anyway? He'd been ev-erywhere, and seen nothing. Lived half a lifetime and never been alive. He knew nothing. Experienced nothing. Was . . . nothing. Pretty soon life would be over and he would die. The death of no one. A little B-flat burp in the firmament.

Of course, Miss Bjork had said there was something after life. She probably knew. She had read Tolstoy and had a Bible. She'd been somebody.

The sound of Tewksbury picking up the phone salvaged Albert from the compost of himself. "Some of it must have got down around the pilot light."

"What?"

"Some of the soup must have dripped down by the pilot light . . . it'll burn off, I guess. Stinks, though," Tewksbury explained. "Anyway, I've kept you up long enough. I'm exhausted myself. It just hit me. I've been going on adrenaline since Strickland was here. Pretty heady stuff, you know? You go on back to bed, Albert. Put all this behind you. It's a matter for administration now. Nothing more you can do. Time to get on with life, you know?"

"Get on with life," Albert whispered into the void that stretched into eternity. He was afraid to let go of the precious pain he'd wrapped himself around. There was nothing out there but miles and miles of open ocean. Without the pain there was nothing to cling to; and once he let go, it would be gone forever. He'd be alone.

"I'll talk to you tomorrow," said Tewksbury. "Good night, Albert." He hung up.

Chapter Twenty-Four

It was late afternoon when he awoke with a groggy headache that told him he'd slept too long. A lot of half-thoughts bubbled to the surface from his subconscious where they'd plagued him all night. It took a while to distill the facts. It took a while to remember that Tewksbury didn't think Strickland had killed Miss Bjork; or Glenly. All he did was steal a rock and take pictures of it.

There was a knock at the door. Albert draped the sheet around his shoulders and dragged it across the room. He had his clothes on, but somehow felt naked.

"Who is it?" said Albert as he opened the door and saw who it was. "Inspector."

Naples wore a half-turban of the type Albert had reintroduced to fashion. His right eye was black and seemed open even when it was shut. Otherwise he looked all right. Not that this was a comfort to Albert, who was more inclined to close the door than open it.

"Mind if I come in, Professor?"

Albert let him in anyway, stumbled back to the bed and sat down. Naples pulled up a chair opposite him and straddled it backward. Albert sketched him in a glance. His face was the same. His clothes were the same. But he wasn't the same. He didn't smile his thin, knowing smile. His eyes weren't crowded with skepticism.

"I'm afraid I've got some bad news, Professor," Naples said. His voice was quiet. Unthreatening.

"Bad news?"

Naples nodded and looked down at his hands. "There was a fire last night . . . at Tewksbury's place."

Albert looked at the inspector. "Fire?"

"Bad one."

Albert didn't want to ask what he was going to ask. But there was nothing else he could do. "Is he all right?"

The inspector shook his head. Albert knew he would.

"It started in the middle of the night. Everyone in the building was in bed . . . there are four apartments, including Tewksbury's." He sighed and scratched between the turban and his forehead with his thumb. "Most made it out, once the alarm was sounded, some aren't out of the woods, yet. But Tewksbury . . . the fumes got him."

This is where the sobs were supposed to come, weren't they? Albert wondered why he didn't feel anything. Anything at all. He doubted if he'd feel a knife in his back. He shut off his face and hung it out to stare at Naples.

"They say it was an electrical fire . . . in Tewksbury's apartment," said the inspector. "Seems he had one of those little heaters, you know the portable things? . . . left it too close to some drapes and . . . " He threw up his hands, "Whoosh!"

"Whoosh," Albert whispered.

Naples shifted in his seat as the news settled around the room. "Sorry to have to be the one to tell you, Professor." He patted Albert on a knee. "I've got to go. I just thought you'd want to know." He got up and walked to the door. "I wanted you to hear it in person."

Albert followed with his eyes. "He smelled something burning."

The doorknob froze in Naples's hand. "Did you say something?"

"He said he smelled something burning."

"When did he say that?"

"Last night," said Albert. "He called."

"What time?"

"I don't know. I was asleep."

"And he said he smelled something burning?"

"Soup."

"Soup?"

"He spilled soup on his stove. He thought that's what he smelled burning."

"It was the drapes," said Naples. "He should've known better than to keep the heater so close to them." He opened the door, stepped onto the landing and hesitated. His hand went to his head. He turned and stared at Albert. "I was wrong about you, Professor."

"I know," said Albert.

Naples nodded. "I've got to give you credit. You did a good job, finding Glenly's murderer."

Albert stared at his television; that's what it was there for.

"If you ever decide to give up the music game ... " After a moment Naples turned and stepped onto the landing where he stood staring at the floor. The door swung shut by itself. A few seconds later Albert heard his footsteps on the stairs. Tewksbury was dead.

Death was getting crowded.

The darkening room echoed the inspector's words. Albert listened to them as they bounced off the walls in no particular order. Eventually one sentence assembled itself and tapped at his forehead, persistent as a poor relative. "He should've known better."

"He should have known better," he said aloud. Leaving an electric heater by the drapes is the kind of thing Albert would do. But Tewksbury? "Dangerous contraptions" he'd called them.

Tewksbury did know better. Suddenly another thought stumbled blindly into his brain: Strickland was probably the last one to see him alive. Strickland, whose leitmotif surfaced time and again throughout the score of the whole tragedy. Strickland, who already admitted to Tewksbury ... that he was willing to lie, cheat, and steal. Strickland, who stood to lose everything when Tewksbury reported him to the school.

"Strickland started the fire," said Albert.

A wet, heavy sleet, driven by a sharp-toothed wind, had begun to splatter against the window, thousands of tiny, frozen sacrifices appeasing the goddess of encroaching spring. With a sharp breath Albert suddenly stood up and began pacing frantically back and forth. He shook his head and slapped his cheeks. His brain was trying to give birth to a thought he didn't want. He piled heaps of mental refuse on it, but it kept bobbing to the surface.

He undressed and jumped in the shower, but it was too late.

At approximately ten after six the idea was delivered. Since nothing could be proved against Strickland, Albert had to confront him ... face to face.

It was an absurd notion. He'd never confronted anyone about anything. How was it done? With what would he confront him? What would come of it? His heart grabbed his ribs and shook them until he could scarcely catch his breath. Some unfamiliar, determined part of his brain had taken over his body and was propelling him to do that which he never would have considered on his own.

He couldn't find a towel so he dried himself as much as possible on the plastic shower curtain. It was only wet on one side. Then he took some clean clothes from under his mattress where he'd been pressing them, dressed, threw on his overcoat, his socks, and his slippers, in that order, and was out in the night before the saner members of his brain could master the reactionaries.

It was a long way to Strickland's, though. He took some comfort in the knowledge that he couldn't go through with it. There was plenty of time to back out. That he should find himself on Strickland's street without the inevitable having come to pass was alarming, but not yet panic-inducing.

His hair had frozen in a solid, omni-directional mass.

When - shivering, blue, and swollen to twice his customary size with goosebumps - he arrived at the head of Strickland's driveway, panic set in with a vengeance. Suddenly his excuse mechanism sputtered to life: He had no evidence. What if Strickland wasn't home? What if he called the police? But it was too late, he'd already rung the doorbell and his slippers had apparently frozen to the porch. Of course he could leave them there and run home barefoot, but Strickland would probably have them traced. Naples would return them in person, and begin asking questions.

Strickland appeared. For a moment Albert forgot which side of the door he stood on. "Yes?" he said.

"Professor?" said Strickland, genuinely surprised. Something about Albert's appearance apparently amused him. "This is unexpected." He hesitated. "Please, come in, won't you?"

Albert was in. The door closed behind him.

"You look cold, Professor. Can I get you some coffee tea?"

"No."

It was warm in the house. There was an immensely uncomfortable silence as Albert began to thaw.

"Well ... what can I do for you?" said Strickland at last.

Albert had been confident he'd never get this far. He had no idea what to say or where to begin. The torch-bearing throng of gray cells that had initiated the uprising, that had passed him over their heads and deposited him at the door of the monster's castle, fell silent when the beast appeared and now abandoned him altogether. "I know about you," he said at last.

"How's that?"

"I know what you've done."

Strickland smiled with half his mouth but not his eyes. He gestured toward the living room. "Oh," he hung his head. "You must have been talking to Tewksbury. Why don't we go in where it's comfortable."

"You killed Professor Glenly."

Strickland tossed a nervous glance toward the top of the stairs. He was looking for shadows, too. "I beg your pardon? What on earth are you talking about? Are you all right, Professor?" He put a patronizing hand on Albert's shoulder. "How long have you been out wandering in this weather? You're half frozen."

"You framed Tewksbury," Albert continued. "You called him and told him to go to Glenly's office. Then you called the police so they'd find him there. And when he got out of jail, you tried to shoot him with a .410."

The words were sanding through the glossy veneer. Bare wood was beginning to show through at the corners of Strickland's eyes. "Perhaps you'd better leave, Albert," he said coldly. "I don't know what you're on . . . but you don't know what you're saying. I don't even own the weapon to which you refer."

"You parked in the little turn-off just beyond my mother's driveway. You were in your sports car . . . the one you ran over the beer bottle with that day in front of the bank. Part of the glass was still in the tire when you parked there. G-to-D. I saw it. You climbed over the fence, made your way to the edge of the meadow, and shot at Tewksbury. But Miss Bjork got in the way."

A predatory gleam trickled into the eyes which Strickland fixed upon Albert with deadly intent.

"And last night . . . you set fire to Tewksbury's apartment. You killed him, too. You could have killed all those people."

Again Strickland jerked a sidelong glance at the top of the stairs. He tried on his condescending face again, but it no longer fit. "Are you on medication of some kind, Professor?" He reached for the phone. "What's your doctor's name?"

"All those people," Albert repeated.

Strickland put the phone back on the cradle. "Why, do you imagine, would I do such a thing? What possible reason could I have ... "

"The stone," Albert interrupted.

"Stone?"

"Tewksbury told me everything," said Albert. "He called me last night. After you left. He told me everything."

Strickland lowered his eyes to the parquet and, folding his arms behind his back, began to pace in a semicircle around Albert. "Perhaps it would have been better ... if he hadn't said anything."

The idea that he was putting himself in personal danger had never occurred to Albert—he'd be embarrassed, of course, that went without saying—but it appeared now, sponsored by the look in Strickland's eyes when he raised them to underscore his words. But there was no terror, or whatever feeling danger is supposed to elicit. It didn't matter. He didn't care anymore.

"I'm not afraid."

"Well, perhaps you should be. If I've done everything you say. I should think you'd have every right to be." A forced little smile spread across his face like butter on hot bricks. "But the fact is, you have a wonderfully vivid imagination, Professor.

"I understand your being shaken after ... what happened to Tewks. We all are. I mean, he was one of my closest friends. We worked side-by-side for years. Everyone's taking it hard ... they closed the school early.

"That's what got you going; a lot of coincidences." He patted Albert reassuringly and turned him toward the door. "You're distressed. No hard feelings, I understand."

If not for the badger at the bottom of Strickland's eyes Albert's resolve might have been shaken. As it was, he began to comprehend the nature of the beast he was up against, and to realize he was no match. He spun around and threw his back against the door which Strickland had opened. It slammed shut.

"Shh! Professor!" Strickland cried in a harsh whisper.

"You killed Miss Bjork! You killed Glenly! You killed Tewksbury!"

Again the eyes flashed to the top of the stairs. Strickland grabbed Albert by the collar and dragged him into the hall leading to the kitchen. "Shut up!" He struck Albert across the mouth with the back of his hand. "You're delirious!

"Tewksbury died in a fire. Accident. Bjork was shot by a hunter. Accident. Glenly was killed by Daphne Knowlton. Vengeance. Accidents! Vengeance! No mystery. Do you understand? All accidents!" He shook Albert on each "accident" for emphasis and punctuated the sentence by throwing him back against the wall where he landed on the doorframe and bounced to the floor, halfway into the living room.

"You made Daphne Knowlton think you loved her," said Albert through the blood that puddled in his mouth. "You took advantage of her that night, after what Glenly did in the lounge. She told Lane.

"You turned her hurt into hate. And when you wanted Glenly out of the way, you just kept pushing her and pushing her, until she did it."

"Why would I want Glenly out of the way?"

"So you could direct the dig this summer. You were going to smuggle that stone back to Crete . . . and find it all over again . . . and get credit for it. You used Daphne Knowlton to kill Glenly . . . just in case something went wrong. Then you framed Tewksbury for it."

Strickland, in the hallway, couldn't see the motionless shadow at the top of the stairs as Albert could. A tense silence followed the accusations. Albert braced himself to be pounced upon at any second, but suddenly Strickland relaxed. "You can't prove any of this, can you?"

Albert didn't reply.

"Of course you can't, or you'd have gone to the police." He smiled. "You don't have a thing."

Albert wiped his lip. "I know."

"You?" Strickland scoffed. "Who cares what you know? Without proof, you've got nothing. Zip. You go around spreading stories like this ... you could end up with a lawsuit for defamation. Might get someone in trouble."

"Another accident?"

Strickland shrugged. "I was thinking about other innocent people. That .410, for instance? What if police start digging around in that business again, and find out the gun belonged to somebody like ... Terry Alter? What then? People start putting two and two together, you never know what they might come up with."

"You used Terry Alter's gun to ... " Albert got to his feet.

"Don't get carried away, Professor. I'm speaking hypothetically. There are other things, too. Accidents, like you said. Could happen anytime. Someone gets hit by a car while they're crossing the street. Someone falls down the stairs."

Albert started. "Daphne Knowlton."

"Daphne Knowlton?"

"We heard the front door that night, at Lane's ... I thought it was Lane coming back." He paused, the truth of his words striking home as he said them. "It was you, leaving."

Strickland shrugged, and smiled. "It's amazing how devoted a girl can be. If I'd only known, I could have saved myself a lot of trouble."

"You pushed her."

"Proof, Professor."

"You did everything!" Albert cried, shaking his finger defiantly. Strickland shot another glance at the top of the stairs. But the shadow was gone.

"Proof," he repeated, pushing Albert across the hall. "Proof." He opened the door. "Proof!" With a final blow to the side of the face, he sent him sprawling down the steps into the mud and dirt. "You should watch your step, Professor. You've just made yourself a loose end." He slammed the door shut.

Albert was abandoned to the cold, the night, and the rain. He'd landed on his hip and pain shot through his legs as he struggled to his feet. He'd hit his head, too, and his cheek smarted from the blow. Still, he was alive.

But what had he accomplished? Strickland was right, as Tewksbury had been, there wasn't a breath of proof. Nothing. Strickland had committed not one, but a series of perfect crimes, and if Albert started making waves, other people would be implicated. People who had enough problems of their own, like Terry Alter whose .410 Strickland had used to kill Miss Bjork.

He thrust his hands deep into his pockets and scuffed homeward. Tears welled in his eyes and the rain came down in torrents. As he reached the end of the street, the brooding night was shattered by two distinct but almost simultaneous blasts, one weak the other deep and percussive. In an instant he pictured Strickland standing on his porch, musket to his shoulder, the look of evil triumphant in his eyes. How long would it take before the bullet hit? Or had it hit already? Maybe he was dead. If so, it wasn't as painful as he'd imagined; not even a very jarring transformation, seeing as nothing had changed. Then he realized he was still cold. His head and face and hips still hurt. If this was death, it wasn't a significant improvement. He turned around.

The doorstep was barely visible through the deluge, but no one was there. Slowly, thoughtlessly, he walked back to the house and up the steps. He peered through the dining-room window into a room thick with blue smoke. He could smell its sulfurous aroma even outside. And dressed in the smoke, like a queen of ashes, stood Catherine Glenly. She looked up at him as if she knew he was there. But she didn't flinch when their eyes met. Her expression didn't change. Her eyes, set in bloody-blue caverns, betrayed no horror, begged no mercy. They were hollow . . . almost as dead as Strickland's. The musket stock rested against her shoulder. The barrel pointed toward the floor.

She knew how to use it.

Albert turned from the window and walked home. There was nothing to sort out. No judgments to make. No one to call. Justice had been done. He was wet and cold.

Somewhere in the reaches of himself he felt the distant cries of music again. It would come, eventually, whether he wanted it or not. But it would never be the same, because it echoed through a broken heart.

Epilogue

My goodness! Such a year we've had at our little . . . my word. Haven't we though!"

The entire school was speaking exclusively in exclamations these days, and Miss Moodie, far from being the rule's exception, was its exemplar. Administration had called a meeting to Summarize and Clarify Certain Recent Events Involving the School and Members of Its Faculty. The meeting had been rousingly well attended, leading one administrator to postulate that, while murder was not to be applauded, of course, it certainly did wonders for bringing faculty together. Even the tenured attended.

The meeting concluded, a number of the faculty repaired to the lounge to discuss it. Not uncommonly, Miss Moodie was the vortex of these little conclaves, as was now the case. "It was in this very room I said 'that man will come to no good; he's in something sinister up to his . . . well. You could see it in the eyes, of course. I believe I was talking to

Albert at the time. What, dear? Oh, my goodness, yes. He's Albert to his friends, you know. Plain Albert. Hardly any affectation a'tall apart from his . . . eccentricities. Well, but even I didn't imagine Strickland capable of cold-blooded . . . I mean, Glenly, the young lawyer woman, poor Tewks, then, who knows where it might have ended? . . . but where was I?

"Oh, yes. Well, she turned herself in, of course. You know that. Not that anyone seriously thinks for a moment they'll convict the poor . . . my word, yes. Such a hard life . . . especially the last few years. Enough to drive anyone to . . . I mean, the way he treated her. It all came out at the trial, didn't it? What? Oh, yes. Justifiable homicide. Temporary insanity. Something to that effect, I'm sure. That's what Professor Clarke of the Law School thinks the verdict will be. Juries are sensible about these things.

"I beg your pardon? Oh, that's absolutely right. I've said so myself, of course. If it hadn't been for Albert's testimony . . . turning up that artifact in the safe-deposit box . . . well, they might never have found the motive for the whole heinous . . . but there. Oh what a tangled web, eh?

"Now everyone's got to sort out their lives, I should think. Of course Lane took the exchange, you know. A year in England will do him worlds of good. What? Well, I know he's asked her to join him . . . he told me so. He said she's going to think about it. I wouldn't be surprised if she does, though. For all the difficulty they've had . . . well 'nothing bonds like sorrow,' they say. And with the Knowlton girl in professional care, I think he can put his mind at ease, concentrate on sorting out his own problems, for a change.

"What did you say, dear? Daphne? Oh, yes. Tragic character, indeed. Tragic. But I shouldn't wonder if she comes through it all right . . . wouldn't seem fair, somehow, seeing her suffer so much, only to be conquered by it in the end, would it? No, I'm sure the poor girl will pull through it all right, if there's any justice in the universe.

"How's that? Oh, yes, well, there are rumors to that effect. I heard about the boy moving in to his apartment, a black woman, you say? Well, I can't imagine . . . not that it means anything to him, though. He's not there. Administration is pitching fits to find where he's got to. They would, of course, seeing the amount of revenue he . . . well. That's all they care about, in my opinion. But they've hired private investigators, put ads in the papers. That kind of thing."

Someone in the rear of the room was carrying on an independent conversation. Moodie fell silent and concentrated the full force of her formidable stare upon the offenders until their tongues clove to the roofs of their mouths. With a majestic toss of her head, she severed the glance and continued.

"Won't do them any good of course. I think people tend to underestimate that young man. Of course he invites it, still . . . I expect he'll turn up again, in his own good time. Quite remarkable, really."

THE END

BOOKS BY DAVID CROSSMAN
from
Alibi-Folio

The Albert Mysteries
Requiem for Ashes
Dead in D Minor
Coda
Improvisato

Winston Crisp Mysteries
A Show of Hands
The Dead of Winter
Justice Once Removed

Photo Club Mysteries
Dead and Breakfast

Bean and Ab Young Adult Mysteries
The Secret of the Missing Grave
The Mystery of the Black Moriah
The Legend of Burial Island

Historical Novel
Silence the Dead

Fantasy
Storyteller

Thriller
A Terrible Mercy

www.davidcrossman.com
davidcrossman@comcast.net

WINSTON CRISP MYSTERIES

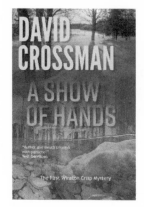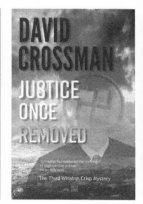

IN HOPES OF IMPROVING THE ODDS in his battle wit dementia, Black Ops specialist and NSA code-breake Winston Crisp retires in search of a quiet life after sixt years of government service. He expects peace and quiet o the island off the Maine coast where he'd spent idylli summers in his youth. Instead, he's confronted with puzzle dark and deadly and must summon every ounce of wit t face them. But first, he needs to untangle the ghosts of th past, with those of the present – and time is running out.

To read *A Show of Hands* FREE, send your request t davidcrossman@comcast.net, and simply enter FRE WINSTON CRISP! in the subject line.

THE ALBERT MYSTERIES

'HE ORBIT OF ALBERT'S TINY, coffee-stained universe was lliptical and only rarely intersected that of the onventional world, generally in the vicinity of a Dunkin')onuts. Some people called him a genius; some called him n idiot. He was inclined toward the latter opinion. To him, othing made sense. He didn't think like most people. He idn't understand how they could spout their age, weight, ocial Security Number, or home address off the top of their ead without looking it up somewhere. He couldn't fathom vhy they cared about celebrities, or sports, or grass, or the veather.

The School cocooned him in penthouse hotel rooms, •rivate jets, and stretch limousines as it whisked him round the world, from stage to stage. It boasted of his ccomplishments: the Noble Prize; "the only one of its ind;" (an excellent coaster) the Pulitzer (too small to be of ny practical use at all, and too large to fit in a cigarette 1achine), and Grammys (paperweights).Music was all lbert knew. He hadn't the sense to know he was clueless, ntil murder came along and tore his cocoon to shreds; but wasn't light that flooded in through the cracks; it was arkness. Still, everything might work out all right – if only omeone would explain . . . everything.

To read *Requiem for Ashes* FREE, send your request to davidcrossman@comcast.net, and simply enter FREE ALBERT! in the subject line.

BEAN AND AB YOUNG ADULT MYSTERIES

 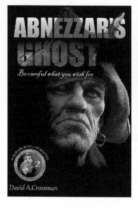 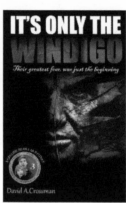

WHEN HE'S BEING AWKWARD, tongue-tied, and, generall overwhelmed, Bean is me as I was at that age. When he' being competent, smart, innovative, and effective, he's wha I wanted to be. That said, I like Bean and, having both grow up on an island off the coast of Maine, have a lot in commo with him.

Ab is based very loosely on Debbie, a dark-eyed beaut from New York City whose family visited the island ever summer and with whom I would love to have had the kin of adventures that Bean and Ab share and, I guess, now have.

Spooky is sort of a composite of a number of guys I gre up with. I love writing these stories because, through then I get to fulfill the fantasies of my youth. But it's not about m – at least not any more – these kids have develope personalities of their own and established themselves a solid, flesh-and-blood, three-dimensional people who hav amazing strength of character and, in the course of thei dventures, reveal traits of loyalty, integrity, grit, and acrifice that challenge me to be better than I am.

To read *Keeping Secrets* FREE, send your request to davidcrossman@comcast.net, and simply enter FREE BEAN AND AB! in the subject line.

STORYTELLER: A FANTASY

PRIVATE PLANCE CRASHES in the south Pacific. The lone urvivor, rap star Rat Badger Junkmouth Flash, washes up n a desert island where he is confronted by a most unex-ected resident. The island's only habitation is a magnifi-ent mansion in which are twenty-two rooms. In each of 1ese he will encounter a dimension of existence – and of imself – that he never imagined.

FANTASY: SUMMER, 2021

FIVE LIFELONG FRIENDS – once the crew of a fishing boat are gathered once again at a hilltop cemetery, overlookin the bay. All of them have been reduced by age to parodies c themselves, Everet is mostly deaf, Kilton mostly blinc Raymond fretful, Alby, the captain, senile, and first mate Ben, just recovering from a triple by-pass.

"They're gonna sink *The Mary* tomorrow, to make breakwater," said Raymond.

"Like hell they are," says Alby in a rare moment of lucidity he may have already forgotten the wife he just laid to res but he'd never forget *The Mary*.

"What do you mean, Cap?"

But Cap, having briefly broken the surface, had
unken once more into the depths of senility. But Ben was
ot willing to let it go. "He means we're gonna save her."
And so begins a voyage unlike any other.

DEAD AND BREAKFAST: A MYSTERY

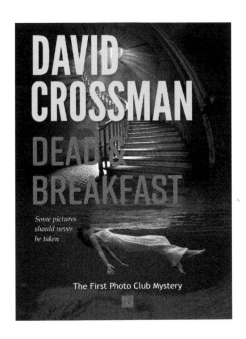

HE IDEA FOR A MYSTERY centered around a peripatetic
hotographer and the classes of well-heeled would-be's she
scorts to exotic locales, came from a visit to Chateau
'Arnac in the Dordogne region of France, where my wife
nd I met such a person, who conducted such a class.
'uring our first breakfast there the owner of the chateau
onducted what she called a "go-round" in which everyone

at the table told their story. When it came to me, mentioned that I was a mystery writer to which one of th other guests – the student upon whom I patterned Mr. Pipe in DEAD AND BREAKFAST – suggested I should write story based upon, well, them. That ignited everyone's inne Agatha Christie and, before the croissants arrived we' killed off half the guests and much of the native population!

For a FREE preview of *Dead and Breakfast*, send your request to davidcrossman@comcast.net, and simply enter BREAKFAST! in the subject line.

HISTORICAL NOVEL: SILENCE THE DEAD

TRAGEDY IS NO STRANGER to the west coast of Irelanc and the old shepherd had seen his share; but he'd neve seen anyone fall off a cliff. Looking down, even from a grea height, he imagined he saw a slight movement; fancied h heard a cry of anguish in the wind-stuffed silence betwee waves. But the man's body – twisted back on itself at a npossible angle – was beyond the skill of a doctor to repair. Christ himself, the shepherd thought, would be hard-pressed to remake a man from such a crumpled mass of human debris. Besides, there wasn't a doctor for twenty miles.

The shepherd ran to the church.

For a FREE preview of *Silence the Dead*, send your request to davidcrossman@comcast.net, and simply enter SILENCE PLEASE! in the subject line.

A TERRIBLE MERCY: THRILLER

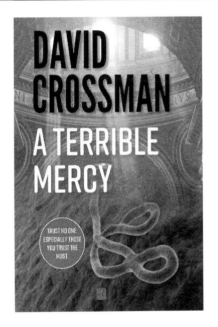

IS CHRISTMAS EVE IN ROME, and the Pope is dying. Among millions of faithful who have come to share in his final Mass, is an American doctor on a mission; to bring the world to an end.

A mismatched quartet of ordinary people are unwillingly stitched together by events over which they have no control, and propelled toward battle with an unseen horror that

threatens to cast the world into an Kitumian darkness i
which only Ebola thrives. As the world crumbles abou
them, one thing becomes certain: trust no one – especiall
those you trust most of all.

For a FREE preview of *A Terrible Mercy*, **send your request to <u>davidcrossman@comcast.net</u>, and simply enter MERCY ME! in the subject line.**

DAVID CROSSMAN

est-selling author David Crossman was once young, is now
d. Once had hair, is now bald. Once was Someone's Prince
harming and, she says, I still am.

With a friend in Chisinau, Moldova
One of us is 8,000 years old. The other just looks it.

www.davidcrossman.com
davidcrossman@comcast.net

Made in the USA
Middletown, DE
25 February 2022

61809732R00170